GETTING OUT

Anthony Bryan joined MI5 in the early 70s and operated in the UK, Ireland, and the Middle East, before being seconded to MI6 to work with the CIA in the USA during the War on Drugs.

He now lives between homes in London, Paris and Manila and runs a successful Private Detective & Corporate Intelligence Agency, *Anthony Bryan Corporate Intelligence and Investigations.*

GETTING OUT

ANTHONY BRYAN

Copyright © 2013 Anthony Bryan
All rights reserved

ISBN: 1-493-76206-0
ISBN-13: 978-1-493-76206-4

Cover by Becky Willingham, BW Designs
www.bw-designs.co.uk

Follow Anthony Bryan on Twitter: @A_Bryan_Author

http://anthonybryan-investigations.com

Acknowledgements

Thanks go to Bryan Vaughan for help with the manuscript. Also to Françoise, Ree Ann, Liz Bailey and especially to Becky for the cover.

Finally to those who contributed that I cannot name for reasons I can't disclose – you know who you are!

Chapter One

The last time I saw Charley Parnarti he punched his fists through adjacent panes of glass in the casement window. Then he twisted his wrists against the jagged edges. I didn't blame him. He wanted to write the end.

I couldn't have stopped him if I'd tried. I was as emaciated as he was and the shellac cane against my soles had left me with watermelons on the ends of my legs where my feet should have been. Hobbling from my cell down the corridor and collapsing on the bench outside the interview room was as much as I could do. Charley was already there. It was the only time we got to talk.

But Charley didn't have a word to say that day. He sat and stared at the casement opposite with its little glass panes framed in metal that made up the only window in the place low enough to see out of. Without warning, Charley launched out of the bench and across the corridor. Next thing I knew there was splintering glass and blood streaming down Charley's arms.

I didn't see them take him away because someone came for me to go and have my turn with Black-Eyed Susan, the name Charley and I had given the impassive bastard who watched while his minions carried out the daily round of prodding. The prodding was designed to help us answer Susan's questions. We hadn't any answers, that was the trouble.

The other trouble was the length of time it was taking to get us out of there.

'They won't be in any hurry,' said Charley.

He'd been around longer than me and knew the ropes.

'Why?'

'We got caught.'

We'd broken rule number one. The longer we were entertained at the pleasure of the Saudi authorities, the more ingrained the lesson. It had been drummed into us. If a field agent got into trouble, he was on his own. Next time we'd cover our tracks. Assuming, there was a next time, that is.

Well, I assumed, I even prayed. Unlike Charley Parnarti, who reckoned if the Saudis wouldn't push him off the edge, he'd take the plunge himself. Dick Frame was going to wait it out if he had to hang on by his fingertips.

'But will they get us out?'

'Yeah,' said Charley. 'Eventually.'

And then Charley had one too many dips in the water tank until his lungs nearly burst. Or maybe the water pouring over the sack on his head drove him out of his mind. Maybe he reckoned his arms were out of their sockets anyway after hanging so long. I don't know. He didn't confide in me. He just took matters into his own hands. Literally. And they took him out of there. Into a hole in the ground? I didn't know. All I knew was I missed the stupid bastard.

I missed our little chats on the bench, and the days got longer. I took to using the memories instead.

I was six months out of the Crazy House and halfway through a much-needed break, listening to the latest Led Zep record when I got the call. Jeannie gave me hell.

'I've barely seen you and now you're off again?'

'It's just a meeting, darling.'

Jeannie stormed into the kitchen of our tiny flat, red hair flying behind a tirade of foul language. 'Some marriage this is.'

'I'll be back before you know it.'

Only I wasn't. When I broke the news, Jeannie exploded.

'Going on a job? I thought you had to do three years training before they'd let you cross the road on your own? That's what the old man told you!'

Turned out otherwise. But I didn't know that when I obeyed the summons to the Russian House, as we called 'The Firm's' HQ. It was a fifties-built shit-hole of an office in the heart of the West End, supposed to be a shining example of post-war reconstruction, but was already falling apart after only twenty years. That's when I met Charley for the first time.

There were three suits in blazers with regimental ties and a woman. And Charley Parnarti. Latin looks, sleek black hair and brown shifty eyes that never stopped moving. I disliked him at first glance. Besides, he was taller than me and better looking, which was enough to make me want to punch him. I couldn't think what the Firm wanted with an operative who wouldn't merge into a city crowd with his smooth good looks and overwhelming smell of some foreign cologne. They might as well have painted him orange.

Charley must have felt the same way about me because he took one look and that was it. For the rest of the meet he concentrated all his attention on the Firm's mouthpiece. She was worth watching, I'll grant you. She was built like a switchback railway and the tight plaid skirt did things to her hips that ought never to be allowed in a boss lady. I spent a few moments imagining her bending over the white oak desk she was using to defend herself with. And she was blonde. Turned out Charley had a weakness for blondes. This one wouldn't waste her time.

'You're taking a crash course in management.'

'Managing what?'

Charley's voice was as rich as his limbs were long and lean. I wondered briefly if he was a fudge packer. All I needed.

'Cleaning services,' said Blondie briefly.

Charley gave an arrogant snort which echoed the thoughts in my head. I'd been busting my balls for six months on taxpayer's money and now I was going to be a damn cleaner?

Blondie fixed Charley with an eye that could've ground meat and he subsided. I knew better than to open my mouth.

'In a few days, you'll take separate flights to Jeddah.'

I got the picture. If we were going to Saudi, this was no routine operation.

One of the suits spoke up. He looked Middle Eastern himself. I later found out he was from Mossad, probably fresh from mopping up the Black September group that was responsible for the Munich Olympics massacre. They had the needed connections into Saudi.

'You'll be shift managers for a company contracted to the Port Authority. They have Yemeni workers cleaning the port area, and you'll supervise them.'

Now the presence of an intelligence officer from the Company made sense. It was their rap to set up foreign deals. They owned lots of business around the world that could be used as cover for agents.

The last guy in the room I already knew. Squadron Leader 'Jack' Leighton-Hart had been my mentor all the previous year when Lord Calveley had been grooming and schmoozing me to get in on the act. I'd had Lord Calveley's patronage so long, I'd got into the habit of doing what he wanted. I was about to regret that big time, but I didn't know it then.

First crack at Jeddah looked promising. Chauffeur fetched me from the airport and landed me in a humongous and well-staffed villa with a private garden and sun terrace on the roof. I basked in unsuspecting luxury, avoiding the fierce heat in plush rooms with lots of ceiling fans until I had to go fetch Charley a day later. I wasn't looking forward to it, and my expectations were not disappointed.

'Hey, Runt,' said Charley, by way of greeting.

Runt? Runt! I felt like trying him on with my newly acquired unarmed combat skills, but I had to work with the jerk.

'Richard,' I told him coldly.

His eyebrows jumped up and disappeared under the mop. The black hair was no longer slick and had taken on a life of its own. He was dressed casual too, in flared cotton slacks and a shirt loud enough to be heard along the rooftops, complete with oversized collars. Did he think we were on holiday?

He eye-balled me for a moment, and then grinned, sticking out a hand.

'Charley Parnarti.'

I wasn't keen but I took the hand.

We got in the car and the chauffeur took off. Charley looked without expression around the sun-bleached landscape that was Jeddah.

'Where we staying?'

'They've given us a villa, fully staffed,' I told him.

He looked round and squinted at me. 'Good?'

'Big.'

'Great. I can do with a rest.'

I made a derisive noise. Charley paid no attention. He looked round and winked at me.

'Got to be better than tailing that Scargill creep day and night.'

'That's what you were doing?'

He didn't answer. I guessed the Firm was looking to discredit the guy who had engineered the Miner's Strike. We'd been warned about the boredom of routine intelligence work. Keeping watch, trying to compromise the target with illegal money traps, find out extra-marital relationships, dig up any dirt. With the Tories in power, current targets would be Left-wing politicians and prominent CND. Or Arthur Scargill and his like. If the government changed sides, we'd be bloodhounds against the Right. The Firm mostly did as it was told and kept its mouth shut. Rumours persisted that it also had an agenda of its own, but I was too low in the pecking order to know about that.

Charley had relaxed into the limo's comfortable leather seat. He glanced at the back of the chauffeur's head, and then flicked a sideways look at me.

'First time they've let you out on your own, eh?'

Loath as I was to admit it, there wasn't much else I could say.

'I'm still training.'

Charley laughed, in that chuckling way I came to know as a mix of mockery and amusement.

'Looks like you're done, Amateur. Or being done.'

Shocked, I stared at him. 'What?'

Charley eyed me again. 'You're here, aren't you?'

Three years, they'd told me. Three years. I'd done less than a quarter of that and I was being thrown to the lions. I seethed, trying not to let Charley know it. But a snake of fear bugged me and I couldn't help asking. I spoke low so as not to reach the driver's ears.

'Do you think it'll be a tough one?'

Charley shrugged. 'Who knows?'

'Don't they ever warn you?'

'Would you do it if they did?'

He was right. Besides, the less you knew about the job, the less you had to tell. But there was one thing I needed to know.

'Have you been around long?'

Charley gave me the once over. Then he laughed lightly and I knew he wasn't going to tell me.

'Richard, eh?' His tone was teasing more than mocking.

'Frame,' I said. 'Richard Frame.'

The next time Charley used my name, he called me Dick. He never used anything else, unless it was Runt or Amateur.

Next day we went to work, reporting to the Company's subsidiary, Poon Saudi, and its manager, a humourless Australian called Rex. If you could call it work. We'd only had one instruction.

'Get embedded into port life.'

We had to get so everyone knew who we were and accepted us. That included personnel from Police and Army. We had ID with twenty-four hour access to the port, though not all the compounds. I'd been taught to keep my eyes open, and it didn't take long to figure out that most functions were under foreign contract; Saudi nationals were lazy buggers who thought the world owed them a living. Skivvy jobs, like shopkeepers, dock workers and cleaners were Pakistani or Bangladeshi. There were US army guys supervising Immigration, and security was run by Egyptians. Little did we guess how well acquainted we would become with the latter's crude methods of gathering intelligence.

I was anxious to know what our real job would be. Charley turned out to be more interested in sex.

'Where is the fucking pussy around here?' he kept asking.

At least I was reassured on his orientation. Not easy in a land where women were so closely guarded you hardly even got close to one. I didn't help him look and tried not to think about Jeannie.

But I finally got sick of his whining.

'Why don't you take a pill or something? What's the matter with you?'

Charley gave me one of his looks. 'I got addicted in Amsterdam. They ruined me.'

It was the first time I'd laughed since we got to Jeddah. My resistance to Charley began to thaw from that moment.

A week in with no further info or contact from the Firm, I began to relax. As well, because Charley organised a party at the villa with the help of a couple of Australians we'd run into. A crowd of nurses from the American hospital turned up and Charley had a field day. One of the Ozzies had managed to organise booze, a miracle in prohibition Saudi, and under its influence, I forgot my vows to my redhead back home and joined in.

We had the most fun since the start of this jaunt, except for the first glimpse of Charley's uncertain temper. As if there weren't women enough for everyone, he got into a fight with one of the guys from Oz.

I hustled him into a corner. Easy, because he was pissed out of his brains.

'Knock it off, Charley. Unless you want to stay dry for the rest of the trip. That guy brought the booze.'

I called him a few choice names, and he stared at me, blinking like an owl ruffled out of his sleep in the daylight hours.

'Okay, Dick, okay,' he slurred. His slow grin dawned. 'Hey, you're more useful than you look.'

I pulled him away from the wall by his polyglot Hawaiian shirt and slammed him back again.

'You know what, you crazy bastard? You're going to get us killed.'

Charley started giggling and slid down the wall. I left him there and went off to apologise to the Ozzie.

The thing I didn't know was that Charley was already halfway to damnation. It wasn't long before he made the rest of the trip.

We were playing pool with our Oz mates when the gong went. Someone from the British Embassy turned up, annoying the hell out of Charley because we had a bet on the game and had to stop.

The brief was simple in theory. Gain access to the shipping containers coming into the newly-built Port of Jeddah. Make a daily phone call to get container numbers. When we had one, find the relevant container and paint a radioactive tracing chemical compound across its ID.

Only trouble was, the container area was out of bounds. We didn't have access. Which meant sneaking around in the midnight hours and climbing a twelve foot fence lit up like a Christmas tree.

This was what we were paid for. To stick our butts on the line because some rich Saudi Prince was alleged to be using diplomatic status on containers to smuggle heroin and cocaine to the UK.

I got hyped up to no purpose.

'Don't get too excited,' said Charley. 'Chances are we'll be on standby for days.'

It took a week before we got word a bunch of suspect containers were expected. We took the serial numbers and the dates they were likely to be in port. We got ourselves two pairs of binoculars and found a vantage point to watch for arrivals. First one came in a few days later. Just before I'd managed to gnaw my nails to the quick. We'd been told the container would be in port at least twenty-four hours, but there was only one way to be sure. We'd have to bust it that night.

Heads down in black, we were plotted up and ready to go by 2300. Our faces matched the pitch of darkness, courtesy of an American nurse who didn't know Charley had kept her black silk stockings after he rolled them off her delectable legs. I'm not so sure why he was wearing her suspender belt though. And some workers who hadn't reckoned on their own generosity were going to miss two pairs of black overalls in a day or two.

Our kit was already hidden in the cars, and the only change of behaviour was to stay in port when the workday ended.

'What if someone challenges us?'

'They won't.' Charley was confident. 'The place is buzzing twenty-four hours a day.'

I wasn't convinced we were unseen, even as we secreted ourselves in the vantage point out of the way so we could monitor the container.

Our controller had instructed a 2340 kick-off and my nerves jangled as we waited for the distraction he was going to organise at the port entrance to draw off security from our end of the action.

At 2330, just as I decided I had to pee, my bladder got shocked into stillness when what sounded like the afterclap of two massive stun grenades hit the front of the port.

'There we go,' said Charley.

I was ready to up and run but Charley held me back.

'2340 exactly. And walk, don't run.'

As we sweated out the minutes, we heard the onset of shouting and the sirens started up.

Exactly at 2340, we shifted out of cover and strolled casually towards the remote edge of the compound. It was the longest hundred metres I ever walked.

'You first, Runt.'

I shifted the rucksack more securely on my back, moved into the glaring light and shoved my fingers through the thick wire of the fence. I'd scaled enough obstacles on the training exercises and the memory kicked in enough to send me scrambling up like a monkey and I was over and down as Charley began his ascent.

We could hear the cars and trucks speeding towards the gates as we raced on silent feet towards the bulk of the containers.

'Three minutes,' said Charley. 'Not bad.'

The lights bugged me and I swore at him to shut up, my attention concentrated on finding the target container as quickly as possible. Close up, the place didn't look as clear as it had through binoculars.

Probably wasn't more than a couple of minutes but after what felt like ten years we finally spotted it. I was hauling off my rucksack even as we made towards it, my ears out like stalks to catch the noise and bustle still coming from the other end of the port.

The chemical delivered to us via a cleaning material store had come in a paint tin and Charley had cursed as we'd done the messy task of transferring the stuff to the spray bottles allocated for the proper job. We dug them out, along with the goggles and surgical masks we'd used for the transfer in hopes of protection. All it had done was stop the liquid from splashing into our mouths and eyes. For all we knew, we'd made ourselves toxic for life.

'What in hell is this stuff?'

'I'd rather not know,' said Charley.

On balance, I thought he had a point. Gingerly, once masked and goggled, I got out my bottle and sprayed across the ID numbers.

'Who are you, fucking David Hockney?' protested Charley. 'Do some damage, Runt.'

Shifting up close, he soaked the serial numbers and the surrounding area until the stuff was running down the side of the container and making me cough despite the mask.

'What in hell are you doing, you raving nutcase?'

Charley was stuffing the near empty bottle back in his rucksack.

'I'm not climbing that frigging fence again in a hurry, I nearly ruined my love life.'

'Yeah, and you'd be doing humanity a favour.'

Charley began to giggle and I aimed a kick at his rear.

'Get on with it, can't you?'

He was still snorting away as we packed our kit and started back towards the line of the fence, moving slow and low and catching what shadow we could find.

Keeping a wary eye out for patrols coming or going in the direction of the guard house about three hundred metres away, I waited at the bottom while Charley shinned up the fence. I heard him swearing and looked up to see his lanky body poised at the top like a bird on a wire.

'Get off there,' I hissed up at him.

I don't know if he heard me, but I heard him descending with a thump as he smashed into the ground, air exiting his lungs with enough noise to send a fleet of birds into orbit. I let out a stream of muttered invective.

'You clumsy bastard, you're going to get us both killed, if you're not dying already.'

I could see the heap Charley had turned into lying on the ground on the other side of the fence and for a moment I went cold, thinking he really had bought it.

I briefly wondered what to do with his corpse. I didn't have time or tools to dig a hole. I looked around for a place to hide a body. And how was I going to explain this slight mishap to the office?

Chapter Two

Then he groaned, and I felt the fury surge into my chest.

My antennae were out, hunting towards the port entrance, my fingers hovering over the Beretta strapped inside my boiler suit. The noises from the guards in response to the explosions were subsiding. Time was at a premium.

I moved about ten metres along the fence before I started my climb, determined not to repeat Charley's cuckoo exhibition. I got over with the minimum of fuss and noise, and ran to pick up my flattened partner. Relieved, I found him already pushing to his feet.

'I'm dead,' said Charley.

'You will be, if we don't get moving. More importantly, so will I. Come on, you dumb-arsed prat.'

I shoved into position under his shoulders to take part of his weight. 'The hide-out,' Charley managed. 'Got to get back there and merge with the works force in the morning.'

'Yeah, good plan.'

As if I hadn't thought of this for myself. If we were spotted after all the shenanigans portside, no one was going to give us the benefit of the doubt.

Moving low again, as fast as I could force Charley to travel, we made it back to our cover spot undetected. It took some effort to get Charley into the hide in the air-conditioning duct in the roof of one of the admin buildings. Without boots we could do it in relative quiet. Heads towards the intake entrance, we were able to see the compound.

All was quiet. As I realised there'd been no reaction to Charley's I can fly stunt, I felt the drop start inside and knew I'd been riding on adrenaline.

'I think I bust my ribs,' said Charley.

'Good,' I retorted.

But I hunted my pack for the regulation first aid kit and shot Charley with a full dose of morphine.

'Cheers, Dick.'

I heard the gratitude in his voice with a sinking heart for the long night ahead. Charley would be out, so it was up to me to stay awake. I dug out my supply of Blues. It wasn't easy swallowing amphetamines without water, so bitter, so indicative of the hit to come. I shoved them down while Charley sunk into slumbering peace.

Part of me wanted to kick him awake. Or to death. The other part knew he had to rest so he could move around next day with normal body language.

I knew about broken ribs. It hurt to breathe. Part of the Crazy House programme was making men of us by lying on the ground while the rest of the team took turns dancing a fandango on your chest. That or the murderous medicine ball bouncing fifteen pounds of solid rubber onto your ribs, causing intolerable pain that stuck with you for weeks. Ribs didn't break that easily after this kind of punishment. Except Charley's had somehow.

At 0600, I covered his mouth when I woke him, in case he was delirious. I reckoned if we moved out now, we'd have a chance to get to the cars, switch our desert boots for shoes, grab towels and hit the showers to freshen up before the morning shift. We both had lightweight safari suits, customary for daytime wear in the Saudi ninety degree heat in our backpacks, ready for the switch.

I planned on giving Charley a second shot when we got to the showers, so I made him shove another morphine syringe down his underwear.

'I could ruin my future with a needle in my dick,' he complained.

'Yeah, if you had a future. Which right now is debatable.'

'Good point,' said Charley.

And he was off giggling again as we made our move by way of the external staircase. Only two floors, for which I silently thanked the architect who had designed this building.

'Why didn't you straighten me out, you heartless runt?' Charley twisted to try and rid himself of the pain from sleeping all anyhow with his head awkwardly bent. 'I've got a crick in my neck.'

'If you'd broken it when you had the chance, you wouldn't have one.'

He giggled again as we landed on the ground floor and I cursed the after-effects of the morphine. We had to cross a hundred metres to reach the cars parked opposite our Poon Saudi office, with the showers and catering block for the staff nearby. We started the walk and Charley went into hobble and waddle mode, which wouldn't work at all if anyone saw us. I had him a metaphorical and literal kick up the ass and whispered the magic words.

'Morphine soon.'

This was enough to give him a boost and we moved on more smoothly. Our cars were parked side by side and the stuff we needed was in both. I sat Charley in my car and searched his boiler suit pockets for his keys. Then I gave him another shot from my pack which was easier to reach than his.

'Better,' he said.

'Junkie. You should be put down,' I told him.

Charley laughed weakly, which hurt his ribs so that he started cursing loudly, making enough noise to bring the whole contingent of guards out on us.

'Shut up, you moron, or I'm going to have to shoot you.'

Charley thought for some reason I was joking and snorted again. More pain to his ribs, more noise.

Giving up, I left him in my car and moved over to his, opening the trunk to get the stuff he needed.

That's when I heard the running feet.

I moved for the Beretta holstered inside my boiler suit and turned to find a sea of bodies heading my way at a clip you wouldn't think an Arab could hit. How many there were I didn't know. I hadn't got time to count. Looked like a hundred and most of them could run and point an M16 rifle at the same time. I reckoned pulling a gun at this point would end my problems for good.

I loosened my grip on the Beretta and slowly tried to move my hand out and away from my chest.

Just as I was praying that Charley was taking the same conservative approach, I felt a crunch to my head. Probably an M16, but it didn't introduce itself.

Stars twinkled in the sunshine and I could feel the blood running down the side and back of my head. I didn't have long to enjoy the sensation because some inconsiderate shit kicked my legs out from under me.

As a myriad of boots found their mark, I could hear Charley screaming rude names. The last thought I had before I sunk out of consciousness was that the dope never knew when to keep his mouth shut.

I blinked my eyes open to find a dozen brown faces looking down at me. For a few minutes I stared up at them in mute incomprehension, with no idea of where I was or how I'd got there. No memory either of what had gone before.

On auto I tried to move and a chorus of shrieking protest from various points of my body brought the recent past flooding back. My first coherent thought was of Charley Parnarti. I found myself desperately hoping he wasn't dead.

Trying to override the muscular objections, I made a move to sit up and several pairs of hands caught at me to help. I leaned against something solid and cold and one glance around told me

I was in a subterranean cell with a collection of seemingly normal prisoners. One of them squatted beside me, holding out a mug towards my mouth, nodding and gesturing for me to drink. It was water, tepid and faintly foul, but it tasted good on my tongue until I found I could hardly swallow. What had the bastards done to my throat?

It was then I recalled the crack to my head and the kicking I'd been given. I knew I should inspect the damage but my mind fastened on the water and whether it was going to make me sick. Where had it come from? What in hell was in it? Was it safe to drink?

Nuts to be worrying about that in the condition I was in. Not to mention the likely worse condition I would be in when my captors came for me, as they undoubtedly would. We'd been told what to expect, and I wasn't looking forward to it with any degree of appreciation.

My fellow inmates' concern for my welfare abated now I was seen to be alive and they settled into desultory groups around the crowded cell, giving me a chance to take stock.

The place stank even more than I did and that was saying something. My hosts had found time and opportunity to whip off my black overalls and stick me into some sort of military outfit, which was stained and rank with sweat and urine - mine or someone else's, I didn't know. All I knew was it was filthy, like the dirty grey walls around me. A steel door complete with prison bars opened onto a narrow corridor. The only other ventilation came from a meagre window two metres up. With help, I might reach it, but it was too small for escape and barred besides. At least I could tell it was daylight, though there was no way of guessing the time.

Someone was squatting over a hole in the corner which, from the smell, I took to be the only form of toilet. There was a bucket nearby and I thought it was for throwing down the hole until a couple of prisoners dipped mugs in it and drank. I retched a bit, glad I hadn't been up to drinking more than a mouthful or two.

After an unfathomable time, which I whiled away by counting the places where I ached, a guard opened the door and shoved a platter of food into the cell. It skittered across the bare stone floor and the metal door slammed shut as a tangle of arms and legs made for the offering, loudly vying for a share. I stayed put, torn between the ravening hole in my belly I hadn't noticed before and indignation that nothing had been provided for me personally.

Now I came to think about it, why the hell had they put me in with twenty-odd common or garden jailbirds? It was a downright insult. Surely I'd be an A Category prisoner with a high level of security? Unless there was an agent among the crew inside? You couldn't expect them to bunk me up with Charley, for fear of collusion. But they'd obviously busted us and knew we were up to no good. And I was a foreign national. I'd got to be entitled to a private cell at least, even if they reckoned starvation was a way to loosen my tongue.

An odd odour under my nostrils brought me out of my distraction. One of my fellow inmates, the same who gave me water, was now offering to share his meal with me. With a nod of thanks I accepted the handful of rice and what looked like rotten fruit of some kind. I tried to smile, but it hurt and turned into a grimace. The guy nodded and grinned, gesturing to me to eat.

I made an effort with the rice and the minute I began to chew realised one of the bastards on last night's happy feet show had dislocated my jaw. The damn thing screamed at me and I groaned back, thinking hard thoughts of Charley Parnarti and his trapeze antics on the high wire fence. How else had they cottoned on to us? Some eagle-eyed guard must have seen us. What's the betting they'd been hunting us down all night, never dreaming that all they had to do was wait for dawn and we'd walk straight into their welcoming committee? Though I'd been awake throughout and seen nothing in the compound.

No point in dwelling on the why because the facts told me I was in it up to the neck and then some. An image of the female suit back at the Russian House crept into my head and I wondered how soon my captors could kill me so that I didn't have to face her. Not that I wouldn't shop Charley and his bird imitations in a heartbeat if it would do any good. But I hadn't spent six months getting the shit kicked out of me without learning to zip my lip with the men in charge. No excuses. Take the pain and sweat it out.

According to Charley, as I later learned, Blondie wouldn't need to haul us on the carpet. The Egyptian security forces would do the job on her behalf.

The tiny patch of sky beyond the window was just beginning to darken and I was trying to reckon up the hours I'd been a guest of this no-star hotel when a guard rattled the keys outside.

By the time I got my head turned, the sack of shit was standing over me, barking in Arabic.

'He is saying get up, dog,' translated my new friend of the water and food.

'Cheers,' I said, my eyes fastened on the ill-dressed barker who repeated himself, reinforcing the command with the toe of his boot.

I winced and slowly inched my way upwards, using the wall for support. Every muscle had seized and the aching wounds were in high-level rebellion.

When I was finally on my feet, I saw that my status was at last being acknowledged. There were three soldiers behind the guard, all armed with M16 rifles.

The guard opened the door, and my cell mates shifted back in a body. Not a good sign. If they preferred to be inside, what the heck was waiting for me out there?

Stepping through the door, I nearly ran into an officer who popped up like a wizard from a trapdoor in a seaside pantomime. His insignia resembled that of a US major, but his side-arm was holstered. A sign of friendship?

The soldiers got pally, grabbing me on either side and dragged me along with painful intensity. Their intensity, my pain. I made my views known, but they didn't seem to value my distress.

Down concrete steps - how much lower could I get? - and another strip-lit corridor, and I found myself inside another concrete cube.

For several moments I was occupied with recovering from freshly churned up agonies. Being pitched onto the floor didn't help. The officer's voice finally got through to me.

'Take off your clothes, you goat.'

Confusion caught. Fuck me, there must me some mistake - they eat goats here.

I did as I was told with some difficulty and humiliation. My fingers were swollen and my vision was blurred. I took my time, trying to think and get a handle on the space. A large room, with no window and a solid metal door. Open at the moment, but I couldn't think of any way to take advantage of it.

Damp had made the clothes stick and the officer seemed to think I was taking too long peeling them off. He swiped me round the head with his cane. Rocking back and forth from the force of the blow, I caught sight of a concrete tank, something like an animal trough. More unpleasantly, I noted a rack on the wall with various unidentifiable items hanging there. Straps? I was to get a more intimate acquaintance with the gear as time went by. It went by very slowly.

My efforts to untangle myself from my clothes made me fall and it seemed easier to finish the job on the floor, despite the mocking jeers from the waiting onlookers. Finally I finished and obeyed an impolite injunction to stand up again. At which point, I was knocked over by a blast of water from a hosepipe the size of a fire hose.

I needed a shower, but I could have done with something a little less like a battering ram. My audience thoroughly enjoyed the show while I slipped and slid like a cow on skates.

Before I completely drowned, the power jets stopped and I fought to get my wind back. My ribs were killing me. Then I heard water running from a tap. Wasn't I clean enough for my new friends for fucks sake?

Apparently not. They dragged me to the trough and strapped my body to a board. A quality piece of wood obviously, because it took my weight as they lifted it and me over the edge of the trough and tipped.

It didn't take a genius to guess what was coming next. Yes, they'd decided to give me a shampoo. A bit like my grandmother used to do it, in a way that you can't breathe.

This was where Dick Frame bought it, hook line and sinking ship. Next moment I had balloons in my lungs and string round my throat and panic shrieking in my head. Last thing I remember was the fleeting realisation I'd been suckered into a game I didn't want to play.

Waking up from a nightmare, I was in pitch black, freezing and alone and assumed it was hell gone wrong. Naked on a cold stone floor? Nice. I wondered if Charley was enjoying similar luxury. I pictured his face as he gave that mocking chuckle of his and for the first time in this fairytale adventure felt the sting of bitter loneliness. Out of the blue I thought of Jeannie and how she'd look if she could see me now. The nakedness bothered me more than anything. I felt so vulnerable.

I hadn't cried since the day Gran locked me in a cupboard under the stairs when I was four. This was the same stark feeling of isolation and I blubbed like a baby. The weird thing was I wanted Jeannie, but I wanted Charley more. Charley was in the same boat and he would understand. Jeannie, even if I told her, which I couldn't, would never believe me.

It hit me suddenly that Charley wanted out. I didn't know how long he'd been in the Firm, and I didn't know if he'd been through this kind of thing before. But he'd reeked of attitude from the off. He'd got so he couldn't care less. Right this moment, everything in me echoed him and I wished I'd drowned in the bathtub, because I knew this was only the beginning.

Chapter Three

The first time Charley and I rendezvoused at the bench, he was sporting a brand-new beard and a pair of blue-ringed sunken eyes. I hadn't seen a mirror, but the rough stubble under my fingers told me I probably looked the same. I didn't care. Joy shrieked through my chest at sight of the closest thing to a friend in a friendless world.

'Charley!'

'Hey, Runt,' was his greeting. I could have kissed him.

He shuffled along the bench and I sat down beside him. I was aware of my guard dropping back, but I didn't bother to look round. I only had eyes for Charley Parnarti. I asked the dumbest question.

'You okay?'

'Ace,' said Charley and the mocking tone shoved warmth through the ice that had settled in my guts days since.

A smoking fag appeared in front of my face and I looked up. Charley's guard was holding it out to me. I glanced at the guy's face, seeking in his eyes for the secret stealth I'd grown used to. Wasn't the first time I'd been offered a smoke. One drag and the jerk who'd given it to me would yank it out of my mouth, hyena jeering as he threw it down and stubbed it out with a vicious boot.

'Take it,' advised Charley sotto voce, and blew a smoke ring into the brightness streaming from the window opposite, with its six by six inch panes.

Only now did it dawn on me that he had a fag too. Still wary, I accepted the offering, waiting for the guard to back off before I put it between my lips. The drag rolled comfort all down my throat and into my lungs. I held it there, savouring the heady sensation wreathing around the dark of my brain. Then I released the smoke and a mass of tension escaped along with it.

For a few minutes we smoked in silence, and the close companionship of Charley beside me filled me as full as the calming fog of nicotine. Almost too close, as it turned out. I forgot caution.

'What do we do, Charley?'

'Stay shtum, What the fuck else?'

'Yeah, I know, but-'

'Shtum, Dick, you hear me?'

It was sharp, and Charley's hollow eyes burned into mine. I glanced along the walls. Both guards were out of earshot. The door to Black-Eyed Susan's office, set a couple of metres along from the bench, was shut. This might be our only chance to grab a word. Who knew how long before one of us was pulled in for another dose of whichever high-jinks was on today's menu? Black-Eyed Susan liked to keep us guessing. His favourite was the cane across the feet. He told me once - he spoke good English and used it with gusto - that the cane was soaked in brine.

'This way the salt releases slowly, you see, Dog.' He never called me anything but Dog, unless it was Dog Spy with a few choice adjectives thrown in. 'It is designed to inflict more pain, but it also helps you because it cleans and disinfects the wounds.'

How lucky can you get? I didn't say it. Policy was to maintain 'Grey Man': no response beyond the basic lie, no reaction to insult, question or torture except to scream blue murder and turn on the waterworks. No stiff upper lips. You don't want them thinking it doesn't hurt enough.

From his appearance, I could see Charley had been enjoying as much tough love from our hosts as me. But he was alive and I rejoiced. Too soon, as it turned out, but I didn't know it then. I lowered my voice to a whisper and flicked a glance at his guard.

'They can't hear us.'

'Someone can.'

The morose tone caught me and I looked round.

'What? How come?'

'Ears and walls, Runt. Work it out.'

It took me a minute, because I was all but brain-dead after Black-Eyed Susan's kindly ministrations, but I got it. I sucked in too heavy a drag when it hit me, which made me cough. How they were doing it I don't know, but we were bugged. Charley hadn't talked any more than me, or we'd both be dead. They still didn't know what we'd been up to, so they'd decided to let us meet hoping we might give it away.

And I'd nearly fallen for it. The thought made me sicker than Black-Eyed Susan's studied insults.

'I'm a wanker,' I said.

Charley let out an echo of that laugh of his, the one that spelled mockery between friends.

'You can say that again.'

So I did, and he laughed louder. So did I. It felt good. Take that, you bastard. Make of it what you will, you smarmy sadistic shit.

Black-Eyed Susan, as we came to call him was in his fifties, with a head of thick black hair greased back and a moustache that looked like it had been painted on. Charley came up with the nickname, on account of the contrast between his skin and eyes, just like the flowers in his great-aunt's garden. I didn't know what evil looked like until I looked into those eyes. He was always well turned out in civvies, a safari suit like the one they'd found for me when they eventually gave me back some clothes. It made his laid-back attitude of pseudo-British politeness the more macabre. He'd been almost friendly the first time we met.

'Good morning, Dog Spy.'

I went into the routine.

'There has been a terrible mistake. I'm a cleaning supervisor and my mother will be missing me. I want to speak with my Embassy.'

Susan smiled. 'Don't worry, Dog, they know where you are. They are not interested in scum like you. There are excellent relationships between the Kingdom and the British Government. Why would they worry about a piece of shit like you?'

The insult was delivered with meticulous care, like the words were a compliment.

I was there in body, but in mind I was already far away, just as I'd been trained. All that time with the long-haired, Doc Martin-booted, weird psychologist was paying dividends. I hadn't dropped LSD without learning to 'travel'.

Someone threw clothes at me.

'Get dressed, you dirty dog. Your body makes me sick. Why are you sickly white with all these black and blue patches? You should be more careful, those wounds could become infected. Prison is not a healthy place, Dog Spy.'

I wanted to swear at him, but my training and survival instincts kicked in. Don't forget the 'Game'. Don't fuel them. Let them burn out. Don't fuel their hate. We'd practiced the Game time and again at the Crazy House, the instructor's voice in my head.

'Get it right. This is not a rehearsal.'

I hadn't expected to be on stage so soon, but here I was and there was nothing I could do about it except stick to the routine.

'Tell me the truth.'

'Just tell me what you want me to say and I'll sign a letter.'

'Tell me the target, Dog.'

'I don't know what you want from me.'

'Dog Spy, what were you looking for?'

'I don't understand.'

'Did you come to murder a member of the Royal Family?'

'I told you, there's been a mistake.'

'Who are you working for?'

'I'm just a cleaning man.'

Black-Eyed Susan and me, we could have earned good money as a cross-talk act. Even the punctuation with an umbrella over the head was replicated on the soles of my feet with that murderous cane of his.

But he hadn't let on about my partner, and to find Charley out of a coffin so boosted my morale I could have burst into song. From then on I took my punishment as if I was an old hand, fantasising about the sweet taste of revenge. Susan got nothing out of me and was reduced to threats and inducements.

'Dog, if you talk there is no need for too much more pain. Little more, not a lot more. Regrettably for you and pleasurably for me, this is a training school for interrogating dogs. We all have to learn our skills somewhere. I'm sure you understand, Dog. Guess where I learned my skills? It's true, I learned very well. The British, Dog. The British taught me to do what I'm doing to your body and mind. Truly I was a good person until the British trained me.'

Accompanied of course by doing the unthinkable. When this failed, he started in on Charley.

'Do you want to hear your friend screaming? Your fellow Dog Spy, he is talking good. We work with him more because he is so good looking and some of my colleagues like to visit him in private. Do you understand, Dog?'

I understood, but I didn't believe him. If Charley was talking, why would they keep on giving us time together on the bench? There was always a cigarette, sometimes coffee and Arab sweets. We took everything they gave us and returned them zilch. If they'd been less than morons, they might have got something.

Charley and I developed a code. Short cryptic questions. Innocuous answers.

'Do they know?'
'You bet.'

'They' might be the guards, the embassy or the Company here, or the Firm back in London. Somehow we always knew which one was meant.

'No sign of the cavalry.'

'Mislaid their horses,' said Charley.

I managed a weak laugh, but I was getting to be bitter as the days passed. Had we been forgotten? They'd only spent six months on me. Maybe they thought it wasn't worth the trouble and meant to leave us here. I was bothered by small things. The rattling of keys that told me they were coming for me, flicking down my nerve endings to set them on fire. What had happened to my watch? Why did I suddenly get sick with hunger when my body was in so much pain and distress?

'How's the food?'

'Hot.'

Originally, Charley was talking about the sparse meals we got of rice and peppers with a little meat. We argued whether it was goat or camel or Yemeni. After a while, 'food' became a euphemism for the torture, which was either hot, cold or warm, depending on how severe it had been.

'Visiting hour' was your time in the concrete cube. We talked about Black-Eyed Susan like we were discussing a whore. I told him she loved to tickle my feet, and Charley said they usually did it in the shower, easier to hose down before the next guest, which made me think he had the worst of it. I didn't know if that was true, but it began to dawn on me that our meetings on the bench were having an opposite effect on him than they were on me.

He looked more gaunt each time I saw him and he talked less and less. I worried when he started refusing the treats. Except the fags. He seized those, sucking up the poisonous smoke like it would be his last.

When Charley finally lost it and pulled his stunt with the window, I was too shocked to think straight for days. I sat in my cell and stared up at the square of window near the ceiling, watching legs go by. I didn't know I was grieving until Black-

Eyed Susan commented on the tracks of my tears through the grime on my cheeks.

'What, are you a woman, Dog Spy? Weeping for your friend? Come on, you can forget about him.'

But I couldn't. The little world I inhabited had grown bleak. I didn't even notice there were intervals of days without visiting hour. I no longer recognised the passage of time. When I finally came to and paid attention, I found my routine had undergone a change.

It took me a while to realise they'd left the cell door open. I eyed it with disbelief. If I tried to creep out, would the unseen guard behind it slam it in my face?

I was lying on the cot they'd wheeled in a few days ago. My straw-like mattress had been shifted onto it but it was less comfortable than it had been on the floor. Maybe I'd got used to the hard surface underneath. But I liked being high enough off the ground to avoid the rats.

The lure of the open door proved too tempting and I dragged my aching limbs to sit up, swinging my legs to the floor. As the swollen soles touched base, I hissed in the usual breath against the first point of pain, but I wasn't paying it much attention. I tried to see through the bars to the corridor wall in case anyone was hiding there, but it was impossible at this angle.

At last I got up and hobbled to the door. Warily I inspected the corridor either side. It looked empty. I placed a couple of fingers on the half-open door and pushed. It swung gently outwards and I stepped hurriedly out of range. Nothing happened. No infuriated guard came sweeping in with handgun poised to crack against my head.

Was it safe? There was only one way to find out.

My heart thumped crazily as I inched towards the opening. Cautiously I peered out, throwing a hasty glance both ways. The corridor was empty.

Half convinced that the moment I set foot outside my cell, I would hear the battering of running boots, I took my first tentative steps along the concrete walk. I got all the way to the corner, noting the empty cells as I passed, without a sign of misadventure. Growing bolder, I turned and retraced my steps, moving on past my open cell door and heading for the other end. I must have done about ten paces when the Arab appeared around the edge of the wall.

I froze, half poised to run back to my cell and throw myself inside. The sight of the white thawb and headdress stopped me. This was no guard.

The man stood still, centred in the corridor, watching me. He was a handsome brute, possessed of chocolate brown eyes that brought Charley's face vividly into my head. But this specimen had all the assurance of rank and status. As he started walking towards me, he smiled and held out a hand.

I backed a step or two, but he made like he didn't notice, coming right up to me and taking the hand that rose automatically from my side.

'I am sorry for your situation,' he said in fluent English, and beckoned to someone behind him.

Only then did I notice a couple of guards at his rear. The man barked a command in Arabic and the guards saluted, turned and went smartly off in the other direction.

'Come, let us sit at our ease while these dogs clean up your quarters.'

Too amazed for speech, I turned as he directed and followed along. Dazed, I found myself sitting at a table in an office with windows and chairs. Chairs just to sit in. The last time I'd used a chair I'd been strapped in and upended so Black-Eyed Susan's minions could get at the soles of my feet more easily.

A white-uniformed Saudi brought in a tray and set it down. He spoke English too.

'Anything else, your highness?'

I was staring at the contents of the tray: a covered silver dish, cutlery - which I hadn't seen since my incarceration - and a bottle of coke. But the servant's words brought me slewing round to stare at my host. I found my tongue at last.

'You're a prince?'

His highness smiled and inclined his head, muttering a name I didn't catch. Then he turned back to the servant.

'Dates, fruit. And cigarettes.' He looked at me. 'You'd like a smoke?'

I nodded with fervour and the Saudi bowed and disappeared, while I blinked at this inexplicable prince. He gestured to the tray and lifted the cover off the dish. A rich aroma drifted into my face and my mouth began to water. It was some kind of stew on rice, but of a cuisine far superior to the fare I'd grown used to here.

At the back of my mind hovered the thought that this was an attempt to soften me up, and I was sure I would regret it later when the reckoning came. But I didn't care. Without pause for word or thought, I ate, using the knife and fork awkwardly, unused as I'd become to civilised meals. It was manna from heaven and my taste buds went into overdrive.

The prince opened the coke and I slurped it down along with the food. He didn't speak as I wolfed the meal, but I caught a faint look in his eyes now and then that I couldn't interpret. Or perhaps I could, if I hadn't been too intent on satisfying my greed.

By the time I finished, the servant had returned with a bowl laden with dates, figs and squashy fruits. He laid down a pack of cigarettes and my host produced a lighter from the recesses of his Arab gown.

My fingers shook as I accepted a fag from the proffered pack. The prince lit it for me and then flicked a finger at the bowl.

'Don't forget your sweet. The English like sweets, don't they?'

'Do they?' I said absently, preoccupied with sucking in the nicotine. I hadn't been given a cigarette since Charley's window jaunt and I felt like a man on the edge of a precipice, anxious to enjoy every last vestige of pleasure before they pushed me off.

The prince laughed. 'Apples. Apple pie and custard, isn't it? I tried it at Oxford.'

It was no news to me that this prince had been educated in England. It was common practice, I'd learned in the few weeks I'd been in Saudi, for the royals to be sent abroad for a little polish. Oxford in England, Princeton in the States.

Without thinking, I reached for a date, munching between puffs. The prince leaned towards me, his voice soft.

'I am sorry it has taken so long to do something about your situation, but now I am going to sort it out.'

Open-mouthed I stared at him. What was this about?

'I am going to get you out of here.'

'I like the sound of that,' I said without thinking, and dragged at my cigarette.

The prince smiled. 'Yes. I am going to get you out - for a while at least.'

That was a less pleasing thought, but I didn't say so. The good food had put heart into me and I was suddenly open to possibilities. If I was out of this hellhole, who knew what I could do? I wasn't in any shape to run away, but maybe there would be other options.

I thanked him politely and he gave me another cigarette. I hoped he might leave me the pack and some matches, but he got up to leave a few minutes later and the Saudi servant gathered up the pack along with the remains of my meal and the tray.

The prince stopped him with a command in Arabic and my hopes rose again. But the servant merely handed me the fruit bowl. I wasn't going to refuse anything, so I took it, assuming this would be the last I would see of the prince and his largesse.

When he had gone, a guard came for me and led me back to my cell. It had been swept and mopped, and there was a bucket of water standing inside. A wash kit and fresh clothes were laid on the bed. The guard left, leaving the cell door open again.

I went over to the bucket and discovered it was filled with hot water. Hot! I threw off my filthy clothing, grabbed the wash kit and set to. My skin was bruised and sore in so many places, it took time to clean up. When I'd done, I felt more like Dick Frame than I had for many a long day.

But this was a Dick Frame with a mission. Aside from the obvious desire to get out of this and home, I only wanted one thing. To get out, period.

I didn't know how you resigned from the Firm. I didn't care that Lord Calveley was going to blow his stack. Dick Frame was in the wrong job, and that was all there was to it. I didn't want to tread the path Charley had trodden and end up damned to hell and gone. Jeannie and me, we were going to have a life.

And that's what started the whole fucking shambles.

Chapter Four

I had to ring the doorbell because the bastards at the Embassy had stolen the keys to my flat. Or someone had. But as the official who escorted me to the airport had my case, I suspected them before my Saudi hosts.

If Jeannie was in rehearsal somewhere I'd be waiting it out down at Harry's café on the corner. At last I heard slopping footsteps and knew she'd been in bed, which meant she was in performance at night, sleeping into the day.

The thought woke up my lost libido. How many weeks since I'd last had a woman? A jeer rang in my head. I was still so bruised it would probably kill me but I wanted to drill her until she screamed for mercy.

'Richard!'

The door was open and Jeannie, all tousled and pink, sleep in her eyes, was staring at me like a moron.

'Yeah, it's me.'

She didn't say anything for a moment. Her eyes woke up fast and I twigged. Last time I looked in a mirror I was a guest at a personnel villa along with my erstwhile guards and the rest of Saudi security services. I reckon it was politics. They wanted me to look relatively normal when I left, not too many bruises. I'd been chuffed with the improvement. Now it hit me how different I must look from the last time Jeannie saw me.

Her face crumpled as she stumbled into my arms.

'What did those bastards do to you?'

Didn't matter which bastards. Jeannie would've called it whoever inflicted the damage. I pushed her inside the flat and shut the door, changing the subject.

'I'm gasping for tea, lover.'

Jeannie wasn't a wet and she sniffed up the tears and went into the routine as we headed for our little kitchen.

'No bloody word for weeks and then you turn up looking like yesterday's dinner. What the hell happened to you? Where have you been?'

She whirled round, waving her hands in my face.

'Don't answer that. I don't want to know.'

I watched her dive for the kettle, slamming things around. Some kind of mental boot kicked into my groin and I forgot my prediction of the likely outcome and grabbed for my Jeannie with both hands.

Later, when we were smoking in bed and I finally got that cup of tea, she staked her claim in no uncertain terms.

'Richard, if you make me a bloody widow, I'm going to kill you.'

'Hey, lover, I'm here, aren't I?'

'Just about.'

I tried to settle my arm more comfortably around her shoulders but she shrugged it off, sitting up and turning on me.

'Don't pretend you didn't nearly die out there, wherever you were. I've got eyes and I can see what's what.'

She had eyes all right. Sparkling big eyes in a kind of tawny green colour. They'd knocked my brains in the first time I saw her in that sit-in in the middle of the square. I was static guard on the government building she and her CND mates were targeting. Sitting there shouting 'ban the bomb', looking like a gypsy, the wild red hair tangled around her pretty little face.

The police started carting bodies away and I lost my head. I raced in, scooped up Jeannie, and carried her screaming into my building. She'd given me hell right there and she hadn't stopped since. I was instant mush inside and I loved her down to my bones.

'I don't want you to do this any more,' she said. 'I liked it better when you were just a guard.'

'Funny thing, Jeannie. I feel the same way.'

She perked right up. 'Then you'll leave?'

I dragged at my fag and swallowed tea. Jeannie's eager look began to fade and danger crept into her face. I found a fast response.

'I have to find out how.'

'How? What do you mean how? Can't you just hand in your notice?'

'It's not that simple.'

The thick red brows lowered. 'It better be.'

I pushed up in the bed, nearly spilling my tea. I shoved the cup on the bedside table.

'Look, Jeannie, if I could just walk away, I'd do it like a shot. Do you think it's fun ending up like this?'

She shuddered, reaching out. 'Who did it?'

I evaded her grasp and swung my legs off the bed.

'You know I can't tell you.'

'I hate all that hush-hush stuff. It's like a lousy B-movie or something.'

Too right. But she gave me a way to smooth things.

'It's like your contracts, lover. You can't leave a show once you sign.'

'Yes, but that's a matter of weeks. Months at most. What, did you sign up for life?'

For death more like. Or a short life, if I didn't get out fast. I shut my mouth on that one.

'I have to check it out.'

Jeannie's pout turned down. 'You mean you have to go and beg Lord Smartass to let you go.'

It happened to be the exact truth, but I didn't like hearing her say it.

'I owe him, Jeannie. He's been like a father to me.'

'Some father. Didn't send you off to Eton like his real son did he? Instead he sent you out to get killed.'

'That was an accident. It wasn't his fault.'

'He got you into it.'

'Yeah, and if anyone can get me out, he can.'

Jeannie's eyes went wide on me and I knew I'd said too much. Time to turn the game. I made like I couldn't keep my hands off her until she was too soft and distracted to think about my future. We didn't talk again until we were soaking in the bath together and I kept it light.

'What are you in, lover?'

Jeannie lit up. 'Got a cameo.' She named a West End hit that had been running for some years. 'Only a few lines, but I'm understudy too.'

'Do I need to break somebody's leg?'

Jeannie grinned. 'A good soaking in the rain should do it for a couple of nights. They'd bring in another name if it was that bad.'

'Consider it done.'

Jeannie was laughing, but she threw the sponge at me that she'd used to soap my wounds, in that gentle way only a woman who cares can handle. I felt more like a prince than the Saudi who'd finally got me out of the holding centre.

After the first time, he'd taken me out a couple of times. Swimming in the Red Sea, which was soothing to the bruising and the mashed brain both. Sea air and freedom was a heady mix, but the restaurant food sat heavy on my shaky digestive system as I wondered if I was going back to prison. Black-eyed Susan had vanished off my radar and no one was bothering to interrogate me. But I was still inside, though my quarters improved almost daily, presumably due to the prince. I guessed they were waiting for the worst of the damage to fade before letting me go.

Now I was home on recovery time and I meant to use it to find the exit door.

Jeannie had got herself up in some of that gypsy style Indian gear she and her actor friends were into, ready for the shops. I gave her some of the cash I'd been handed and she demanded more.

'Got to build you up, Richard. You're stick thin.'

I counted out more bills from the fat wad and caught her staring at it with a look I read without too much trouble. The thing with having an actress for a wife is you get the whole package. They were all the same, the ones I'd met. Extrovert. Let it all hang out. They train it into them at drama school. Where I'd been bludgeoned into holding back, Jeannie never hid what she felt or thought, though she'd learned when to shut up about it.

'Paid leave,' I told her, waving the wad of notes.

Jeannie was delighted. 'How long?'

I told her and she threw her arms round me.

'You mean I've got you for a whole three months?'

She bought wine and cakes to celebrate, and made me promise to bus into the West End and pick her up after she finished at the theatre. She was halfway out the door when she dropped the bomb.

'Shit, I nearly forgot to ask. Who's Charley?'

All the way down on the train I thought about nothing else. Charley was alive. The kick it gave me was almost better than my reunion with Jeannie and I could hardly wait for him to pitch up again. Operatives don't have contact except via Control. Charley didn't know my address. I didn't remember telling him about Jeannie, but he'd turned up at the theatre one night.

'Tell her I'm a friend of Dick - sorry, I meant Richard.'

The stage doorkeeper had refused to give out Jeannie's address, and I thanked Christ these people had rules. Not that I didn't want to see Charley. I was burning to see him. But I went cold when I thought of all the people that could have been asking for my wife. Mr Denman for one.

Denman had told me when Lord C would be at home. Tantamount to telling me I'd better present myself then and at no other time. I both admired and respected Lord C, but Denman, that slimy ass creeper, I hated with a passion. He never let me forget I was a charity case Yid.

Small town Sussex didn't like me or my family. They didn't like Jews, and I reckon they didn't much care for the criminal fraternity that came with a couple of my uncles. I never figured out if Gran was involved or not, but she knew people. Politicians I think she worked for once, and odd names from entertainment, some of them mixed up in intelligence. Visitors came and went, and some of the names only made sense when I moved into Calveley House.

How I ended up in Grammar school was a mystery known only to Gran. I was thirteen when she died and the aunts and uncles kicked me out of the house so they could sell it. The head must've taken pity on me. Next thing I knew he'd arranged for me to work for Lord C after school and weekends. Lord C was patron of the school and lived a short bike ride away. By the time I was fifteen, I was parked in a wing of Calveley House, not quite a member of the family, but accepted as if I belonged. Except by Denman, whose butlering kept me distanced and out of the stupid idea I'd been adopted.

Lord C bought my ticket into the agency. Took some persuasion. I had other ideas but Denman shopped me. When I mentioned joining the US army and going to Vietnam so I could get on the citizenship program, Lord C cut in fast.

'If you want to do something for your country, Richard, there's a better way.'

I thought I was going into security. Security guard services was a passport to running my own company, until I went up for the training and twigged on the real deal. The dosh was good and I had Jeannie to think of, so I reckoned what the heck. I didn't know it would be hell on wheels, steel fences and a boot in the face.

And now there was Charley, all six feet of him still intact and looking for me outside of the Firm. It didn't smell right and if we were caught fraternising, watch out, Dick Frame. I ought to be shaking, but elation gripped me.

How had he done it? The moron had looked like a suicide nut. Now I questioned if it hadn't been a plan. I was on fire to know why Charley was looking for me and Jeannie had nothing. She hadn't even seen him.

'Then how do you know what he looks like?'

The description she'd given told me he'd recovered a bit.

'I asked Joe.'

The stage doorkeeper had a good eye for faces.

'Well, tell him if Charley asks again, you want to see him.'

Jeannie eyed me with suspicion. 'Why do I?'

'So you can give him this address.'

'Was he with you?'

I sidestepped the question. 'You'll be late, lover.'

That was enough to send Jeannie racing for the bus. She was the first woman I'd ever met who was never late for anything. Actors can't be late, Jeannie says. You're liable to get the elbow if you miss curtain up.

I knew Charley would have the sense to call when Jeannie was out of the way, so she wouldn't get to meet him past the necessary hello just to get him to the flat. No using the phone. The damn thing was unlikely to be clean and a juicy recording down at the Firm was the last thing we needed.

He didn't show before Denman gave me the go-ahead. I tried to switch to what I needed to say to Lord C, but I kept thinking about Charley. Not just how come he was walking around. But how come he was after me. I couldn't get the sneaking hope out of my gut that his mind was jumping with mine and he was looking for an ally.

'Good to see you, Richard.'

We shook hands. I'd put on formal wear because it's what Lord C liked. I waited to see if he would comment on my mess of a face as there was little to see under the suit. Unless he'd noticed my limp. I could no longer walk straight and it seemed to me like Black-Eyed Susan's minions had broken a couple of bones in their enthusiastic engagement with my feet. They'd healed but set wrong.

'Coffee?'

He waved towards the tray Denman was setting down. In the old days, I would have got up and poured it myself, but I wasn't about to take liberties with the butler around. I accepted the offer and waited, mentally drumming my fingers. I wasn't going to speak my piece with Denman in the room.

Lord C kept up a flow of general chitchat about the state of the house and grounds and the latest from the children from both marriages. I was only close to the two younger children Lucy and Charles, two and four years younger than me respectively.

I heard less than half of it. My heart got tangled up with my vocal chords as the moment of truth came closer. I'd meant to rehearse what to say, but with Charley on my mind I hadn't remembered.

The coffee was too sweet. I'd got used to doing without sugar in Saudi, but Mr Denman had chucked four lumps in because that's what I used to take when I was living here. Much to his disgust. I sipped at it, nodding from time to time in hopes of convincing my host I was paying attention.

'What's the trouble, Richard, my boy?'

I jumped, nearly spilling my coffee. Glancing round, I discovered Denman had finally quit the big room Lord C used for a study. We were sitting in the wide alcove which overlooked the front gardens and driveway. I'd never got used to the sumptuous sofas and the mahogany surrounds. Always felt out of place. If I had money, I'd have made a cosier job of it. I cleared my throat.

'Thanks for taking time to see me, my lord.'

'Always welcome, Richard, you know that.'

Smooth bastard. Knew just how to hone in on the obligation. He never once told me direct that I owed him. But it was in every utterance, every nuance and I rode shotgun with him on the guilt.

He asked nothing about the job because of course he already knew. Probably on his say-so the powers-that-be left me in that hellhole for so long. But he'd pretend to his grave he knew zilch. The thought jerked me into speech.

'My lord, I don't think I'm cut out for this type of work.'

His brows rose. They were bushy and had a tendency to bristle. In my teens I'd had to fight off an urge to go at them with a toothbrush.

'You don't?'

It was mildly said, but I heard the edge beneath and it hardened me.

'No, my lord. It's not my style of thing.'

For a moment Lord C said nothing. He leaned back in his chair so that the good living paunch showed more and his gaze went off me towards the windows. I could see he wasn't looking out. He had that kind of glaze that says he was staring at nothing while his mind worked. I'd noticed it before. Working out how to deal with this?

Now it was said, my guts quietened down a bit. I thought of Jeannie's face when I told her what was in my mind and I determined to hold my position no matter what.

When Lord C turned back to me, he was wearing his expression of benevolence. It had fooled me to begin with. I thought it was kindness and meant support. It did, but on his terms. I braced. He was a clever bastard and he'd tricked me before.

'You do know this is only a prelude, Richard.'

To what? I waited. No guessing games for Dick, thank you, my lord.

'There will be the management role at the end of it. I've promised to set you up in security and I'll keep my word.'

He'd set me up all right. For security read secret. Security service, secret service. Big difference. I opened up.

'I thought you meant like Securicor, my lord.'

He did surprise very well. 'Oh, I did, Richard. That's exactly what I meant. Just like Securicor.'

He laughed in a way that shot me back in a split to my interviews with Black-Eyed Susan. I went cold inside and cursed my grandmother for dying when she did.

'Then can I switch over now, my lord?'

Lord C set down his cup and saucer on a nearby table and leaned in towards me. Another of his poses. Confidential, reassuring.

'Experience, Richard, is everything. You'll make a far better manager in the business when you've a few more assignments to your credit. Don't you think your operatives will trust you more if they know you've 'pushed it' yourself?'

Yeah, if I live that long. But I said nothing, just nodding vaguely.

He got up and moved towards the big old-fashioned desk in the centre of the room. Honour-bound, I stood too and followed a little way in. He went to his side of the desk, sat down and unlocked a drawer. Glancing up, he waved at the chair opposite.

'Sit down, Richard. I want to show you something.'

He dug some papers out of the drawer, shoved it closed and laid them on the desk. But he didn't look at them for the moment. Instead, he folded his hands together on the desk and leaned a little towards me. This time, he chose the nice uncle expression. If he'd known my uncles, he'd have known I could see through it.

'You've had a rough ride, my boy, I know that.'

Lately? Or was he talking about my childhood? He was apt to refer to it when it suited him. I wasn't going to deny it.

'Yes, my lord. Very rough.'

Lord C nodded, the steel keen gaze narrowing with sympathy. I didn't believe in it for a second. I'd been had too often.

'It's understandable you would be dismayed. But you're an intelligent young man, Richard, and I think you can do better for yourself than the mundane type of Securicor world. But you need experience of a particular kind if you're going into private investigation.'

I was totally thrown.

'Private investigation? But you never said...'

I faded out. Lord C didn't speak, just watched me as it sunk in. I'd swear this was the first he'd thought of such a thing if it didn't explain why he'd bundled me into the Firm. Shock tactics? But what if he left me stewing for years?

'How long, my lord? Before I could get into that line of business, I mean.'

He smiled. 'That's probably up to you, Richard.'

The hell it was. Did I dare call his bluff? I reckoned I had nothing to lose. If I didn't say now, I probably wouldn't get the chance again.

'Why couldn't it be now, my lord?'

This time he didn't bother hiding his hand.

'On mere weeks? On one assignment? Come, come, Richard. If you were running the show, would you take on an operative with so little experience?'

I wouldn't, of course. Dumb-arsed question. As if I hadn't known the answer.

Lord C turned his attention to the papers he'd fished out of the drawer. It was obvious he thought he'd won. I could feel a stirring of rebellion bubbling away somewhere inside, but I kept quiet, telling myself I didn't have to do what he wanted. I could walk away. All right, I'd lose the pay-off, but what the hell? Other guys found their own way. Why not me?

'This is the deed for a house, Richard.'

I shot back to attention. 'My lord?'

'You're a married man, my boy. You can't keep a wife in a rented flat.'

Charley met me in a dingy café uptown. He wouldn't take my address though Jeannie had written it down for him, instead handing her a slip of paper with a date, time and place. He'd smiled at Jeannie, told her Dick was a lucky beggar and left.

All the way in the tube I was on edge. Lord C had turned me inside out and I didn't know any more which way was up. I didn't have to ask myself why he'd bought me a house. When I was seventeen and itching to spread my wings my way, he'd bribed me with a mini. Last time it was a visit to a gent's suiting establishment in Jermyn Street. This time he didn't stop with the house. Along with the deeds, he handed me a card.

'Go to my man in Harley Street, Richard. He'll fix you up. I'll get Denman to tell him to expect you.'

I was glad of the chance to get checked out and fix the crap my body had been through in Saudi. But the house was something else. I knew without being told it would come fully furnished and I knew I'd hate it. The décor would be suffocating and I'd never feel at home. My only hope was Jeannie. I thought she'd be over the moon, but I guessed she'd change everything to suit the crazy gypsy style she chose to live in. That wasn't my taste either, but better than the stuffy formality of the world of Lord C.

Jeannie wasn't over the moon. I should have remembered she'd never approved of Lord C. He'd never asked to meet her, and Jeannie said it was because she was a theatrical.

'People like him think we're vagabonds.'

The news made those eyes spark lightning.

'Why has he bought you a house?'

'Calm down, lover. He's always looked after me.'

'Who wants his damn charity?' The eyes narrowed with suspicion. 'He's shafted you again, hasn't he? He won't let you out of the horrible shit he's stuck you into.'

Sometimes I wished I didn't have a wife with a mind like a ferret. I took refuge in Lord C's excuse.

'He wants me to get more experience.'

Jeannie looked me up and down. 'How many bruises does it take to get this precious experience?'

'It won't be for long.'

'No, because you'll be bloody dead.'

Suddenly Jeannie flung herself on me, sobbing like a baby.

'Get out, Richard, please! Please, please get out!'

I couldn't deal with it. I didn't know how. No one ever taught me the basics. I'd never seen close up an example of how you did relationships. I was flying blind the whole time and Jeannie's heart was breaking.

Next day she came home with Charley's bit of paper. She hadn't forgiven me, I could tell, though I'd told her don't worry. I'd told her it'll be okay, knowing it wouldn't. She didn't say anything when she gave me the message, but her eyes said it all. I knew haunted when I saw it. Impulse kicked in.

'Charley will help me, lover. Charley knows the score.'

Jeannie didn't ask if that meant I'd changed my mind. She just nodded and went off to the kitchen to make the late night snack she needed after performance. We made love and she snuggled. But I could feel her distance and I couldn't take it.

'Fuck Lord C, okay? Fuck him.'

Jeannie slept in my arms and I pinned my hopes on Charley.

He'd put back flesh but his cheeks were still hollow and hell was still sitting in the brown pools of his eyes. He grinned at me and the old mockery lingered in his voice.

'Are you crazy, Dick? You're not supposed to meet another operative outside of instructions.'

My chest warmed up. 'I'm not here. And you're a ghost.'

The giggle I'd heard in my dreams sounded.

'A skeleton with skin attached.'

I looked him over. 'You're more or less in one piece. How come? I thought they dumped you.'

Charley's mouth twitched. 'They did. Right in the Embassy forecourt.'

It hit me straight off. Last thing the Saudis needed was an MI man dying on their patch. Better to stick him where he'd either get rescued or perish on what amounted to British soil.

'I hope you bled all over that lousy prick who pitched us into that mess.'

Charley's eyebrows shot up into the flop of hair on his forehead.

'I like your thinking, Amateur.'

I took the plunge.

'I think I'm thinking what you're thinking, Charley, or we wouldn't be here.'

'When did you get to be such a smart arse?'

'You taught me, moron.'

Then we were both laughing, doubled over the table like a couple of adolescent schoolgirls. When we sobered, Charley gripped my hand.

'Pact, Dick?'

'Pact.'

He leaned back in his seat and lifted the coffee cup to his lips, eyeing me over the rim. I guessed what was coming.

'How, right?'

Charley nodded. 'How is right.'

Remembering, I let out a sigh. Then I told him about my discussion with Lord C. He agreed it looked dicey. But he cocked an eyebrow.

'Is that what you want? The gumshoe game?'

'Dunno.' Gloom descended on me. I pushed for change. 'You?'

Charley showed his teeth and his eyes gathered an echo of amusement.

'Can't you guess? I want an island in the goddamn sun where the beer and women are free and easy.'

Yes, the life of Riley was Charley's style. On the surface. I didn't know him all that well but I knew him better than that.

'You'd get bored.'

'I'll take bored big time if I know my arse isn't on the line.'

The bitter note got to me.

'How the heck did you get into this, Charley?'

He looked sour. 'Same way anyone does. No family. Reckless. Nobody to miss me. Then some jerk caught me using my brains instead of my dick.'

I got it. He'd been too clever, whatever he'd been doing before. The Firm have eyes and ears out everywhere on the lookout for recruits. Lord C told me that once. Charley was likely in the armed services. I didn't ask. Most of the men at the Crazy House had come through the military. Ideal fodder for the life we'd been let in for.

But Charley had a streak of rebellion or he wouldn't have kicked himself down the road to perdition. Indoctrination hadn't set in hard enough. You can't be in this game and human both. I'd learned that already. I chose human.

'So what do we do?'

Charley shrugged. 'Get dumb and dangerous enough so they don't want you but don't need to clean you away.'

My heart sank. A difficult balance to find. 'I thought we did that already.'

'We cocked up. We weren't that dumb.'

'What's the difference?'

A devilish smile split Charley's face.

'That's what we have to find out.'

Chapter Five

Hours of driving through narrow winding roads rapidly moved up my list of personal hells. But it didn't overtake the penalty of working with Charley Parnarti, who was showing his less endearing side.

'Take over for a bit, will you?'

'Nah.'

'Why not, you selfish prick?'

'Seniority,' said Charley, adding before I could speak my mind, 'Anyway, I can't drive. Got cramp in my left leg.'

I fumed in silence. If bullshit was a pound a ton the guy would be a millionaire. To tell true, Charley had been narking me from the off and I was almost ready to stuff his pact where it would do most good.

The call for the new job had put my guts in overdrive. I'd just about started feeling human again after weeks of Jeannie's tender care and the ministrations of Lord C's Harley Street quack. My feet would need an operation to fix fully, and he told me I had the body of a man twice my age due to the beatings, but physio had done a treat for the rest. Then I got recalled to training.

After I'd mastered my fifth new firearm it dawned on me there was method in the madness, signalling exactly the kind of job I was anxious to avoid. Was this Lord C's punishment for daring to ask for an out? I wouldn't put it past the bastard to shove me into the worst scenario the Firm had going.

By the time my Motorola Minitor pager bleeped the summons, I was in near as many knots as Saudi had tied. Cursing, I hit a phone box and dialled the number.

'This whisky has a tang to it,' I told security, adding, 'And my car is rusty.'

I slammed the receiver back in its cradle and waited, churning up inside. The instant it rang, I grabbed it up.

'1700 hours,' said the voice at the other end. '123 Pall Mall. Pack a bag for city and country tourism. You're for the dark stuff. Ask for Mr White.'

That was it. The phone clicked off and I was left with the dial tone in my ear. I stood there for a second, absorbing the shock.

The 'dark stuff' meant bloody Ireland, for shit's sake. Like asking for a bullet in the head. Right now, with the IRA and Brit troops at each other's throats, it was exactly the place to avoid. 'City and country tourism' told me I'd have to make like city workers and country bumpkins. In other words, we'd be in the thick of it. The rest - time, address and contact - was already tucked in the back of my memory. We'd done plenty of practice instilling data for instant recall at the Crazy House.

I had about three hours and Jeannie would still be home. She'd quietened down once I told her Charley and me were pledged to get out. She'd even agreed to look over the house Lord C had bought for me.

'Gotta look willing, lover. Won't hurt to check it out.'

We hit suburbia to find the place, and my expectations couldn't have been more wrong. A neat terraced joint in a quiet cul-de-sac and nothing in it bar the fittings. Jeannie had started out mulish, but she ended full of plans like a regular little homemaker.

'I hate to admit it, Richard, but it's perfect.'

She didn't even mind the railway line out the back. Said it made her feel at home. I gave her the keys and told her to do what the heck she liked.

'But we'll keep the flat. Don't want you coming home from the theatre all the way back here at night.'

Especially when she was on her own, but I kept that bit to myself, along with the real reason. If things went the way I wanted, I might have to give the house back. If it all went ape-shit, the place wouldn't be part of my estate.

When I got home after the call, Jeannie took one look at my face and hers fell ten feet.

'Shit. You're going, aren't you?'

I wanted to make light of it but I was too sick about the whole thing.

'Yeah. Gotta pack.'

Jeannie followed me to the bedroom and watched as I shoved the basics into a holdall and dug out boots and a waterproof jacket. I wasn't paying too much attention to my needs. Probably have to buy stuff out there, new or second-hand. 'Always dress and smell local' was the Crazy House dictum. I'd have plenty from the Firm to cover expenses, and if I ran out, I'd been told to take it from anywhere I could. Lack of resources wouldn't cut it as an excuse for not doing the job.

I could see Jeannie trying not to ask where I was going, her eyes big with dread. Instead she did the wifey bit.

'Make sure you eat properly. I don't want you coming back a skeleton again.'

I dragged up a grin and slapped my stomach. 'No chance. You been stuffing me like a turkey for Christmas, lover.'

Jeannie's lashes trembled and her eyes gleamed water. But my Jeannie was a trooper. She fought down the tears and started to bustle me.

'Come on, you don't want to be late. And bloody take care. If you get yourself shot, you'll have me to reckon with.'

'Yeah, I know, scary bitch.'

She laughed then and my heart twisted. Her kiss goodbye stayed with me until I hopped the bus on the corner. And then all I could think about was the upcoming brief and I wasn't any too hopeful.

My instincts proved out. If it hadn't been for getting caught and the aftermath, the Saudi operation was a picnic in comparison.

Charley was already in evidence and I could see the way his mind was working as he eyed up Blondie. He'd shag the boss in a whisper, if he wasn't already. The way Blondie smiled at him, it looked like a done deal. She had no smile for me. Maybe she hated Lord C. Or maybe she could feel the glare under the neutral mask my face had assumed on auto.

'Have either of you heard of the Smallwood brothers?'

I shrugged but Charley looked like he had a clue.

'That pair of northern monkeys? Couple of crooks.'

'They're our crooks,' said Blondie.

'And the IRA's too,' put in the suit who'd been introduced from Special Branch.

Double agents then. The assignment was already lousy and it began to look as full of worms as a fisherman's knapsack.

'They've overstepped the mark too many times,' interrupted a tall rake of a man in a pinstripe suit. I recognised him from the evening news. Peter Short, Right Honourable MP and cabinet minister. Unlike a minister to dirty his hands in operational briefings like this. He must have some personal interest. I didn't ask.

'We're going to use them up,' said Blondie.

Charley's brown liquids swept over her and for once there was no lust. He knew as well as I did what that meant. Whatever they'd fixed for us to do, the crooks would end compromised and eliminated. Not by us. We'd be the fall guys who had to work with them and fix up the sting. If they didn't fix us first.

The plan stank even more than if we'd been going to Belfast, but it was typical work for the Firm. Driving a wedge between two parties was fun and games to MI6, its purpose in this case being to smash the credibility of the IRA. Make it look like they reneged on an agreement with the Republic of Ireland not to commit crimes there, and thereby create distrust.

We got a history lesson on Smallwood Bros, appropriate passports to pass muster in Eire, driving licences, two thousand quid and a vehicle that on the surface made us look like ordinary businessmen.

Blondie waved us out the tradesmen's entrance to 123 Pall Mall and we headed off to a pharmacy to get our scripts from the tame doc for wake-up pills. They were officially legal, but had to be plugged somewhere in the car.

The other plug was coded telephone numbers in case our memories failed. These were stuffed in rubber and shoved where the monkey put the nuts. I was quick to pass on that one.

'You can take the plug, Charley. You'll probably enjoy it.'

'As long as you put it in for me.'

He laughed, but I reckon it's why he let me do all the driving as we headed for Fishguard to catch the ferry. We'd checked the vehicle for a tracker and found nothing, but that didn't stop me keeping an eye out for anomalies in any traffic coming up behind. I felt like I was on red alert the whole time and was knackered and craving wake-up pills well before we finally made it to the coast.

Predictably, the plain clothes police stopped us as we were ready to drive onto the ferry. They ought to have been tipped off to leave us alone, but the Specials and the Firm were vicious rivals and never lost a chance to screw each other if they could.

Not that the bastards would nail us. I had the cash in my jocks while Charley had put paid to the codes and scripts for more amphetamines before we reached the port. It was a cinch they wouldn't find the stash we already had. Charley had a knack with cars and he'd shoved the pills in a remote section of door and sprayed sealing foam behind.

While the search was ongoing, Charley shot off his mouth as usual.

'This is what Anglo-Irish relations have come to, is it, harassing honest British citizens? Why don't you try to catch some real criminals?'

I gave him the glare and nudge to shut him up, but Charley never knew when. He kept up a running commentary all through the search. When the Specials finally let us go, looking disappointed, I put in my request for his balls.

'I'm going to kick the shit out of you if you don't knock off messing around.'

Charley wasn't fazed. 'Relax, Runt. Talking throws their attention off.'

'Yeah, and there's bells on my leg.'

'Let's go chat up the best-looking women.'

Why did I bother? A law to himself was Charley. He was off without waiting for me, heading for the bar. When I caught up, I found he'd already sussed a target and had started with the charm and chat-up lines. I cased the area on auto but didn't recognise anyone, so I left him to it and went to find the men's loo. Even if I'd been in the mood, I couldn't have joined in because the crossing was choppy enough to make my stomach curl, threatening to rid itself of the last meal I'd had when we stopped in Bristol.

I dug Charley out when we were about to arrive. The ferry dumped us in the Republic at Rosslare, and though we'd no reason to be jumpy yet, I hit counter surveillance mode the instant we docked. I could feel my neck prickle as I scanned every person I could see from hair to shoes. Any little detail seen twice would trigger an alarm. I'd not been in the game long, but the habit was already ingrained. My antennae were ten times more active than they'd been in Saudi.

Who knew where word of our activities might've reached? MI6 was as traitor ridden as Special Branch. For all we knew, informers on either side had shopped us to the Smallwoods or the IRA or both.

Worse, we might be the target for the Firm's set-up rather than the Smallwood brothers. It was just the kind of elaborate scheme they'd use to be rid of us. Except I couldn't really believe Lord C would condone it after putting so much effort into his protégé. But this might just be my test run, and here I was planning to make good on a pact with Charley to screw up big time. Was I off my head or what?

Along with constant watchful glances in the rear view mirror, uncertainty kept me from enjoying the drive up the picturesque coastline of the Irish Sea towards Dublin. Charley only made me the more sore by falling asleep and snoring. I found a pit stop at the halfway point and took pleasure in breaking into his dreams.

'Shake a leg, Charley. Food time.'

He yawned and sat up. 'Already?'

'Yeah, and you'd better drop some pills. That's the last nap you're getting for a while.'

Charley didn't argue. We were due to drive to Cork after we'd met our contact in Dublin. For a wonder, he even offered to drive the rest of the way so I could sleep and pick up a pill as we neared destination.

That was the thing with Charley. Just as you ticked him off on your hate mail list, he turned the tables on you and made it all go away.

It took a while to find the phone box opposite a Garda station. We made the call to the contact and a woman's voice said to rendezvous at a pub in Terenure Road North at 1200 hours. We were early, so more hanging around, but what was new?

This time around Charley was the relaxed one while I chewed my nails. Unless he was faking it. I didn't think so. On the surface he was the same old hail-fellow-well-met joker, and I couldn't feel the angst beneath it that had sent him to hell in Saudi. Should have been glad for him but it made me sour.

'Don't know what you've got to be so happy about.'

Charley grinned. 'Prospects, Dick. I've got me a future planned.'

I couldn't let this pass. 'Yeah, if we get out of this with our heads intact.'

'Are you kidding? Working with northern monkeys and Irish slags? Bound to be a cock-up.'

'But that doesn't let us out.'

'It will, Runt, it will.'

'How come you're so confident all of a sudden? Know something I don't?'

Charley eyed me sideways.

'You're strung up like a fiddle, Dick. Take it easy.'

I'd have said something cutting if I could have thought of anything. And if the mick we were waiting for hadn't walked in right then.

He came straight up to us, a good-looking bloke, around forty with a twinkle in his eye.

'What are you drinking, boys? Are you on the pink gin?'

Charley's eyebrows did a spider imitation.

'How did you recognise us? Was it the way we walk? How do you know we're not a couple of fags on a short break from the wife and kiddies?'

'You mean you're not?'

Charley gave him the grin. He knew as well as I did that the mick and his mates watched us arrive, park up and walk into the pub. I cut in with the password.

'If I may interrupt, how is Shirley?'

The mick looked at me for the first time, and I braced as the shrewd eyes appraised me. If this was Charley's idea of an Irish slag, he was in for a surprise.

'Busting my balls as usual.' The mick held out a hand. 'Patrick O'Leary, but you can call me Paddy.'

I shook the hand, throwing a glance at Charley who returned it with a cool look, like I was being too friendly. Paddy's glance went back to him.

'How's that cow, Blondie?'

'Great, mate. Best shag I've had this week.'

Paddy roared and I wanted to kick Charley's arse. I kept my trap shut and Paddy went off to get the drinks. Fruit juice for me and Charley because of the pills. Paddy was on the Guinness and I chafed while he and Charley swapped jokes like old friends.

Under the banter I could tell Charley was as leery as me, but the mick had charm and more bullshit than Charley himself.

I endured until we finally got down to business.

'Just follow me, boys.'

We headed out of the pub, even Charley on alert at these words. To be asked to follow anyone, especially in the dark country in these uncertain times, was enough to give me a dose of the squirts. Being captured by micks was no way to die for man or beast.

Charley looked relaxed but I knew his mind and every sinew of his body would be working overtime like mine. For all we knew, as we headed for the car park, we might as well have been riding in a tumbrel.

No sign of other bodies, which was a relief because we weren't tooled up yet. The car was clean and so were we, or we'd never have got into the country.

Paddy made for an old, beat up Opel Rekord station-wagon which looked like it had just come off the farm. A collie's snout was sticking out a crack in the rear window. It looked so normal, I relaxed a little - was that good?

We politely rejected an offer for one of us to ride with Paddy. Better together and in our own vehicle. We followed to the Temple Bar hotel and parked. Paddy got out slow, but Charley and I could've cut seconds off the world record. Sitting ducks in a car in that location, we didn't aim to be. We moved away from Paddy, ready for anything. So far nothing was going down, but my heart was doing a drum roll in my throat.

'Come on, boys, let's have a drink.'

I glanced at the hotel, but Paddy took off down a side road and we followed, suitably wary of outside action, along a block to a row of large terrace houses in Adair Lane.

At Number 23, Paddy rang the door bell. It opened to reveal a brunette, a looker of foreign origin. Seemed about in her twenties, I thought, but I was less keen when I noticed she was holding a pistol at her side.

Chapter Six

Charley, just as I could have predicted, lit up fast, moving in ahead of Paddy. I checked the street before I went in after them. Empty. The lounge was surprisingly upbeat with soft music playing and the wafting smell of cooking. My nose caught a whiff of spices, and I looked again at the female operative, who was ogling Charley.

'My name is Samira.'

Charley nodded at the pistol, a little Italian job - Galesia Brescia 635, .25 calibre, if my recent upgrade on weapons told me true. Sleek looks, but that model never met a full magazine it liked.

'Isn't that a little rude?'

Samira gave him a look any man would recognise and tucked the pistol into the back waistband of her jeans. I reckoned she was from anywhere but Dublin, which mattered zilch to Charley, whose desire was palpable. We'd been there ten seconds and already I felt like an intruder. The atmosphere was electric and I found myself waiting for shit to break out.

Paddy seemed entertained, while I was deciding Charley needed to be locked up for the good of the community. Or mine anyway. I broke the spell.

'Paddy, can we get down to business?'

'Just what I was thinking,' said Charley, widening his eyes so that we all knew exactly what he was thinking.

'You English fuckers never relax,' said Paddy.

But he led the way out of the living room and I followed. We were going down some cellar steps by the time I realised Charley wasn't with us. It didn't take much imagination to work out why.

The cellar was stacked out with wine and brandy which probably hadn't paid duty at any port.

'Trade is brisk eh Paddy?'

Paddy laughed. 'Ah, you know how it is. The worse it gets, the better it gets for us. Would you be helping me shift this?'

Together we moved a wine rack to one side, exposing a trap door. Paddy heaved it up and below was a double door to something like a pit for a vehicle bay. The sight of the folding doors threw my reflexes into gear and I kept well back while Paddy hauled on the handles. To my fraught mind, anything might spring. If I had to I could disarm or even take out the older man in seconds. I might even enjoy it, though what the Firm would say to overcooking the game was something else.

The doors came up and Paddy's face looked like a kid opening his Christmas presents.

'Feast your bastard English eyes, son.'

Keeping one eye on Paddy, I looked down into the pit. One glance told me I was about to make acquaintance with an arms cache sufficient to supply a platoon.

'Take this, will you?'

I seized one half of the metal doors while Paddy lowered the one on his side. I did likewise and Paddy eased down into the pit. Next thing I knew, he was handing up toys like he was Santa Claus. My recent training kicked in as I took the first one and checked it out. An AK47 with bayonet attached.

'Chinese?'

'Type 56 copy of a Kalashnikov 7.62mm,' announced Paddy.

To my mind it was a little over oiled, but pristine otherwise. Next up was a Winchester pump action shotgun, sawn off at both stock and barrel, but I could see some jerk had been overenthusiastic.

'It'll take an hour to degrease this bastard, Paddy.'

'British are never happy,' he mumbled, handing up another AK47.

Time to put him straight.

'Our brief is to help some morons go over the counter of a country bank, not start a bleeding war. You do know, Paddy, what the job is, I take it? Just let me have two older revolvers and two sawn-offs for our friends in Cork. And a couple of automatics for me and lover boy up there.'

Paddy didn't appreciate my candour.

'Do you know how much trouble it took to get this lot sorted? And you're not even grateful, you shite English prick.'

'I'll be happy to check out your whole toy store another time, Paddy. Right now I just want to get tooled up.'

He grumbled some more, but found the rest of what I wanted without a fight. I picked Walther PPKs with two boxes of shells for myself and Charley, and we added ammo for the other pieces, plus gun oil and some fresh leather cloths.

'Does this arsenal of yours have any stun grenades and smoke bombs, Paddy?'

'Not in this lot. But I'll bring them down south for you before things kick off with the brothers.'

We closed up the stash doors and moved the wine rack back into place. I loaded my PPK and took off the safety. I wasn't that relaxed. Who the heck knew what was going down upstairs while we were gun-hunting down under?

Not wanting to show Paddy my back more than necessary, I encouraged him to go upstairs ahead of me. Soon as we hit the lounge, we discovered something had gone down. Samira, to be exact. Charley, on the other hand, was well up. Like my PPK, he was cocked in the fire position.

To my relief - never was a comfortable guest at this kind of party - Paddy led me through to the dining room and shut the door on all this free love. Charley would have been right at home in a hippie commune.

'Where's the girl from?' I asked, laying the armoury down on the table.

'Iranian Jewess. She was working for our Yid friends in Iran and the shit hit the fan. The Yid got her and family out and now she's on loan to the company. Working off a debt.'

The info didn't do anything to lessen the growing prickle that told me things were not as they seemed.

'When's the off, Paddy? Aren't the brothers waiting for us down in Cork?'

'They'll keep.'

This didn't fit with the brief.

'London gave us the impression this job was ready to go.'

Paddy laughed. 'According to that stinking crew, everything is ready to go. Have a drink, son. You never know when it will be your last.'

Guaranteed to make me feel totally confident, I didn't think. I pushed it.

'How are we supposed to make contact?'

'All will come to light in a few days.'

'A few days?'

By now I was chafing big time. I'd envisaged being in and right out again in a few days. The longer we were kept hanging around where anyone could jump us, the worse my future was looking.

'Relax, son,' said Paddy, sounding so like Charley I began to feel like thumping him good and hard. 'You're in one of the best cities in the world for a party.'

The veins in my wrist were doing a scintillating dance like a river of cars moving on a night time highway. I felt sick and immediately regretted closing my eyes as a million dayglo dots and stars patterned across the inside of my eyelids. Intensely beautiful, but my head was tripping so much I couldn't appreciate it.

I tried to focus, kicking my brain into a semblance of memory. What the heck had happened escaped me. I had a vague picture of downing a strange drink and could hear an echo of Paddy's voice.

'It's the way the Mexicans do it, son.'

It was piecing together. Salt on the hand. Pinch in the mouth. Suck a piece of lemon. Down the drink. Or was it the other way around?

Tequila? Yes, Tequila. Paddy was teaching me how to drink the stuff. I couldn't remember how many I'd had. But however strong the liquor, it couldn't have struck up these lighted coloured amoeba blobs plastered around me.

I could hear hazy murmurs in the background and tried to voice the question in my head.

'Did one of you bastards spike my drink?'

Silence hit, but I could feel the presence of others in the room. Who they were didn't register.

'Get some sleep,' said a voice I didn't recognise.

It struck me that if it wanted me asleep, it wasn't about to make me dead. Why anyone should want me dead was a question I couldn't answer, but I felt sure someone did. The sleep suggestion seemed good to me and I let myself fall back on the pillows.

Pillows? Then was I at least on a bed? This struck me as sound strategy. Slip me an acid tab and stick me on a bed. Safer.

The idea surfaced in full. Someone had given me LSD. Outrage swept through me, but I felt powerless to do anything about it. I could hear mumbling in the background. After a while it shifted into the rhythm of my dreams.

I was playing music but the sound kept moving up and down. I had a good memory for favourite album titles but the songs didn't make sense. I was going in circles, hunting for something, though I didn't know what, all the while becoming more and more disoriented and scared. I was going to die and I had to remember what I needed to say to God to rationalise my short life, but the words wouldn't form. Underneath me the floor was undulating and everything I looked at took on massive significance in light of the last moments of my life.

For a while there was oblivion. When awareness began to knock on the walls again, the sounds outside me formed into words I could recognise and concepts that finally made sense.

'Did you change the Brit plates?'

'All done. Made it look more beat up as well.'

'Right. Let's get them both inside.'

Both? All at once I remembered Charley. When last seen he was getting it on with the girl Samira, while I picked us a stash of armour from Paddy's arsenal.

The clarity of my thoughts astonished me. My head was busting at the seams, but there was a cold shrill vein of sharpness doing my thinking.

Hands grabbed me under the armpits and yanked. Instinct made me play sicker than I was. I let my head loll and gave out a groan, allowing the strong-arm fraternity to take my weight. It hurt to open my eyes even the slit needed to take in the action, but the rewards were worth it.

Paddy was at the door, seemingly directing operations. A couple of heavies had Charley, who looked to be in much the same state as me. The traitor Samira had her pistol trained on him. If she'd been Charley's lure, it struck me Paddy must've had forewarning about his habits and preferences. Did that mean the Firm was behind this bitching mess?

No time for more. The heavies manhandled us out and we were bundled into the back of our Toyota. I'd got a look at the plates and saw they'd been switched from British to Republic of Ireland. I slid against Charley's long form, which lay awkwardly across more than half the back seat. The doors slammed. The front doors opened and the car tamped down as the heavies got in. More slamming and the engine revved.

I stopped trying to see which way we were headed and closed my eyes. Until I was fit enough for action, no point in advertising my condition.

After a while, I felt a finger poking into my ribs. Was Charley awake?

Trying not to make too much fuss about it, I shifted my position in the seat and swivelled my head so I could see his face. Half-lifting a lid, I discovered Charley's bloodshot brown eyes looking into mine. He wiggled an eyebrow. I wiggled back. He mouthed and I read the curse on his lips. We'd been had.

I listened to the drone of the Toyota engine and the soft Irish burr of the voices in front. If we dared to whisper, would they hear us?

Charley very slowly turned his head until his lips were close to my ear. The whisper reached me through the external noise.

'Play dead and wait our chances.'

My hackles rose. Oh yeah? Hadn't thought of that one, you moron.

'Can you move?'

Like a jangling puppet probably, but I tried a motion close to a nod.

'Split second timing, Runt.'

Thanks. I needed that advice. If Charley hadn't given way to animal instinct, we wouldn't be in this condition. Pity I had no means of letting him know what I thought of him.

He didn't speak again and I shifted in a bid to throw him off, besides making myself more comfortable. It wasn't easy maintaining the pose. All kinds of discomfort surfaced in different places from keeping still in an awkward posture.

Worst was the ceaseless ache in my head and the parched mouth crying out for water. Having Charley all over me wasn't helping. I spent miles mentally raging against Blondie for lumbering me with this cock-eyed nutcase for a partner. After a while though, I remembered I'd been just as easy to hoodwink. I cursed myself for falling for the oldest trick in the book, like an innocent chick with a fancy pimp or seducer. I whiled away the next few miles cursing Paddy and his blarney instead. Where was the bastard now? And who the heck were the hoods driving our car?

Right on cue, the duo in front gave tongue and I tuned in.

'Overtake the shite, why don't you?'

'Sure I will, when the miserable shite stops weaving left and right.'

Silence for a moment. Then the first voice came on again.

'Will you look at that? Fecking farmers.' Then a shout. 'Get your fecking beast out of the road, dickhead.'

'He's got one over the eight, if you ask me.'

'Get past or we'll be here all day.'

The car revved and I felt Charley brace against me. On instinct, I did the same, putting out a surreptitious hand to grab the edge of the seat.

Our driver was obviously going for it. The other guy was swearing blue murder as the car swung wildly to one side. There was a screech of tyres, a warning yell and then a terrific bang.

Chapter Seven

I lurched sideways and couldn't have stopped the urge to save myself if my head was on fire. The car juddered to a stop, and I kept enough savvy to let my body sag where it had fallen, tangled as I was with parts of Charley's anatomy.

'Fecking shite.'

'Shut up and check on them, will you?'

I heard the driver's door open and felt the motion as the passenger turned in his seat and looked over at Charley and me.

'Still out of it.'

There was no answer. I could hear movement as the driver got out, from the sound of it already under fire from the guy in the other vehicle. I lay still, begging the second heavy to get out too. My heart thumped as I heard his door open and the car lightened in weight. The door slammed.

Neither of us moved a muscle. I could hear our second escort cut in on the acrimonious discussion going on outside. I opened my eyes.

Charley was peeping over the seats.

'For Christ's sake, they'll see you.'

'Shut up.' He looked round at me. 'Do we take them now, or make a run for it?'

We could take both of them on, no question. But why risk it? We had the advantage right now.

'Don't know about you, Charley, but I'm not at my best.'

The familiar grin dawned.

'Too right. The other bastard will keep them busy for a while. Let's go.'

I was already climbing over the seat, my guts pumped for action despite my lazy muscles which didn't want to shove me around at speed. I slid into the driving seat and punched the ignition.

It roared into life and I reached to grab the handle of the still open door beside me, pulling it shut. The heavies were busy thumping shit out of the other driver, but they turned the instant the engine fired. I didn't wait to check their reaction, but one glimpse of their stymied faces as I hit the accelerator was enough.

I swung the wheel wide and the car lurched crazily over the rough edge of the roadway. I held the speed and flung the vehicle out into the main road, my foot flat on the floor as I crunched the gears up and up again.

'Get down!'

I dived just as a bullet slammed into the back window. The car swerved violently. Adrenaline surged into my veins as I came up again to grab back control, forcing the vehicle into the centre again.

'Jesus!'

Another bullet pinged somewhere off the back wing. Then nothing.

I struggled to hold the crown of the road at seventy miles an hour. The Toyota wasn't built for speed and this was the best I could get out of the thing.

'They're commandeering the brute's Datsun,' Charley announced.

'That lumbering thing? Thank Christ. They'll never catch us in that.'

'Keep your foot down.'

'What do you think I'm doing?'

Charley wasn't paying attention. He was still checking out the situation through the rear window. Incredibly, he started to laugh.

'What's funny?'

'The Datsun won't start.'

I was cheered for the first time since I'd woken to find my brains mashed. Though the delay might only be temporary, at least it gave us a sporting chance. I kept up speed until we were so far ahead, they couldn't have caught us in anything less than an E-type Jag. I dropped to a more comfortable pace and my jangling nerves began to settle.

'Problem,' said Charley.

'Shit. What now?'

'Where are we headed?'

I thought about it. 'Cork?'

Charley spent some time scanning the side of the road for milestone markers before we could be certain the heavies had indeed been driving us to Cork. It was where we were supposed to go, but it made no sense. If the Firm was behind this, we shouldn't have been heading for the Smallwoods' lair.

My headache couldn't deal with the implications. I hit a side issue which was beginning to be urgent.

'Did those bastards bring any food or drink?'

'This is no time to be thinking about your stomach, Dick.'

But Charley hunted around the back. Finding nothing, he leaned over between the seats and opened the dash. He slammed it shut again.

'Zilch.'

'Bet they stuffed their faces with breakfast before leaving.'

The sour note caught Charley's attention as he manoeuvred his lanky frame into the front seat.

'Remind you of anything, Runt?'

'Yeah, Saudi.'

'Except we got away this time.'

'To what? Where do we go, Charley? How do we get home?'

He nodded, his eyes trained on the road ahead.

'Good question. For my money, I think we find a phone box and call up Blondie.'

Shock made me throw the car into a swerve and I earned a curse from my laconic partner.

'Are you crazy? She's got to be behind this.'

'But she won't admit that. She'll have to make like it's news and do something.'

'Yeah, get us killed outright.'

Charley shook his head.

'Nah. Doesn't smell like Blondie to me.'

If the Firm didn't set this up, who did?

'Could Paddy and the girl be working for the Provos?'

'Anything is possible,' said Charley, turning to look out the back over his shoulder. 'Do we have company?'

I checked the mirror and swore. A large black car was coming up on us fast. My pulse shot into high gear and I cased the road for a turn-off.

The scenery was exceptional but I wasn't in the mood. Ireland's green was everywhere when all I wanted was a track off this tarmac.

'It's gaining on us.'

I'd already put my foot down, but the sinking in my gut told me there was no way we could outrun the vehicle behind.

'It's a bloody Mercedes,' mourned Charley, swivelled half-round to watch.

'What I wouldn't give for Paddy's arsenal,' I said, thinking longingly of the guns I'd chosen with such care.

'I don't think they'd make a present of them, Dick.'

I swept the side of the road, looking for an opening between the trees. Any opening. But Charley's gaze shifted to me.

'Don't even think of it, Runt. We'll be taken for sure if we crash.'

I kept one eye on the rear view mirror, watching the oncoming Merc as Charley rapped out a series of terse instructions. I wasn't about to argue. As the Mercedes came up behind and shot past, I slammed on the brakes, jerked the car into reverse, shot backwards about twenty feet and then swung the Toyota sideways across the road before hitting the brakes again.

Charley and I were out of the car and hunkered down behind our improvised barrier before the Mercedes had come to a stop. Now they'd have to come for us and we'd be ready.

The sleek black car rolled smoothly to the side of the road and pulled up. We waited. The pounding in my chest caught up with the rhythm in my head. I felt sick, my legs were jelly, and I couldn't remember a single thing about unarmed combat.

'They're getting out,' said Charley, who was just able to see the other car.

'How many?'

'Two.'

One on one. Maybe I could manage that.

'Armed?'

'May be packing. Neither is carrying.'

Neither of us were either. I could see them now. Two large men in sharp suits in keeping with the car they'd arrived in.

'They don't look Irish.'

'Who cares?' said Charley, and I could feel him brace beside me. 'Shit.'

'What?'

'Two more.'

I swore, feeling the blood rush to my head. Then Charley sighed.

'Just back-up. They're waiting by the car.'

Which didn't make me feel any better. There was no time for further speculation.

'Come on out, boys.'

The voice was definitely Irish. Charley's eyebrows flicked up as he glanced at me. I shook my head.

'No way.'

'Put your hands up and come on out.'

This was a different voice. Authoritative and thick. The stooge. Then the other must be the brains of the outfit.

'Make them come to us.'

I wasn't about to come out of cover anyway. Like Charley, I got ready.

'Are you coming out?'

We kept shtum. I was starting to feel faintly hopeful. Puzzled too. Why hadn't they started shooting? They must know we had no weapons. A few warning shots and we might have been spooked into running for the trees, an easy target. Or else they could've fired under the car.

Footsteps sounded, slow and even. They were coming for us.

Charley crept to one end of the Toyota and I went to the other. They were bound to split up. Sure enough, we saw the shadows divide. I don't know what Charley did, but as my target came around the nose of the car, I was up.

The guy was armed, but my open-hand cut to the throat took him before he could do anything and he crumpled where he stood. I seized the weapon and ducked, hearing the other body fall. I looked round to find Charley on his feet, gun in hand.

'What about the others?'

We looked through the windows of our improvised barrier. The stalwarts by the other car hadn't moved.

'What do you say we take them down and steal the Merc?' said Charley.

'And look conspicuous, you moron?'

'Good point.'

We eyed the opposition. They looked like two black-clad statues standing there. But we knew that would end the moment we made a move.

Charley opened the Toyota door on our side, keeping a wary eye on the two by the Mercedes. He jerked his head.

'Get in.'

'Why don't you drive?'

'You're smaller. You can get in quicker.'

Yeah, and have my head be the nearest target for our no doubt pistol-toting friends over there. I couldn't see any better plan if we were going to get out alive. Staying low, I got into the car and shoved across to the driving seat, slipping the gun into my lap. Charley got in beside me and shut the door.

'No move from our friends.'

I turned the key and the motor fired up. As my head came up a bit, I felt it. Cold, hard steel at the back of my neck. The voice was perfectly friendly.

'Come up nice and slow, sonny.'

Charley was half turned, his gaze fixed on the fellow in the back. Ice in my veins, I rose with care and looked into the rear view mirror.

The man behind the gun was of middle age, small and compact, with the same air of bonhomie that had fooled us with Paddy. His eyes were on Charley as he spoke. His brogue was thick.

'Will you be giving me the pistol, sonny?'

Charley looked as if he preferred to answer in the negative, but prudence won out and he handed it over. The man in the back seat dug his barrel into my neck again.

'Ah, sure, you'll be switching off the engine now, will you?'

I turned the key and the thrumming died off.

'That's the way now.'

I looked at Charley and saw his glance flicker towards the Mercedes. From the corner of my eye I saw that the statues had at last come to life and were crossing towards the car.

'You'll be getting out of the car now, boys, and over to the limo. Easy now.'

I saw Charley reach for the handle of his door and did likewise. The statues were not noticeably armed, but close up they looked like something out of a boxing ring. Remembering Saudi, I decided to come quietly. No sense in getting myself beaten up unnecessarily. At least our captors didn't seem to have any immediate intention of killing us.

'Hands on your heads now, boys.'

How in heck the little weasel had managed to sneak into the car without us seeing or hearing anything I couldn't guess. Out of the car, he proved a small man. Either of us could have taken him with one blow, except for the silent escorts who saw us across to the Mercedes. Unlike the first two, this fellow was not at all smartly dressed. He was sporting a flat cap over short grey hair and a mackintosh that looked both dirty and creased. He got into the front and we were prodded into the rear by the statues. One of them climbed in behind us and the other got into the driving seat.

'What about your friends?' asked Charley, regaining his customary laconic tone.

Our captor turned his head. 'Ah, they'll be finding their own way.'

In our Toyota presumably. I couldn't resist looking back as the Mercedes took off, the driver treating the car with as much respect as if it were the Queen's. The two men we'd felled lay where we'd left them. So far there hadn't been any other traffic, but what if someone found them before they woke up? A careless ending, it seemed to me.

Then Charley spoke up.

'I suppose you've got another vehicle on its way to pick them up.'

The small man turned around in his seat, grinning like a monkey.

'Sure and you've a head on your shoulders, sonny.'

'For how long?'

That drew a laugh from the other man, but he made no answer. The whole episode was beginning to look weird. Like some kind of charade. What the hell was it all about, if they didn't intend to kill us? We still had no idea of the identity of these jokers, but we were headed for Cork all right. The Mercedes hadn't turned, but continued on the road in the same direction we'd been headed.

My thoughts were interrupted by Charley at his most ironic.

'I don't suppose you thought to bring a picnic? We haven't eaten for more than twenty-four hours.'

The grinning monkey face looked round again. 'Ah, now would I be forgetting a thing like that?'

He lifted his chin at the fellow in the back. Next moment, a covered basket appeared between Charley and me. I looked at it with a good deal of suspicion, and even Charley seemed wary.

'And this is?'

'Is it not a picnic, sonny, just like mother made?'

The juices in my stomach started writhing and I decided what the hell. I grabbed off the cover to find a stash of Tupperware boxes and a flask. I seized the latter and unscrewed the lid, uncaring if it was poison I was so parched. It was lime juice of all things and I drank deep before handing the flask to Charley, who had opened one of the boxes and started devouring a chicken leg.

We ate like it was our last meal on earth. For all we knew, it might have been. The monkey found it highly amusing. The statues remained silent.

The trip to Cork took hours and I gave in to the fatigues of the day and slept. There seemed little point in battling against the odds.

It took a while to figure out what the hell was going down when I eventually woke and found Charley asleep beside me. Remembering, I glanced into the front to see if the monkey was awake and found him as alert and upright as he'd been at the start. He seemed to know I'd come to.

'Not long now, sonny.'

If that was meant for reassurance, it had the opposite effect. Darkness had fallen, but we'd hit a lighted city which I assumed was Cork. The thought of what might await us here wasn't any too inviting. We had no idea who our host represented, whether IRA, the Firm or some other faction connected with the Republic. We didn't know what had happened to our brief to aid the Smallwood Brothers, or whether our cover was blown, which seemed likely. By now Blondie must be worried, if she didn't know already. I had the job of checking in daily and I'd never made the call. Would they bother to find out what happened to us? Or just assign new operatives and rethink the game?

At last the Mercedes moved off the main street and took a convoluted route through a number of back turns, presumably covering its tracks in case it was being followed. It stopped outside a pair of wrought-iron gates and as I watched them open, I realised Charley was awake. He caught my eye in the glare from a passing headlight and I thought I saw him throw one of his mobile eyebrows to the ceiling. Que sera sera.

We drove through and I looked back to see the gates closing behind us. The Mercedes cruised quietly around the shadow of a large building to the back and pulled up next to a pair of double doors.

'Journey's end, boys,' said the monkey, grinning round at us.

We didn't need telling it was time to get out. It was good to stretch my legs, despite the sudden hammering that had started up in my chest. I made like I was carefree, yawning wide and flexing my elbows and hands.

The statues motioned us to follow the monkey who was already walking through the open double doors. Charley waited for me to catch up before going in, and as I entered, I turned my head and caught sight of a familiar shape across the yard. Without thinking, I nudged Charley and he looked round.

'The Toyota,' I muttered, jerking my head towards it.

Charley's eyebrows flew up as he took in that the vehicle was indeed our pretended businessmen's car, somewhat battered after its adventures.

'Sure, and will you be dawdling all night?'

The monkey had come back into the doorway. One of the statues jabbed me in the back and Charley and I crossed the threshold.

The place was dimly lit, but it looked to be one of these old colonial mansions from way back, all dark panelling and ancient landscapes with chandelier style light fittings.

We followed the monkey through a series of corridors and into a large living room where the light was bright enough for us to see two men standing in front of a wide old-fashioned fireplace. Both men looked to be short - one chubby, one wiry - like a couple of ferrets with their ginger hair and foxy faces. Incongruously they were both in shabby-looking brown suits that fit them badly, but I'd never seen eyes so keen or figures of such supreme confidence.

The monkey grinned back at us as he waved a hand at the two men.

'Sure, and you've been itching to meet our Sean and Seamus here. Boys, allow me to introduce you to the Smallwood Brothers.'

Chapter Eight

I stared at them, wondering how deep was the shit we were in. Charley was ready to say something and I hoped he would change the habit of a lifetime and keep his trap shut. Luckily, before he could launch into one, the shorter, skinnier Smallwood, Sean started laughing.

'Welcome to Cork boys. Don't look so mardy there. If you can't take a joke you shouldn't have signed up now?'

Charley and I exchanged a glance.

'You set this up to amuse yourselves did you?' I said. I was getting pissed now. I'd gone from bricking myself, expecting a kneecapping, to anger in about three heartbeats.

'We had to be sure you wouldn't crack under pressure,' said Seamus. 'We know what you soft Southern poofs can be like.'

Sean giggled again, like a little girl. That was going to get old really quick.

Charley shrugged and stepped over to the brothers, 'Fair point. No offence. We'd probably have done–' He didn't finish his sentence. He'd only been speaking to distract them while he moved close. I'd seen him do this before, its always amazing to watch. Just one flick of his wrist in the middle of Skinny Smallwood's chest and Sean crumples like he's dead.

'What the fuck d'you do that for?' screamed Seamus, torn between checking on his brother and not wanting to put his back to Charley. His brother lost out. Charley stepped away and flexed his fingers.

'If he can't take a joke then fuck him. He'll live.'

I was wound up tighter than a kitten at a dog show, and started sizing up the oppo. I'd got as far as deciding we were sunk when a voice I recognised behind me chirped up, 'Evening boys. Making friends I see.'

It was Paddy, with sultry Samira at his side. The look in her eyes was pure smoldering lust. Unfortunately it wasn't directed at me. Charley broke into a smile and flashed it back at her. The tension was replaced by another sort, but at least the goons in the suits weren't going for their guns. They followed the monkey out, and I almost relaxed.

'Come on now. Let's have a drink and make nice,' said Paddy.

I ignored Charley, who was reacquainting himself with the taste of Samira's tonsils.

'Okay. What's the plan?'

'Typical Brits,' said Paddy, 'There always has to be a plan.'

I looked at the Smallwoods. Seamus had convinced himself that his brother would live and straightened himself out. He gave Charley a look of hatred I didn't like, but Charley was too busy to notice.

'Do you have a phone around here? Someone has to report in and we've already missed a couple of appointments.'

'Alright, calm down,' said Seamus. 'I got a phone just through there.' He pointed to a doorway. I circled around the room towards it. No way was I putting my back to any of them. Charley could turn it on and off like a switch, but I was always on duty. Maybe he just didn't care any more?

Through the door was an office containing a couple of desks, covered with dog-eared bits of paper and over-flowing ashtrays. Oh, and a drop-dead gorgeous blonde sprawled out on a sofa in nothing but her jewellery and lipstick. Things were looking up.

'Hello,' I said when she opened her eyes and looked at me. 'I'm here to use the phone.'

She pointed towards one of the desks and sat up slowly.

'Who are you then?' I picked my way over to the phone.

'I'm Jenny.' She wasn't Irish. Scottish.

'Jenny what?' I didn't care really, but I liked the way her tits wobbled when she spoke.

'Just Jenny,' she said, and started looking around for her clothes.

I picked up the phone and dialled the number from memory while I watched Just Jenny squeeze herself into some stilettos and totter over to pick up a silk robe. I waited until she'd left the room before I completed the password ident process and put the phone down to wait for the ring-back. It took a while, but I had no problem with this. The job taught you to be patient.

Blondie called back after about ten minutes. I gave her a quick sit-rep. I said we had been on a retreat for two or three days, which meant we had to lie low. I didn't bother to mention the fiasco with the Smallwood brothers. I'd decided by now Blondie personally had nothing to do with it, or if she did, I wanted her to sweat it out wondering what had happened.

'Okay, that's fine. Just remember to keep your friend out of trouble,' she said, and hung up.

I'd had a quick look around before Blondie called back, but I didn't find anything interesting. By the time I'd finished, Sean was back on his feet and Charley and Samira had found a room.

'Charley will be down in a minute if that wailing means anything,' said Paddy.

I was busy watching the brothers. They seemed okay. Smiling even. Just Jenny was sitting in a corner sorting out her nails.

'I've brought your toys down for you,' said Paddy. He jerked a thumb towards a sports bag. I went over and checked it out. He was as good as his word, which was unusual for a mick, but there were the shotguns and the pistols. I slipped a PPK into my waistband and felt a whole lot better.

'So Paddy,' came Charley's voice from the other side of the room, 'What's the pussy situation round here?'

'Dejesus, have you not had your fill? What have you done with her son?'

'I left her in bed, smoking. She sent me to get some fags though.'

We all laugh at that one. I toss Charley the other PPK and he pockets it.

'Now then boys,' he said, turning to the Smallwoods, 'We brought you some gear too.'

They perked up at this and I passed over the bag of shooters. They spent a bit of time checking them out. I wasn't worried. They were still too slathered with grease to be dangerous.

Paddy brought us back to business, 'Okay you langers, we're going to start the evening with a jaunt to the best club in town. The best food your dulled English pallets ever tasted served by goddesses in g-strings who dance themselves naked between courses. Always your boss's favourite when she visits. Is it true she's a dyke?'

'You'd love that, wouldn't you, you perverted mick,' said Charley.

'What about the girl upstairs?' I asked.

'No time for that son,' said Paddy. 'She's got to stay back and guard the place anyway.'

Paddy took us to a strip club that served food. The Smallwoods joined us too. The room was upstairs with big windows that looked out over the dance floor so we could watch the girls and still hear ourselves talk over the music. Seamus took the head of the table right from the off. I could tell Charley was rankled by that, but we were in their manor so I let it slide. I made sure I sat with my back to the window. The girls were cute, but we were here on business. Charley didn't notice or more likely ignored my pointed hint and got himself a seat with a good view.

'Now then gentlemen,' Seamus started off the proceedings. 'I invited a few friends over too.'

Charley turned at stared at him, 'What kind of friends?'

'The kind that are going to help us out.'

'Isn't it a bit public here?' I asked. We were pretty visible to anyone in the club below.

'Don't worry. No one is going to fuck with us here.' Seamus leaned back in his chair and his shirt nearly popped a button as it stretched over his belly. He had that physique that had once been stocky and ripped, but was now running to flab. He was not to be underestimated though. He pulled out a fat cigar and stuffed it in his mouth.

'Have no fear,' Paddy said, smoothing over the building tension, 'We've got a little cottage just south of Cork. You'll love it. We'll use that to talk over the plan.'

Before I could say anything else, the door opened and a man came through, sporting a old, purple scar that ran across his cheek and under his chin. He gave us the once over with eyes that were dark slate and missed nothing. He made no attempt to hide the pistol sticking out of the front of his trousers. I sat still and tried to blend into the scenery, became the grey man, just like I'd been taught in the Crazy House, but Charley went completely the other way. How he ever graduated I'll never know.

'Ah John, come on in,' said Seamus, standing up. He waved his arms towards us and said, 'here are the boys from over the water like I told you. Here to help us out on a little job.'

John didn't smile. I never once saw him smile, even with girls draped all over him. Charley thought he might have been one of 'them', meaning that he batted for the other side, but I reckon he was just a miserable sod.

Charley broke into a big grin, 'We're going to teach you yokels how we get things done in the civilised world. But how about a drink first?' A heavily fragranced waitress strutted up, nearly falling out of her string bra, and brought along another round.

'John here is an expert bomb-maker,' explained Paddy, 'used to do a little work for the Provos.'

'No offence Paddy,' I said, 'but we're not planning to start a war down here. We don't need bomb-makers.'

'We may as well have him on standby. You never know what you might need, until you need it,' glared Seamus. I must have hit his soft and tender side.

John still hadn't said anything. He just picked up a pint of stout and took a large swallow.

Charley ignored all this and started discussing the merits of the dancers below with Paddy. It was okay for him, but I had Jeannie to think about. I got up and excused myself. John stared at me as I left. That guy gave me the creeps.

When I got back more of the crew had turned up and were deep in their cups. Everyone was practically singing. Charley too. I drank slowly. No way was I going to let my guard down in this place. There were six of them, all rough-looking men who stared at me when I came in. I didn't say much. I kept my eye on Charley, made sure that no-one slipped him a mickey. These boys didn't like us, and they didn't try to hide it. It occurred to me that my function in this little escapade was to keep Charley out of trouble and on track, and lets face it, happy. It reminded me of when I was a teenager and worked for Lord C. I often had to play nursemaid to his children. Seems nothing had changed.

I called time on the proceedings at about ten. 'Come on Charley, I don't want to be carrying you home.'

'It's still early. The best girls haven't come out yet.'

I dragged him out of there. We'd picked up the Toyota when we left the Smallwood's and now got into it out of the cold air. 'Where to?' We didn't have anywhere to stay yet.

'Go to the Imperial,' said Charley. 'Only the best for servants of the Realm.'

The Imperial looked imposing and lived up to expectations inside. The cash we'd carried stuffed down our smalls on the way over easily covered the cost of the rooms for a couple of weeks. I could almost have bought a small cottage with my share.

'Up at six tomorrow,' I said. 'We've got to get off by seven to make the RV.'

'No problem Dickey-boy, don't oversleep.'

I made sure I had a good nights sleep. It was going to be the last one I'd have for a while. Charley and I met in the restaurant and stoked up on a full cooked breakfast.

'We'll keep the rooms here,' said Charley around a mouthful of black pudding.

'Good idea. If anything goes wrong, split up and meet back here.' I took a swig of coffee and said, 'I checked in with Blondie last night. She said under no circumstances are we to harm a member of the Garda.'

Charley snorted in derision, 'I'll do whatever I have to do to get out of this.'

'She was pretty insistent.'

'She can insist all over my dick and it wouldn't make a difference to me.'

I didn't push it. I'm sure I'd ignore her instructions if I had to. She'd been out in the field in her day. She knew the score. We finished up and headed out to the Toyota with our gear.

'Did you get under this car son?' Charley arrived a few minutes after me.

'Yes, no problem. Clean as a nun's snatch.' I said.

'Oh, convent brat are you?' Charley tossed his bag into the boot.

'Yep, time served and all that.'

'Me too.'

I wondered about that. 'So we had similar upbringing. You're an ex-soldier and I wanted to be. Is that what attracted the Firm to us?'

'You think too much about what you can't control,' snorted Charley. 'It's no coincidence. If you're looking for people to train up, to control, to do with what you want and dispose of, what type of background would you choose? When we meet the inevitable who's going to miss us? Maybe wifey will blubber a bit and then take the payoff. The kids will get their school fees paid and be told Daddy died in a car crash. The wife will re-marry and the kids will forget you.'

'Nothing to worry about there then. And another thing-'

'For fucks sake, just get in the car or I'll be forced to shoot you on principle.'

Charley took the passenger side before I had a chance to.

'How come every time I get in a car with you there's a steering wheel in front of me?'

'Told you. R-H-I-P'

'Rank may have it's privileges, but we're the same rank dickhead.'

I started the engine. Even though I'd checked the car out thoroughly I muttered a silent prayer as I turned the key. The IRA loved their car bombs and what with being introduced to Smiling John the bomb-maker the previous night, we were definitely going to be on someone's hate list. I drove off through the empty streets. I'd memorised the address and route before hitting the hay.

'So who the hell are we working for anyway?'

'What do you mean?' Charley wound the window down and lit up a fag.

'We're supposed to be working for the Firm, for Five, right? But this job stinks of the Company. Why don't they use their own personnel?'

'Look runt, I've told you before we work for a right-wing cabal that hovers in the background of British society. We've been loaned out to Six because they have the cash and the relationship with the Zionists.'

'Samira.'

'You got it. That fuck was on Six.'

I was quiet for a while as I navigated us out of the city. Then I muttered 'I hate this.'

Charley laughed humourlessly, 'That's why we're ditching this outfit at the first opportunity. If we can make a big enough cock-up, maybe they'll fire us.'

I didn't think that was going to happen somehow, but I didn't ruin the dream.

The cottage was a single storey, white-walled affair with knackered old tiles and stone chimneys. It was right under the flight path of Cork Airport, so every half an hour or so we were treated to roaring jet engines and rattling windows so loud we had to stop talking and wait until we could hear ourselves again. No wonder the roof was wrecked. All around were grassy emerald fields and the horizon was a long way off. It also rained almost continuously. No wonder Ireland was so green.

We got there before the Smallwoods and their people, which gave us a chance to do a thorough recce. I'd have preferred to have sorted out the house myself rather than rely on Paddy, but needs must and all that.

'Did you find anything?' Charley asked after checking the perimeter.

'Nope. Did you find any booby traps?'

'Do I look like I'm hopping around with my legs blown off?'

I didn't have time to reply to that, as we heard a car pulling up outside.

Chapter Nine

'Look lively Dicky-bow,' Charley pulled out his pistol and checked it before sticking it in the back of his trousers. I took up position behind the door and waited.

Sean and Seamus Smallwood led the way and waltzed right in without bothering to check where they were going. Amateurs. Still, it would make it nice and easy to hang them out to dry.

'Morning boys,' chirped Charley, 'nice of you to join us.'

Seamus Smallwood waved his cigar around, 'What do you think of the place?' His crew followed him in and made themselves at home. Smiling John came in last and spotted me straight away. I gave him a friendly wave which he ignored. Maybe he realised I was taking the piss?

'Not bad for a northerner,' said Charley. 'Get a brew on and we'll get down to work.'

We got an introduction to the Smallwood crew. Apart from the brothers and Smiling John, there were five others. They were lowlife Irish crims, typical of the breed, but they were amiable enough. They were like kids at Christmas when we handed around Paddy's toys. After cooing over the guns for a bit, Charley got down to business.

'So you're probably wondering what the fuck you're doing here, other than getting to walk off with a shit load of cash in your back pockets?'

That got their attention. He took a moment to look at each of them and continued, 'What we're after are some documents stashed in a safety deposit box in this bank.' Charley pointed out the location on a map spread out on the kitchen table. 'Now we don't want to let the owners know that their papers have been compromised, so we need a diversion, which is where you boys come in.' Charley grinned, 'You're going to rob the place.'

That got them smiling too.

'Anything you find in the other safety deposit boxes you get to keep. We'll also help you get into the main vault, which could contain upwards of fifty grand or more. It's all yours, as long as we get those papers.'

Sean rubbed his hands and I could see he was already spending the cash. Seamus was a bit more switched on though.

'How do we know what to look for?' he asked.

'We know the number of the box,' said Charley smoothly. He was making it up on the fly, and I was impressed with him all over again. 'A good crowbar should get you into the boxes, or if you feel the need, a bit of Semtex courtesy of your mate John here will do. A *little* bit though,' he stressed. 'We want to be able to read the bastard things afterwards.'

Seamus relaxed a bit and checked his team was up for it. Their eyes were all shining with excitement and the bait was well and truly taken. Except for Smiling John of course, who just stood at the back and stared at the map through narrowed eyes.

'We're going to need four cars and a van,' said Charley. 'We'll split into teams of two, and rotate between the vehicles.'

'I thought we were robbing a bank here,' protested Skinny Sean Smallwood, 'Not having a road trip.'

'You haven't heard the rest of the plan yet,' said Charley. 'We'll find out all about the bank manager, then hold his family hostage and make him open the vault for us. Before we do that, we have to do a little thing we like to call surveillance. I know lads, that's a big word for your sort, so I'll break it down. It means spying on them and following them to find out what they do and where they go.'

'When do we get to use the guns?'

I stepped forward and gestured to the map, 'We don't know where he lives yet, so the first thing is to recce the bank, find out what he looks like, then wait until closing time and follow him home.'

Eventually the penny dropped, and they settled down a bit. The Smallwoods told us they could get the cars and the van and we sorted out a routine.

'Two of your boys go in and ID the bank manager.' Charley explained. 'Then we follow him home and find out where he lives. After that, we'll set two teams off to follow him and two teams to follow the wife. Hopefully we'll find out she's having it off with the gardener or something which will give us some good blackmail material.'

'How soon can you get the cars?' I asked.

'We'll have them before the bank closes, no worries about that,' Seamus said.

'Let's get going then,' Charley said. 'We'll be parked outside all night, so all of you tell your missus not to wait up. If anything goes wrong, meet up back here. Clean.'

There was a round of okays, then everyone left, leaving us alone again.

'What do you think of them?' I asked.

'Bunch of tossers,' replied Charley, 'but who gives? As long as they hold it together long enough to get the Smallwoods into the bank. Then we make a call to the Garda, they get caught, and we bug out and head back to Blighty.'

'Sounds simple if you say it fast,' I said. But something was bugging me. 'So how are you planning to cock it up? That is still the plan, right? Our plan I mean?'

Charley frowned in confusion. For once he didn't have anything to say.

'It's all plans on top of plans isn't it?' I said. 'It's probably making your tiny head hurt.' I counted out on my fingers. 'The Smallwoods think they are doing over a bank for us. Blondie thinks we're going to get them caught, so she can use their Provo links to make it look like the IRA are knocking off the national coffers, which will piss off the Irish government.'

'I do know all this runt,' Charley said sourly. 'Get to the point.'

'The point is if we do our bit and call the cops, Blondie goes to bed with a smile and we become people she can rely on instead of kicking us out. I don't think that's what you'd intended, is it?'

'I'll think of something,' Charley grumbled.

The fact was the whole situation left me feeling like I wanted to scrub myself down with bleach, just to get clean again. Bringing in the bank manager and his family had been the idea of one of the guys from Six. It hadn't sounded that bad in a cosy London meeting room, but now I'd met the Smallwoods and their little gang of psychos, I could see all sorts of ways for it to go wrong.

We had few hours before they'd get back with the vehicles, so we went to town to stock up on supplies. We bought ourselves a large stock of props; hats, coats, fishing gear, waterproofs and the like. Keep changing your clothes so it made it difficult for people to remember you. We also got a stack of two-way radios, torches, ropes, duct tape. Everything a budding bank robber might need.

We got back to the cottage to find half a dozen cars pulled up outside. They were old bangers mostly, dull colours. The kind of cars you see all over the place without noticing. The Smallwood's boys did good.

The whole crew were inside, with a couple of large black and white photos of the bank manager, a Mr. Harold Grossman. He was just what you'd expect a bank manager to look like - pin-striped suit, salt and pepper hair, horn-rimmed glasses and a huge beak of a nose, just right for looking down on poor saps who went begging to him for money.

'Bank closes at four-thirty,' said Sean. 'He probably won't leave until near six.'

'Let's not take chances,' said Charley. 'Everyone take a good look. We'll all go. Use your radios if you spot him, and let's not do anything stupid.'

Charley and I took one of the cars. The Smallwoods wanted the van, and I wasn't interested enough to argue. We'd rotate around the vehicles anyway, so we'd get our turn.

Near the bank I parked so that the sun was behind to make it more difficult for Grossman to see us. Charley sent the other vehicles off onto cross streets around the bank to cover other exits.

We reclined our seats until we could only just see over the dashboard, flipped the sun-visors down and put on wide-brimmed hats to cover our eyes so it looked like we were sleeping. Then we just lay very still. People spot movement better than anything else. The hard part is staying focused. That's where the little blue pills help out. We waited until the bank staff started to leave. He wasn't among them. It was another hour before he came out and locked up. I made a note of the time in a notebook. I made it look like a price list for car parts. Everything in code in case I lost the book.

Charley got on the radio. 'Wake up ladies, we've got our target. Heading west.'

Grossman climbed into a shiny new baby-blue Cortina and I scribbled down the number plate as Charley tossed the radio into my lap and pulled out behind him. Charley kept back a fair distance, closing up fast when he turned a corner so we didn't lose him, then dropping back when we got sight of him again. Rule number one of surveillance - never take your eyes off the target.

Grossman was driving like he was completely unaware of us, but we were still careful. I gave a running commentary into the radio of where we were going and the other vehicles leapfrogged ahead of us. Good job too, because Charley let a car get between us at some traffic lights and forgot to leave a decent space behind it. The lights turned green, Grossman pulled away and turned at a junction, but the car in front of us stalled and we were sat there, pinned in traffic.

'What is this dick doing?' fumed Charley, but he couldn't lean on the horn in case it attracted Grossman's attention. I got on the radio.

'Team two, take over. Target is heading south over the river on Parnell Bridge.'

'Got him,' came the reply. Tailing someone is easier with teams. Less chance of being spotted too. Rule number two of surveillance - if the target spots you three times, you're burnt. We crossed over the River Lee into the leafy posh suburbs of Douglas and Rochestown.

'I hope these micks know what they are doing,' Charley was never happier than when he was moaning.

It wasn't long until we got word over the radio that he'd stopped.

'Hope he went straight home,' I said.

'Did you get the route logged?'

I waved the pad at him, 'What d'you think this is? My fucking shopping list?'

'All right Dicky-boy, keep your hair on.' Charley grinned.

Grossman's house was a two storey red-brick set back from the street in its own grounds, which were dotted with trees and bordered by hedges. The other houses in the street were similar, with driveways big enough for half a dozen cars each. All were jealous of their privacy. The kind that were also overly interested in the goings-on of their neighbours. So, good for us that the house was nice and shielded, but bad for us that we'd have to watch out for the snoopers. Our knackered old cars looked a bit out of place, but that couldn't be helped.

'I'll park between the properties,' said Charley, 'That way everyone will think it's their neighbour who has visitors.'

I got on the radio, 'Let's not crowd the property. Any sign of the wife?'

I got a round of negatives. Charley shrugged and pushed his seat back. Then he reached behind him and pulled out an empty bottle.

'What's that for?' I asked.

'Too much tea,' Charley grunted, and unzipped his fly. I looked away and tried to ignore the sound of running water.

'That's better,' said Charley, 'Want a go?'

'I'll pass for now, cheers.'

Charley screwed the top back on and stowed the bottle behind the seat. We settled back to wait for the wife. She wasn't long. She drove up in a convertible E-type Jaguar, parked on the drive to the house. We couldn't see her get out because the hedges blocked our view.

'We need to do a walk-by,' Charley said.

'Great. I'll do it. I could do with stretching my legs.'

Charley looked out of the window at the darkening sky. 'Looks like rain. Help yourself.'

I got out of the car and pulled on a brown leather jacket and a cap. Hats are marked items - anything out of the norm. Like very short or very long hair, tattoos, stylish clothes and so on. They draw attention to you and are normally to be avoided, but they can also work to your advantage. If I was spotted people would remember the cap, so on the way back, when I'd taken it off, I'd have effectively disguised myself.

I did a slow walk-past and got a good look up the drive at the house as I passed. The downstairs lights were on to drive out the deepening spring dusk and the curtains were closed. I walked down to the end of the street and round the back where they stored the bins. I returned to the car and got in beside Charley.

'There's an alley behind the house. Not big enough for a car but they could get out on foot that way.'

'We'd better put watchers at each end.'

I hit the radio and relayed the message.

'You got it,' came a reply from Smallwood, and he sent his boys to cover the exits.

The only other way out was the front drive, which we had covered, but we couldn't get in a decent position to view the house. Charley pulled out a coin and flipped it, 'Heads you go first,' he said.

So five minutes later I was picking my way through the hedge, trying to stay out of sight of both the target and the neighbours. Bloody Charley. I'm sure that coin was rigged somehow.

I did a couple of hours' stint. Enough time to see the lights go off downstairs and come on upstairs. Then after only ten minutes the upstairs lights went out too. They'd gone to bed. I checked my watch. Not even ten.

I went back to the car and kicked Charley out to do his bit. He was predictably reluctant, but he got out and I got in. I was starting to feel tired, so I popped a couple of blue wake-up pills. I had to smile about ten minutes later when the heavens opened and rain came down so hard it bounced a foot back off the ground. Charley would be hopping mad. It could be worse. It could be me out there. Charley did better than I expected. He stayed out there for the full two hours, until the rain had subsided to a slow, persistent drizzle. I was watching when he emerged from the driveway and walked towards me, his shoulders hunched against the rain.

'Bloody country,' he said as he got into the car, dripping all over the place. 'Monsoon season out there.'

'Anything to report?' I asked, trying to avoid leaving the nice dry car.

'Not a peep from them. Might as well stay here for a few hours.'

I couldn't believe my luck. I didn't even mind when Charley shook his head, sending droplets of water all over me.

'Shit,' muttered Charley. He was looking through the windscreen at something. I followed his gaze towards a slow-moving Ford Granada coming towards us. It passed under a streetlamp and I saw the sign on the roof with the conical blue lamp on top.

'Someone must have called the cops on us,' I said.

'You should have moved the car around a bit, amateur.'

I couldn't argue with that. Charley wound the window down as the police car pulled up alongside and the officer wound his down too. Ireland's finest didn't want to get out in the rain either.

'Are we doing okay, boys?' The garda asked. He had a partner beside him who was scrutinising the inside of our car.

'We just woke up from having a nap,' replied Charley, injecting a yawn into his words. 'Wanted to find a nice quiet place to rest.'

The officer shone a torch into Charley's face, then mine, and peered into the seats behind us. 'Just the two of you?'

'Yeah. Do you want to see our passports?' Charley reached into his pocket. The officers stiffened and jerked back as Charley's hand reappeared with his fake ID. I guess I'd be twitchy too if I lived here.

'Not necessary, sir, but if I could be asking you to find somewhere else for the rest of the night? There's a public car park about half a kilometre back towards the centre of town.'

'Understood,' Charley waved, and started the car. The garda stayed put and we were forced to drive away. Charley put us round a few corners out of sight and made a slow double-back over the next half an hour.

'We'll have to swap this car,' I said.

'And keep moving around this time,' Charley scowled. 'I honestly don't know what they teach you these days.'

I let him have that one. But I wouldn't make the same mistake again.

We switched cars with one of Smallwood's team and watched the place from a distance for the for rest of the night. Very little traffic passed and no pedestrians. At about six in the morning, Charley elbowed me in the ribs.

'Out you get. They'll be waking up soon.'

I groaned, but climbed out. The rain had stopped but it was bloody cold. I put on one of the overcoats I hadn't worn yet and checked on the others. In the first car, the two goons were both asleep, so I rapped on the window. They jerked awake and had the decency to look embarrassed.

'Wakey, wakey chaps, they'll be getting up soon.' I left them to it and went to the next. Every one of them was asleep apart from Smiling John, who was looking weary, but sat up straighter when he saw me.

'See anything?' I asked.

'Not a thing. Boring as fuck.'

'Wake up Fergal over there. We're back on.'

I got back to Charley and used the radio to brief the other teams. We'd split up as agreed. Two teams would follow the bank manager, two teams would follow the wife and one team would stop here and watch the house. Charley and I decided to tail the wife.

'Maybe she'll stop off for a shag?' Charley said.

'You planning on watching or joining in?'

'Whatever my country needs, shorty.'

Harold Grossman left home at eight, and the wife left half an hour later. It turned out she was the head-teacher at a Catholic girls school. You can imagine what I had to put up with from Charley about that. We took up a post across from the school and waited to see if she would nip out to do something interesting over lunch. She didn't.

Half-way through the day we switched cars with the other team and changed clothes. By this time I was getting really uncomfortable. I found pissing in a bottle in front of Charley difficult. Don't ask me why. Shy bladder syndrome or something. Surveillance was also mind-numbingly tedious, and the blue wake-up pills gave me a weird buzzing behind the eyes, like an itch except I couldn't scratch it. I kept thinking I could see something out of the corner of my eye but it was always gone whenever I looked.

'It's the pills,' said Charley when I finally mentioned it to him. 'They make you paranoid.'

'And you've let me keep popping them like humbugs? Are you out to get me or something?'

'Very funny.'

The wife left the school at six and went home without any detours. The bank manager was already there when we arrived.

'Like bloody clockwork these two, I bet they even shit on time,' said Charley after we checked in with the others by radio.

'Good for us, isn't it?'

'Yeah, but we still don't know much about them.'

I noticed movement in the mirror and elbowed a warning to Charley. Two men were approaching the car.

Chapter Ten

The men split up either side of the car. It was the Smallwood brothers.

'What the fuck do you think you're doing?' demanded Charley, 'You're not supposed to be seen with us.'

They climbed into the back of the car and made themselves at home.

'This is getting us nowhere,' said Seamus.

'We know you boys have ways to bug their house,' said Sean.

'We think we'll learn a lot more if you got in there so we could hear what they're doing.' Seamus again.

'What are you, a double act?' I asked.

'Just bug the fucking house.' Seamus glared at me and his hand drifted into his pocket. I had to bring the tension back down or someone was going to get slotted.

I looked at Charley and shrugged. 'We'll have to go out of town to get the gear.'

'For how long?' Seamus was clearly not impressed.

'Couple of days maybe. Dublin and back.'

'You'll not be leaving us on our own here now will you?' Sean cut in.

'Don't worry your pretty little head,' said Charley with a smirk. 'I'll stay and hold your hand. Dick can hike up to get it.'

I didn't say anything, but I was annoyed. Driving alone through bandit country wasn't my idea of a jolly good time. Still, you don't argue with your partner in front of the opposition.

The Smallwoods muttered something about commitment and got out of the car. We waited until they had disappeared back to their van, then Charley let out a theatrical sigh. 'Well Dick, you'll have to get your little legs up to Dublin safehouse tonight. They'll be able to sort us out with the surveillance gear. Get on the blower to Blondie and set it up.'

'I don't like splitting up. It's a bad idea.'

'No choice Dick. I don't trust them on their own. They'd go in there mob-handed and fuck everything up, and not in a good way. One of us is going to have to stay here and make sure they behave, and quite frankly, I'm the one they'll listen to.'

'You just don't want to drive around all those windy lanes again,'

'Well that too,' admitted Charley.

I checked my watch, 'It's about time to check in with Blondie anyway. I'll make the phone call and tell her what we need.'

I got out and left Charley to it. The evening was slowly drawing on to night and the setting sun behind the trees had painted the bottom of the clouds a stunning pink. I had to just stare at it for a moment. The nearest phone box was half a mile away and by the time I got there the sun had dipped below the horizon and it was dark. I dialled the number, left the coded message and waited for the call back. It didn't take very long.

'How are things?' That was Blondie-speak for things had better be going smoothly. I told her things were going smoothly.

'There is one thing though,' I said casually. The silence on the other end of the phone was more cutting than flint. 'The natives are getting impatient, so we could do with some surveillance gear to speed things up.'

'That's not a problem, but you're going to have to cross the border. Our Dublin assets are in use.'

Shit. This party was getting better and better. She gave me a name and an address in Lurgan, County Armagh, south-west of Belfast, one of the most troublesome of the troubled areas north of the border. Charley pissed himself with laughter when I told him.

'I'd love to go with you Dick, but like I said, I need to chaperone the girls here. Besides, someone your size will be able to get in and out without being seen much easier than us normal-sized folk.'

I muttered something uncomplimentary about his mother, but the decision was made and I had to deal with it.

I spent half an hour studying a map, plotting the best way up there. It would take the best part of the rest of the night if I drove without stopping. Bollocks to that, I thought. Smallwood and Smallwood could wait. I could take the opportunity to have a nap. Besides, it would be easier to get over the border in daytime rather than at four in the morning, when the Brit squaddies would be tired and skittish.

'Right,' I told Charley, 'in and out. I'll be back in twenty-four hours. Do you think you can manage until then?'

'I've been managing just fine for the past ten years without your tender lips around my cock.'

'Fine. I'll take the Toyota. I'll radio in when I get back.'

It was nearly midnight before I got going, and the roads were blacker than the inside of a coal miner's jock-strap. There was hardly any traffic on the roads and I took full advantage to push the limits of the Toyota, which weren't that high. I deliberately didn't take any wake-up pills as I drove. My plan of taking a nap on the way wasn't going to do me any good if I was wired. Explains why I nearly wrapped myself around a tree several times on the winding Irish roads. I opened all the windows and chewed the inside of my cheek to keep awake, but when I realised I was driving with my eyes closed more often than open, I pulled into a lay-by to rest. I had enough energy to get out and pull some branches over the car to shield it from sight, before I crawled into the back seat and took a well-deserved rest.

I woke up far too soon, freezing in the dawn mists which hung above the fields in every direction. Only four hours of sleep so I was tempted to grab a few more, and to hell with Charley, but my annoying sense of duty took charge and made me get up.

I must do something about that. I took a few pills and grabbed a quick breakfast of cold hard-boiled eggs, then broke the car out of cover and continued north. I was only an hour from the border, and by the time I got there the gear had done its stuff and I was alert and buzzing. The border patrols gave the car the once over, but since I was alone they were pretty relaxed. I opened the boot when they asked and let them look inside the cabin. I wasn't worried. I'd agonised about leaving the gun behind, but I couldn't risk it being discovered.

'What is the purpose of your visit?' A humourless corporal asked me.

'I've got a business meeting. I'm in the import-export business.'

'What do you import?'

'Anything that will sell,' I said glibly. 'Right now I'm going to talk to a guy about two hundred blow-up dolls he wants to shift. I can drop one off for you and the boys on the way back if you like.'

'Very fucking funny,' he growled and shoved my moody passport back at me.

I drove slowly between the barriers and entered British soil again. It didn't feel as safe as it should. My counter-surveillance radar was spinning like crazy, even though I had another hour drive ahead of me. The Provo's liked to watch the borders and keep tabs on who was coming and going. I hoped that by pissing off the border guard back there anyone watching me in my Irish-registered Toyota wouldn't be thinking I was cosying up to them. It was subtle, but you'd be surprised how little things like that helped to keep you alive.

Lurgan was just like I'd expected from seeing it on the news every night. Huge colourful murals depicting masked gunmen adorned every other end-terrace wall and people shuffled though the streets as if they expected to get smacked on the back of the head with a batton any second. The cars were faded and beaten, and litter lay abandoned, hugging the corners of buildings like no one gave a shit. But what really struck me and set my teeth on edge was how quiet it was. Even at nine in the morning when people were out and heading to work, hardly anyone dared to make a sound. It made me think of a mousetrap I'd set up once. I knew it was behind the couch, but when it suddenly snapped shut late one night I nearly crapped myself and jumped a foot in the air. The mouse was pretty annoyed too.

I was getting suspicious looks from everyone I drove past, and it eventually dawned on me that driving round in a car with Southern Irish number plates wasn't such a great idea. I found a public car park and left the car tucked away at the back. I didn't bother buying a ticket. I wasn't planning to return to it. I made my way to the address Blondie had given me. I walked past it the first time and circled the area, checking for anyone following me or taking an interest. Luck seemed to be with me as I didn't see anything. Either that or whoever following me was better than I was. I took up a position at the end of the street and flicked through a paper for half an hour, watching the house. It looked empty, but that was the point. They were supposed to be expecting me, but Blondie hadn't given me a phone number to give them the heads-up when I was going to be there. About mid-morning I decided to make contact. This was the most dangerous part. Either they'd be twitchy inside and give me a hard time, or the house could be watched and I'd be giving them away to the neighbours.

I went straight up to the house without bothering to pantomime being lost and asking for directions or anything. That kind of thing just draws more attention. Better to act as if you have every right to be there and people will just ignore you. I knocked on the door quietly, using one of the rap-rap-rappity-rap patterns I'd learned at basic. The door was opened immediately by someone who tucked themselves out of sight behind it. I stepped in quickly and it closed behind me. I tensed, half-expecting to be tumbled, but instead a Geordie voice beside me said, 'Wondered when you were going to come over. We bin' watching you out there.'

The man behind the door was thin and wiry, with a bushy black moustache, smoker's teeth and when he gestured for me to lead the way into the kitchen at the end of the hall I noticed he was missing his middle two fingers.

'I'm Dick,' I volunteered.

'Steve,' he said, and indicated his head to another man sitting at a table pouring over a crossword. 'That's Mike. It's just the two of us.'

I took a seat at the table while Steve put the kettle on. Mike looked up and reached across to shake my hand. 'Heard you were coming. Welcome to the fucking madhouse.' He was in his late fifties, but still had all his hair, even if it'd lost its colour. He had that tired, stretched out look I was starting to associate with long-term operatives.

Steve dumped a large mug of tea in front of me. 'Sugar?'

'Eight please,' I said, lighting up, 'but don't stir it, cause I don't like it too sweet.'

That got a chuckle and I took a few moments to relax.

'So what d'you need?' Steve sat down in the third chair and pulled out a fag of his own.

'Got a couple of rooms to kit out,' I said. 'Domestic house. Civvies.'

'So they won't have snoopers or anything?'

'They don't even know they are targets.'

Steve grunted. 'Easy enough. How are you getting in?'

'Probably pick the lock while they are out. Detached property so we have to get inside rather than go in from next door.'

'You're going to need radio transmitters then. We've got a couple of kits here you can have.'

'Appreciated.'

I took a large mouthful of hot tea. It was high on the list of one of the most wonderful things I'd tasted. 'So how long have you been over here?' I asked.

Mike snorted, 'Too fucking long.' I waited for him to say something else. He just stared at his mug.

'Don't mind old Mike here,' said Steve, 'He's been here so long he's forgotten what normal feels like.'

'They're fucking animals,' said Mike unexpectedly. 'I'd just as soon nuke the whole fucking lot of 'em. They got no limits.'

'You must have seen some pretty fucked up shit,' I said quietly. I didn't want to know, but he felt the need to tell me anyway.

'You'll have heard about the beatings and the knee-cappings?' he said. 'Well that's what they do if they like you. A couple of months ago they got hold of one of our boys in green. He was only eighteen. About a dozen of the bastards shared out his arms and legs and pulled him apart. He was still alive. At first. Helicopter nearby saw it all, but couldn't do anything about it.'

As much as I tried, I couldn't prevent the image of that playing out behind my eyes. 'They must hate us a lot,' I muttered.

'Nah, we're just a convenient target.'

'Well the job I'm on will give them a bit of trouble.'

'Amen to that,' Mike tilted his mug at me in salute.

'So who do they save the beatings for then?' I asked, 'I thought they just had grief with us.'

'Mostly it is their own people who don't sing to the same hymn sheet,' said Steve, 'Sometimes literally. The UDA and the pro-British. They call them traitors.'

'I heard they didn't like drug dealers either.' I said. 'Always struck me as a bit funny really - them getting all preachy over drugs but thinking nothing of murder.'

Mike barked out a laugh, 'Bollocks. The only reason drug dealers get a beating is if they don't pay their dues. The IRA loves drugs. It's a huge money-maker for them. All that public outrage nonsense is just so much shit. A smokescreen to make them look like fucking freedom fighters.'

I must have looked like a constipated fish or something because Steve burst out laughing at me.

'Christ you've got a lot to learn, mate,' he reached out and ruffled my hair playfully. I closed my mouth and tried to look professional.

'Everyone's on the make over here,' Steve explained. 'IRA, UDA - doesn't matter. It's all just a big joke to them. A bloody good reason to go anarchic, break as many laws as they can and have a bloody good time doing it. It's not about some noble war, or the right to self-governance or individual freedom. It's about money and kicking the shit out of anyone they don't like.'

'They're basically organised criminal gangs scrapping over turf,' said Mike. 'They get thousands from extortion and robbery, but that doesn't get close to the millions up for grabs trafficking drugs from Afghanistan or South America.'

I sat back and had to think about that. It shouldn't have surprised me, but I guess I was still wet behind the ears in a lot of ways. I'd always thought that the paramilitary groups over here were totally out of order, but basically fighting for something they believed in. It was depressing to find out they were just as hypocritical as the rest of us. Another slip down the ladder of cynicism for Dick Frame.

'When do you want to get off?' asked Steve. 'We can offer you a mouldy old mattress if you need a rest.'

I perked up and downed the rest of my tea, 'That is my idea of heaven right now. I could do with a couple of hours, but I'm going to need to pick up a new set of wheels, and head off by nightfall.'

'We could sort you out with a little runabout if you like. Just enough to get you over the border.'

'That's decent of you.'

Steve grinned, 'Anything for one of the lads.'

They showed me into a small room upstairs with the promised mattress, which wasn't half as mouldy as it might have been, and I crashed out immediately. I wouldn't have been able to do that if I hadn't been confident someone was watching out for me. I was woken up once by a distant explosion, the staccato-crack of Armalites and British SLR rifles returning fire. It was over in less than a minute and I rolled over back to sleep. Most people didn't even bother looking out of their windows at that sort of thing in Belfast any more.

I got up again far too soon, but it was dark already.

'I've loaded the car up with a couple of kits,' said Steve, 'R2's and transmitters. I wasn't sure quite what you'd need.'

I rubbed the sleep away and took the mug of tea he was waving in front of me.

'One thing, though,' he continued, 'You'll have to walk a bit to pick up the car. Can't risk parking it outside this place.'

'No problem,' I shrugged. He gave me directions to where he'd left it and handed me the keys.

They were good blokes. God knows how they did it, living here so close to the enemy, knowing that one slip-up would mean a painful dismembering. I'd be crapping myself the whole time.

I ducked out of the house, head down and tried to look as downtrodden as everyone else. I'd got about two streets away when I realised I was being followed. I caught movement behind me and another parallelling me on the other side of the road. The rows of terraced houses didn't allow me a lot of options, but I cut up the first alley I came to and broke into a sprint.

I glanced over my shoulder as I left the alley and saw a couple of playmates enter and break into a run. They were both wearing ski-masks. Shit. It didn't matter who they were. I couldn't let them get me. I didn't have a weapon either.

I hopped over a low chainlink fence and raced through someone's garden, ducking under a sagging clothesline and dodging kids' toys. Someone opened a window and shouted. They were letting my pursuers know where I was. I ran through another couple of gardens, and back out into another alley. The two boys behind were still with me, spurred on by the baying of housewives hanging out of doorways, throwing curses my way.

I rounded a corner and nearly ran into a couple more friends wearing balaclavas. I recovered first and took out the first with an elbow to the neck, using the Krav Maga-style martial arts that had become instinctive. The other raised a short, stubby shotgun, which I took off him with quick flick of aikido and then broke his arm backwards at the elbow to encourage him to leave me alone. He went down, screaming and I took off. Now I had a shooter, but it would be useless for anything further than ten feet away.

I heard a curse behind me as the first two came across their downed comrades. I ran across the road and vaulted over a tired wooden fence into a stretch of unlit wasteland. They'd seen me go in, but I was hoping to fade into the darkness and lose them. The ground underfoot was treacherous and rubble-strewn, probably the half-cleared remains of an old bombing site. Here and there were rusted-out shells of cars, and I crouched down behind one and listened. I heard them clambering over the fence and crunch across the rubble, moving carefully and spreading out. They were doing the right things, but not doing them well enough. They let themselves get too far apart.

One drifted in my direction, but was looking in completely the wrong direction. I sprang up behind him, wrapped a hand over his mouth to stop him shouting out and dragged him down, jerking his head over my knee so his neck snapped. He was dead in seconds, but I kept my hand over his mouth to stop his death rattle giving me away. I pulled up his mask and swore silently. He was probably only sixteen. Well fuck him. If he's out here, he's here to play.

I kept quiet and reacquired the other target. He was twenty feet away with his back to me, but he was getting nervous. He hissed a question out to his friend, torn between keeping quiet and wanting to communicate. He had a revolver in his hand that was bigger than he was and I could see it shaking in the dim light from the quarter-moon. After another ten seconds and a couple more calls to his mate, he lost his bottle and scrambled back to the road. That suited me fine.

I moved out in the opposite direction I'd entered, rejoined the street and spent half an hour in counter-surveillance mode, putting distance between me and the wasteland, before doubling back to find the car.

It was on a wide main road in a commercial area. I scanned the street for it and spotted a patrol of soldiers heading my way. They were doing their usual thing. Eight-man Brick in full cabbage gear with packs, radios and rifles strung out along the street. The man at the rear walking backwards for half a minute, then replaced, leap-frog fashion by another.

They were looking at the car suspiciously. I pulled back round a corner and tipped the shotgun into a bin. Couldn't risk being searched. Then I wandered around the corner and headed straight for the car.

The soldiers stopped and watched me as I reached it and jumped in. A little Datsun that was on its last legs, but would suit me fine. I started it up and pulled away gently. No surprises. The soldiers watched me go, probably as relieved as I was.

I drove west out of Lurgan and went back over the border at a different place to where I had entered. No point running the risk of meeting that corporal again. Getting across was easier going south. They pretty much just waved me through, and I took full advantage.

I drove about an hour, then pulled over to call in to Blondie. It was late, so I didn't get her personally, but I was expected to leave a message. I told the guy on the other end of the phone that I'd picked up the kit and was heading back, then hung up and carried on driving. I took my time, and checked my rear view mirror frequently. Full counter-surveillance activities. I started to breathe a bit easier after I passed Virginia, and the roads got a lot emptier.

I drove most of the night, and stopped half an hour out of Cork when I saw a line of scrap cars along the road outside a garage. I nipped out to borrow a set of number plates from one of the wrecks and replaced the Northern Irish ones on the Datsun. Probably should have done that nearer the border, but I wasn't planning on keeping the car too long anyway. I had a few hours until dawn, so I took what I considered a well-earned nap before going in to meet up with Charley and the boys.

Chapter Eleven

I got on the radio to Charley.

'About bloody time. I've got a flat arse sitting around waiting for you.'

'I've got the stuff. Meet up at the house?'

'Sounds good to me. I'll bring the van.'

I went to the cottage. The Smallwoods turned up as well. They had left the others to tail the manager and his wife to work.

'So is this it then?' Seamus grinned around his cigar. He was like a kid on his birthday. I had laid out the equipment on the kitchen table, and he reached out eagerly for it.

'Easy does it,' I warned. 'This is expensive stuff.'

I took Charley to one side, 'Why did you bring them along?' I hissed.

'Didn't have a choice Dick. They were hanging around when you called in. Couldn't do much about it.'

'I don't want them tagging along when we plant the stuff. They are going to be a fucking liability.'

'I'm with you on that one, but we're a bit short-staffed, in case you hadn't noticed.'

Normally we'd go in with a team of four. Two to plant the equipment and two anti-personnel types to deal with security.

We turned back to see they were pawing all over the stuff.

'Right then boys,' said Charley, 'Leave this to the professionals. Setting this up takes skill and training, which means it will be me and my colleague here.'

'We want in on this,' objected Sean.

'You will be,' said Charley smoothly, 'I've got an important job for you. We need a couple of pairs of eyes to run interference outside. Give us a warning if anyone comes.'

'That sounds like you're fobbing us off,' Seamus said suspiciously.

'Not at all, my northern chums. If we all piled in there and got caught, it'd be game over. I'm sure a smart man like you can see that?'

I could tell they weren't happy about it, but Charley hadn't left them much room to manoeuvre, so they had to agree.

'Are the targets both at work?' I asked.

'Like clockwork,' said Charley, 'We should have a good five or six hours to set it all up.'

'Let's get going then.'

We moved the stuff into the van and drove over to the house. I pulled over to the side of the road a couple of streets away.

'Alright lads, out you get.' Charley opened the back door and allowed the Smallwoods to climb out.

'Why are you dumping us here?' protested Sean, 'It's fucking miles away.'

'Can't have us all piling out together, can we? The neighbours will have a field day twitching their curtains. Now remember, get on the radio if you see anyone going up to the house.'

Charley climbed back in and I drove away, leaving the brothers on the pavement.

'Pull up around the back,' suggested Charley. I nosed the van up to the alley behind the house, and got as close as I could. We scanned the surroundings, looking for any sign of onlookers.

'Nice and easy,' Charley said, and we casually climbed out and grabbed a bag each. This was the most risky part. Once inside the house we'd be well hidden and could get on and do the job at our leisure. Walking across that thirty foot stretch to the back door seemed to take a hell of a lot longer than it should. Fucking gravel. Should be against the law.

'We should have worn overalls or something,' I muttered.

Charley shrugged, 'Never fear Dicky, just keep your head down and pretend your life is shit.'

'Shouldn't be too hard.'

We got up to the back door, which was out of sight of the nearby houses thanks to a couple of well-manicured bushes. I dropped the bags as Charley got out his lock-picks.

'I'll move the van while you get inside.'

Charley grunted something and concentrated on the task at hand, so I left him to it. It was hard not to run back, but I managed to keep to a gentle walk and jumped into the cab and started her up. I took the van around the corner and made my way back.

Charley was still fiddling about with the mortice lock.

'I thought you were supposed to be good at this?'

'Fuck off, I broke a pick and had to fetch it out. I'm almost there.'

It only took another thirty seconds and then the lock snapped open with a satisfying clunk. We entered the house, pulled the door quietly shut behind us, and listened. You never knew what you might find inside. The only sound was from a grandfather clock in the front hallway, a repetitive clack, clack, clack which for some reason set my teeth on edge.

The first time I'd entered a house like this was during training. Some guys enjoyed it, got a kick out of it, but I never did. I hated the violation. I always thought about someone walking around in my house and looking through my stuff.

Charley and I carefully moved from room to room, checking it was empty. There was no cellar, so we didn't have that complication to deal with. In the main living room there was a small desk against the wall supporting a phone and some papers. I handed Charley a screwdriver and he went to work. There was plenty of space in the base of the phone for the transmission device, and he spliced the phone microphone and power source, connecting them to the device. Three minutes and he was done.

'Right, bedroom next,' said Charley.

'Do you think they'll do much talking in there?'

'I hope not. I just want to hear them get it on. I reckon she's a wailer. The quiet ones often are.'

'You're an animal Charley.'

He just laughed. They didn't have a phone in the bedroom, but we had another device that we could install. This was essentially a tape recorder that could record up to ten hours of audio. It ran off the mains, but the recording could be disrupted by background noise, like running water, so placing it was a bit tricky. Charley spotted the entrance to the loft space and gave me a leg up.

'It's filthy up here,' I grumbled, pulling out a torch. I gingerly picked my way across the support beams to a position over the bedroom. I followed Charley's knocking on the ceiling to get to the best place for the recorder. Right over the bed if I knew Charley. I had a little hand drill and slowly and carefully made a little hole in the ceiling and fed a tiny microphone into it. The microphone had a white face which was supposed to blend in with typical ceiling paint.

The next thing to do was to tap into the electrical cables to power the device. This was easy as the lighting main cables were all up there. I took a wooden-handled knife and cut into the cable insulation to expose the wires inside. I had a set of sharp crocodile clips which each went to a different cable and pierced the secondary insulation to make the contact.

It took about ten minutes to get it all set up, and I flicked the switch to start the recording. I'd have to come back in tomorrow to collect the tape and put a new one in. I shuffled out of the loft door and eased my way out.

I found Charley going through Mrs Grossman's underwear drawer.

'I don't think any of that will fit you Charley.'

'Fuck off. I'm taking a professional interest.'

'Oh yeah? How do you work that out?'

'I'm looking to see if she's got any sex toys to work out how healthy their marriage is.'

'You're just a dirty old man aren't you?'

'Hey, less of the old.'

I had a look around the rest of the bedroom, careful not to disturb anything. There were the same drab clothes in the closets that we'd seen them wearing. By the side of the bed there were half-empty glasses of water. He had been reading a newspaper, she was half-way through a romance novel. His pyjamas were neatly folded and placed under his pillow. Her flannel nightdress was hung over the head of the bed. I didn't think Charley would get any entertainment out of these two.

'Right Dick, take a quick look around for footfall dirt and trace then let's bug out.'

We were about to slip out the back when the doorbell rang. We froze. Charley held up his hand and gestured for me to step into a room out of sight. He looked towards the front door, which was at the end of the hall he was standing in.

'It's the police,' he said quietly. 'I think I've been spotted. Stay out of sight. I'll deal with this.'

'Where the fuck was our warning? The Smallwoods must have fallen asleep. Amateurs.'

Charley unbuttoned his shirt a few notches and I heard him open the front door.

'Hello officer,' he said in a camp voice, 'How may I be of service?'

I didn't hear what the officer said, but Charley responded with a squeal of pretend shock, like a flaming poof.

'Oh my, I didn't realise. Did someone see me sneak in?' he giggled.

'Who might you be?' the policeman had got a foot inside now. I tensed, wondering what to do if he decided to search the house. We were under strict instructions not to harm the local plod, and I couldn't imagine Blondie would be too forgiving.

Charley lowered his voice to a stage whisper, 'I'm going to get into so much trouble with poor Harold if anyone finds out. No one knows about us, you see, especially his wife. And oh, if the bank finds out, it might mean his job.'

The officer cleared his throat uncomfortably, 'Are you saying…sir, that you and Mr. Grossman are, er…'

'Special friends?' said Charley sprightly. 'Yes we are. I thought I'd pop over and surprise him. He said he was going to go in late this morning, but he's obviously changed his mind. I'll have to wait until our regular Friday evening.'

'Well, er… I see,' the officer coughed, 'I won't keep you any longer then, but just be careful next time. And be a little more discreet perhaps? The neighbours don't like strangers in the area. It does waste police time, you know?'

'Of course officer,' replied Charley in his campest voice. 'I'll be a good boy from now on. Unless Harold doesn't want me to be, if you know what I mean.'

The policeman couldn't get out of the house fast enough. Charley and I laughed once he had gone.

'I can't believe you got away with that,' I said when I caught my breath.

'Well you know, Dicky, we are often called upon to do distasteful tasks on occasion in the service of our country.'

'You can keep those kinds of tasks to yourself, thank you very much.'

'I'm getting a bit worried about your operational viability if you won't indulge in a bit of uphill gardening once in a while. It's mandatory if you work for Six, you know?'

'Fuck you. Let's get out of here.'

We checked that the Garda car had gone, then crept over to the back door.

'Hello, what have we got here?' said Charley, reaching for a set of keys on a hook.

'Back door key?'

'Looks like it.' He tried a likely-looking key. It turned and locked the door nicely.

'Result. Bring it along. We can get a copy made and replace it before they come home tonight.'

Charley pocketed the keys and we snuck out, locking the door behind us. We made sure we stayed out of sight of the neighbours and got back to the van without a lot of flashing blue lights descending on us. Another result.

Chapter Twelve

The Smallwood brothers were over the moon when we got on the radio and told them.

'That's good news lads,' said Seamus. 'When the banker and his wife come back we'll have some really good stuff to work with.'

'Don't get your hopes up,' I said. 'Chances are you'll just hear them talking about the telly or what to have for dinner.' They didn't want to hear that.

That evening they climbed into the van with us where I'd set up the receiver. We had to stay within three hundred yards of the house, but that was plenty in this neighbourhood. We had to keep moving the van every few hours, so as not to arouse suspicion.

As I suspected, they were as boring as a vicar's tea party. They didn't make or receive any phone calls that night, and we had to wait until the morning when they left for work before I could nip back in and retrieve the tape using my newly cut key. The bedroom talk was mundane. Most of it was the wife complaining about one of the staff at her school. The Smallwood brothers were probably hoping for the bank manager to tell his wife about a special transfer coming in or something, but he wasn't the type to talk about work.

We carried on tailing and listening to them for a few more days. The weekend was a bit more interesting as we didn't have any clue about what their routine would be, so we had to keep on our toes. They pottered about in the garden, drove to the shops, bought the weekly groceries, and on Sunday went to church, all dressed up.

The best bit was when I got the tape on Sunday morning. We'd not had a chance on Saturday, so the recording was from Friday night. Clearly Friday was their 'special night', much to our amusement. Charley was right, she was a wailer. Grossman impressed us all. He managed to keep her going for nearly an hour, and some of the words coming out of her mouth ought never to be uttered by a headmistress.

The next night, we were summoned to the cottage by the Smallwoods. They had their mob all around them, and were not looking friendly.

'Evening boys,' said Seamus tightly.

The skin on the back of my neck tightened. I had a pistol stuck in the back of my belt, but if it came to a shoot-out in close confines we were toast. Charley strolled over to the kitchen where the Smallwoods were standing, flopped down into one of the chairs and swung his feet up onto the table. I hung back, watching the others.

'What's eating you Seamus?' asked Charley, 'You're looking a bit stressed if you don't mind my saying.'

Seamus leaned over the table and attempted a smile. It was like watching a bulldog break wind. 'My brother and I were wondering how things were going?'

'Things are going about as well as you can expect. We've got ears on the manager and his wife, and your boys are doing a reasonable job of following them about.'

Seamus looked around the cottage meaningfully, 'Are you enjoying the facilities we've provided?'

'Very nice. Could do with a few more birds about the place though.'

Seamus turned to look at his brother, and something passed between them.

'We need to move the schedule up,' Seamus said.

'What's the hurry? We're getting some good stuff, trying to work out how they are going to react under pressure, but you can't rush these things you know?'

Seamus chewed around his cigar and his eyes shifted between us. 'We have...other things to consider. We need that money. I want it done this Friday.'

'That's only a couple of days away. Are you sure your boys are ready?'

The lads behind the Smallwood's bristled a bit at that. Charley had a knack of rubbing people up the wrong way. I think he didn't give a shit whether he lived or died half the time. Seamus just smiled and stood up.

'We'll be ready. Make sure you are.'

They filed out. All their boys strutted after them, puffed up with their chests out, arms swinging, and giving us the hairy eyeball. I didn't hold eye contact for long enough to cause offence. Just enough to show I wasn't scared. I think I fooled them.

We sat in silence until we heard the cars pull away. I watched out of the window, to make sure there were no stragglers hanging around, then gave Charley the nod.

'Fucking wankers,' he said.

'I wonder what's going on? Did you see the way Seamus was acting. He was jumpy as hell.'

'Yeah, something was on his pea brain mind.'

I noticed the bag containing the surveillance kit tucked into the corner and an idea started to form. 'Maybe we should make it our business to find out what?'

Charley followed my gaze and broke into a grin. 'Dick, sometimes you talk like you're a proper operative.'

'Yeah I'm learning really fast. Must be the shining figure of excellence they've partnered me with.'

Charley swung his legs down from the table and heaved the bag onto it. 'This will be tricky to pull off, you know?'

'It'll be a piece of cake,' I said. 'We know where their gaff is, and we know that half of their people will be out watching the Grossmans. We just have to slip in tonight, stow the kit and job done.'

'We can't both go. The Smallwood's are tossers but they're not stupid.'

'You can run interference. I'll head over and set it up.'

'You sure, Dick?'

'You almost sound concerned. I'll be in and out in no time. They won't even notice.'

'I've heard your wife say that about you.'

We loaded the bag into the back of the Datsun which I still hadn't got rid of, and Charley jumped into one of the other cars to take his shift at the Grossman's house. I drove to the mansion we had been taken to when we first met the Smallwoods. It wasn't hard to find. It was in an older part of town made up of the kind of large pretentious houses you secretly wish you owned. The kind that came with golf club memberships and butlers.

I parked up a few streets away and waited an hour or so until it was nice and late. I reclined the seat right back and pretended I was taking a nap, but there was no chance I'd have drifted off. I was shaking too much. I tried to tell myself it was lack of sleep and too many blue pills, but really I was crapping myself in case one of their boys recognised me. I finally got enough of a hold of myself to get out of the car and hoisting the bag over my shoulder, I headed over towards their place.

I avoided the big iron gates at the front and instead checked out the sides and rear of the house. The neighbours were close, but they were all so precious about their privacy they had planted lots of trees and tall hedges. I had plenty of cover. There were walls all around the Smallwood place, but they weren't too smart about making sure the perimeter was secure. I found a tree had been allowed to grow too close to the wall, and it wasn't hard to use it to climb over it. I could have done without the eight foot drop on the other side though.

The house looked dark and quiet, which was just how I wanted it. Too late I hoped they didn't have dogs running loose in the grounds. After a few minutes crouched amongst some climbing roses I decided if there were any, they were asleep too. I waited until the moon was hidden behind a nice big cloud and jogged up to the house.

Charley had given me his lock picking kit so I set to work on the back door. I wasn't as good as he was, but it didn't take me more than two minutes until the cylinders turned over with a loud click. I froze, not daring to breathe, and strained my ears to hear anything. Had someone heard? Nothing. I tried the handle, pleasantly surprised that they hadn't bothered to bolt it.

I slipped inside and took a moment to get my bearings. We hadn't had a lot of time to kick around and explore when we were here before. All I remembered was a bunch of corridors and gorillas in suits waving guns. Funny how small things like that can distract you.

I couldn't hear anyone moving around, so I looked for the big room with the fireplace and the adjacent office. It was as dark as the inside of a barrel in there, but I didn't risk a torch. I had just found the room with the fireplace, when I heard a toilet flush upstairs. I shut the door behind me and minced over to the office to find a place to hide. Whoever it was might decide to come downstairs for a midnight snack. I listened to a set of bare footsteps track their way above my head, then a door closed and bedsprings creaked as someone got into bed. I breathed a bit easier and got back to the task at hand.

I flicked on a small torch, covered most of the beam with my hand and checked my surroundings. I half expected to see Just Jenny laying naked on the couch again, but fortunately she wasn't. I installed a transmitter into the phone base and wired it all up. It was a bit riskier than the basic recorder, but I'd be able to pick up the transmission from outside the walls, so I wouldn't have to break back in and collect the tapes.

I was about to leave, but couldn't resist a bit of a snoop around. The desk was covered with papers. Invoices and receipts mostly. I read a bunch of them and tried to find anything of interest. A couple of shipping manifests caught my attention, but I couldn't tell you why. Something was circling around in the depths of my memory, something familiar I ought to know, but I couldn't work out what it was. I didn't have a camera, so I just memorised their contents and put them back carefully where I found them.

Getting out always seemed to take a lot longer than getting in. Seems to be true of a lot of things in my life. My arse was well and truly twitching with tension by the time I got onto the back porch and set to work on the lock. Always lock up after yourself. Climbing back over the wall was a complete ball-ache. My arms and knees were scratched and bruised by the time I had managed to pull myself over it, using the small mortar lines between the large stones. I dropped down on the other side in relief and took a few minutes to rest. Before I left I set up a receiver and a tape recorder buried under a bush and covered over the disturbed ground with some fallen leaves. It would only turn on the tape if any sound was picked up, and we'd get up to six hours of conversation.

By the time I got back to the cottage I was ready for a shower and a drink. Charley was there. He was pale and his skin was shiny and stretched around his eyes.

'Are you okay?'

He grunted. 'All done?'

'Yep.' I told him about the recorder hidden outside their walls and got a nod of approval. 'When was the last time you slept?' I asked.

'I dunno. Three or four days. I can't remember.'

I felt a twinge of guilt. I'd at least managed to snag a few hours. Charley was relying on pills, coffee and bloody-mindedness.

'Why don't you get some sleep,' I offered. 'I think we know enough about our target's habits for me to cover them for a while.'

'You sure?'

'Of course. I was also thinking we should tell the Smallwoods and their boys to stand down for a couple of days. Tell them that they need to build their strength up, ready for the job.'

Charley frowned. 'I'm having trouble remembering my name right now Dicky. You're going to have to spell it out for me.'

'We need to give the Smallwoods a chance to go home and make some calls.'

'Dicky, you're talking like a fucking pro now. What happened to you?'

'Just go and get some rest. You're no good to anyone like this.'

He didn't need to be told again.

I got on the radio after he'd gone and broke the good news to the Smallwoods. I didn't get a whisper of protest. They were even more knackered than we were.

We took a day off from following the Grossmans. They were as predictable as hell. I could have written down their movements for the day without getting out of bed. I pretended to follow them for appearances sake, but I was more interested in the Smallwoods. I swung by a used car place and bought a cheap banger for cash. Something the Smallwoods wouldn't recognise. I drove over to the mansion and watched the place. Most of the morning everything was quiet. Then just after lunch I heard a horn going off. There was a dark sedan waiting outside their gate. A few moments later I saw one of the Smallwood gang, Smiling John, come out of the house and open the gates. He went round to the car window, which lowered, and spoke to the driver. They spoke long enough that I was sure he wasn't just giving them directions. That and the regular glances across to the house and over his shoulder. Then the car drove inside, and he closed the gates after them and followed the car up to the house.

I was itching to get over there and get eyes on what was going on inside, but I had to be patient. I scribbled the number plate down in my notebook. I could get London to trace it if it became interesting. They were inside for half an hour, then the gates opened again and the car drove out. I couldn't get a good look inside, but I saw four shadowy silhouettes within. I gave it another half an hour for things to settle, then ran out of patience. I left my car and took off round the back of the property to retrieve the tape. It might have picked something up.

It was undisturbed, and I quickly dug it up. I pulled out the tape, replaced it with a fresh one and reburied it. Time to leave. I figured I'd probably seen enough, and I wanted to get back to the cottage and listen to the tape.

Charley was awake when I got back. Groggy and in a foul mood, but awake.

'I've got something to cheer you up,' I said, waving the tape in front of him.

'Let's hear it then,' he snatched it from me and shoved it into the machine. After letting it rewind he pressed play and we settled down to listen.

'Where was the microphone?' asked Charley as it picked up the sound of the door opening.

'In the office.'

There were sounds of a couple of pairs of footsteps walking across the floor. Then Sean Smallwood's voice.

'Do you reckon they'll go ahead this time?'

'They'd better.' That was Seamus. 'Otherwise we're fucked.'

There was general chit-chat for a few minutes - Sean was a whiny bastard - then Seamus swore, and we heard an envelope being opened.

'What is it?'

Seamus grunted. 'Letter from O'Neill.' There was silence while he read it, followed by an expletive.

'He's coming over.'

'Fuck. Does he expect the money?'

'How the fuck do I know? We'd better think of something to tell him.'

'Just tell him about the job on Friday.'

'Don't be a fucking retard Sean. They can't know about the bank job. Not south of the border. Try to pay attention.'

'Oh yeah.'

They left the room and the tape cut out and restarted when the door opened some time later. How much later I couldn't tell.

This time no one said anything, but plenty of rustling of paper, drawers opening and closing. Then footsteps leaving and the door shutting behind them.

The tape jumped once more as the door opened again.

'Come in,' said Seamus obsequiously. Lots of footsteps moving all around the room.

'So you'll be telling me what has happened to my shipment then?' An Irish accent.

'Well you know, we've been looking into that. It never got here.' Someone, presumably Seamus, picked up some papers, 'Here, see for yourself.'

A bit of a pause, and then Seamus started talking again, the way you do when you're trying to fill an uncomfortable silence. 'The container was intercepted. All the merchandise was impounded. Fucking ragheads must have been tipped off.'

'You'll be mistaking me for someone who give a shite,' said the voice. There was silence. Then the voice spoke again, 'You owe us a lot of money Smallwood. If I don't see it by this time next week, I'm going to come back with a corkscrew and a pair of pliers and take it out of your fooking fat arse, an ounce at a time. Do I make myself clear?'

Chapter Thirteen

I looked at Charley. The tape burbled on as the Smallwood's visitors left and then cut out a few seconds after the door closed.

'Sounds like the brothers are in deep shit,' said Charley.

'Yeah, I'm sure we're all really sorry about that. We need to find out who this O'Neill character is. I've got the number plate of their car. I'll call Blondie and get her to trace it. Get her to do something for her pay.'

'Why do we care?' asked Charley with a yawn. 'We're going to hang the slags out to dry anyway.'

'Maybe so, but I don't want anyone coming after us next.' I got up and made the call. The car would take a while to trace. The girls back in London would have to call the Northern Irish police and get them to contact the Southern Irish Garda, negotiate the retrieval of the information and then wait while someone went and searched through the files to find the car. Plus it was night-time. Probably wouldn't get any news for a couple of days.

Something occurred to me. Something I'd heard on the tape made a connection with something I'd seen in the office in that mysterious way the brain works that I'll never understand. 'Saudi.' I said.

'What?'

'I saw a shipping manifest in the office. It was for a container out of Jeddah bound for Cork. The container number was the same as the one we painted.'

Charley looked at me, trying to sort through the connection. 'That can't be a fucking coincidence.'

'Not a chance. How long would it take for a shipping container to get from Saudi to Ireland?'

'I don't know. Months probably.'

'I thought we'd fucked up in Saudi. That they knew we'd identified the container. Maybe they didn't and they let it leave. Then it was intercepted on the way.'

Charley frowned. 'It's possible. Shit, how did we wind up on the other end of this?'

We looked at each other, and we both realised at the same time. 'Blondie,' I said.

'She must have known what was in that container and where it was going.'

'What is she up to, do you think?'

Charley shrugged, 'Who cares? She's not likely to tell us. Maybe she thought it would be funny?'

I didn't like it. Something felt wrong. Like we were being played again. I rubbed my eyes and realised how tired I was.

'We can't let this distract us,' said Charley. 'We proceed as planned.'

I nodded. 'Agreed. Friday the thirteenth we do the job.'

Charley's eyes widened, 'Friday the thirteenth? Why the hell did they have to pick that date?'

I gave him a wry smile, 'Superstitious?'

His reaction took me by surprise. He jumped up and kicked his chair clear across the room, causing shards of wood to fly off it. 'Fuck!' He snatched up a mug and threw it across the room where it shattered into a dozen pieces, 'Fuck, fuck, fuck!'

I didn't know what his problem was, but I didn't want to become a target. I backed up and let him rant. Eventually he calmed down, but he kept whining and moaning to himself.

'Are you done now?' I asked quietly. The kitchen was a mess, and his knuckles were bleeding from where he had taken a few swings at the brickwork. The bricks had won.

'Fucking northern monkeys,' he muttered. 'Some really bad things have happened to me on Friday the thirteenth.'

'We've got a couple of days,' I said, trying to get his head back into the game. 'Let's get the Smallwoods together tomorrow and go over the plan again. Make sure they've got all the stuff they'll need.'

Charley nodded and started to engage. 'Okay, fine. But let's get some sleep first.'

I had no objection to that.

We knew that the next couple of days would be difficult. Trying to keep a reign on the Smallwoods was the hard bit. We came up with some exercises and activities to keep them busy, such as collecting equipment; ropes, electrical tape, masks and so on. The boys were excited by that. They felt like things were moving finally. They were grinning and handling the guns and knives in a disturbingly sexual way.

'What do you reckon we should do with them first?' asked one excitedly.

'You'll not do anything without good reason,' I interrupted. 'We go in there, tie up the wife and make it clear that the husband better do what he's told. He's no good to us if he's a quivering wreck because he's just watched you carve his better half up.'

There were nods, but the gleam still didn't quite leave their eyes.

'I'm worried about the manager's wife,' I said to Charley that night. The night before the op. 'The plan entails us doing the prep and then letting the Smallwood team taking over. We'll have no control.'

'I'm sure the Smallwoods will be very professional,' he said.

'But what about the others? They might be sadists and rapists for all we know.'

'Don't worry son, I'll make sure those scumbags know a slow and painful death awaits them if they embarrass us.'

'Will that be enough?'

'Leave it to me runt. I've got an idea.'

The next day we were all on edge. Even Charley seemed a bit more tense than normal. The waiting was the hard bit. We followed our routine and put a tail on each of them as they left the house and went to work. Mrs Grossman left the Catholic school where she worked at exactly six o'clock, just like she did every day, and Mr Grossman left the bank at half past five and drove straight home. We set the van up and listened to them nattering to each other. Talking about colleagues at work mostly. Charley and I were alone in the van. I was getting restless as the time for the break-in drew closer and I started to think of all kinds of unhelpful things.

'Do you feel sorry for the Smallwoods?' I asked. Charley gave me a look like I'd asked him if goblins existed. I felt obliged to explain myself. 'I mean, they think we're here, sent by their favourite aunt Blondie to help them rob half of Ireland and what is really going to happen is we are going to serve them up to the Garda and put them at the top of the IRA's Christmas wish-list.'

'Keep your bullshit sympathy to yourself son,' said Charley, 'What makes you think the Smallwoods don't already know this? Maybe they are planning to offer us up the the Garda instead?'

'Is that possible?' I wondered if it were just the pills talking. Making Charley think things that weren't true.

'Of course it's possible. Do you think they are stupid? The only thing we know for sure is that the Firm will do what's best for them and fuck us. They won't even pause to think. We're just cannon fodder. If they suddenly decided they wanted to keep the Smallwoods active, we'd be toast.'

'So what do we do to protect our sorry asses?'

'Against the Firm? Not a lot to be honest. Do the job and hope for the best. I've long given up trying to second-guess that barrel of monkeys mate. They know all about us and the op. Against the Smallwoods is a different matter. We can get some leverage against them.'

'What did you have in mind?'

Charley grinned. 'Just follow my lead, son.'

We took the two Smallwoods to dinner that evening. Charley had found a place that did steaks. It was a family-run place made of timber which was supposed to look like an American ranch house. The waitresses wore tight denim shorts and checker shirts tied into a knot under their breasts to show off their washboard tummies. Trust Charley to have found this.

'Well boys, are you ready for tomorrow morning?' Charley asked, wiping steak juice from his mouth and reaching for a pint of stout.

'Fucking right,' said Sean. 'What time do we go?'

'Four in the morning,' explained Charley, 'Then we babysit them until eight when you boys take the manager to the bank to open the place up. I reckon it'll take fifteen to twenty minutes to fill up the bags with as many notes as you can, and then you bug out, your boys leave the wife tied up at home and we all rendezvous back at the cottage to count the spoils.'

'What are you lads going to do?' asked Seamus.

'We'll stop outside and keep an eye out. Wouldn't want the whole thing to go south because some passing Garda got curious.'

Seamus grinned and sat back contentedly.

'Now, we've got a surprise for you,' said Charley. He gave me a wink and I wondered what he was up to. 'Dick, why don't you take Sean here out to the car and show him what we've got for him in the boot?'

Sean looked up eagerly. 'What did you get me?' He was probably expecting a gun of some kind.

'You'll love it. We used something similar in Dartmoor on a training run, remember Dick?'

I stood up. I had a good idea what was in the boot. 'Come on Sean, you'll love it.'

Sean followed me out to the car park. There were a lot of cars out there, but no one was around. I led the way over to the Datsun and got ready to open the boot.

'Stay close,' I said, 'We don't want anyone to see now, do we?'

I popped the boot and gestured to Sean to bend down and take a look. As he did, I stepped up and brought my elbow down on the back of his neck, driving his head into the rim. He went down, and I quickly scooped his legs up and bundled him tidily into the boot. He groaned as I was about to close it. Shit. That wasn't meant to happen. I took a quick look around and then bent over him, turned his head to the side and gave the hollow part at the base of his skull a solid whack with the butt of my pistol. He went quiet instantly. That could have been embarrassing.

I jumped into the car and drove it down the road about a hundred yards and hid it in some bushes. Then I jogged back to the steakhouse to give Charley some backup. They had moved onto coffee and cigars and Seamus looked up expectantly as I entered.

'Where's Sean?'

Charley placed a friendly arm across Seamus' shoulder, which also kept him from moving away. 'He's taken a little trip with some friends of ours.'

'What? Why?'

'Nothing to worry about, Seamus,' said Charley, 'Just a little insurance policy we've taken out. Your little brother is the insurance, just in case you might be thinking about screwing us over.'

Seamus tried to jerk away but Charley held him tightly. Seamus scowled, 'This is hardly the spirit of cooperation I was promised Charley.'

'We know all about northern monkey cooperation, Seamus. I appreciate your anxiety, but business is business, and let's face it, we have no idea who you actually work for or where your loyalties lie. Providing all is sweet this time tomorrow, you will have your sticky money and your brother. If you still want him of course.'

Seamus turned a strange purple colour as he struggled to control himself.

'Remember,' continued Charley, 'if anything happens to us or for that matter to the Grossmans, your brother gets fed to the pigs, and I'm not talking about the police.'

'If you harm Sean I'll kill you, you cunts.'

'Oh Seamus I'm sorry, but I've had the Gypsy warning before.' He gave Seamus another firm squeeze and then stepped away. There wasn't a lot Seamus could do, and he knew it.

'So then Seamus,' I said, 'We'll let you and your boys in at oh-four-hundred. Make sure you're there.'

'You make sure *you're* there,' he snarled.

Charley and I left and made our way back to the car to check on Sean. The car was still where I had left it in the bushes. Charley opened the boot.

'You need to get some oil on these hinges son.'

'Oil them yourself. Is he still alive?'

Charley reached down and checked for a pulse. 'Yeah he's got a strong pulse. He'll be awake in an hour or so.'

'We'd better find some place to stash him. I don't suppose you thought that far ahead did you?'

'Have no fear my little apprentice. I spotted an old farmhouse up near the cottage the other day. There's a decent silo there that will make a great cell for him.'

I shut the boot again and got back into the car. 'Better give me directions then.'

The farmhouse was only a mile from the cottage. It had once been used to harvest crops that grew on the acres of surrounding fields, but now it was run-down and empty. There were several knackered old barns built to store farm equipment and one of them housed a thirty-foot high silo that would have originally contained grain. It was open at the top and had a small door near the bottom to take the grain out, but it was all seized up with rust now and wouldn't open. We dragged Sean out of the trunk and dumped him on the ground. He was still out cold.

'How hard did you hit him, Dicky?'

'Not too hard. He must have a glass jaw.'

'Grab his legs then, we'd better carry him the rest of the way.'

I looked up at the silo when we got him inside and spotted a flaw in Charley's plan. 'So, how are we going to get him inside it then?'

Charley tapped his head, 'I've got it all sorted. All we have to do is shimmy up the ladder on the side and sling a rope over the beam up there. Then we just hoist him up and lower him inside.'

I studied the silo. The ladder welded to the side of it looked as worn out as the rest of the place. 'I suppose you expect me to do the shimmying don't you?'

'Bloody hell, that's good of you to offer,' said Charley, 'what with my bad knee and all.'

I didn't bother to argue. Charley produced a rope and I took one end of it and tied it loosely through my belt. The climb up was about as bad as I thought it was going to be. Every other rung sagged, like it was going to snap through, so I kept my feet toward the outer edges just in case.

At the top I was still well out of reach of the girder.

'I don't think this is going to work, Charley,' I called down.

'It will if you stand on the top,' he shouted back.

I looked. 'There is no bloody top. Just a rim. Plus it stinks down there. Like rotten sewage.' I didn't fancy Sean's next few hours.

'Just grow a pair, would you?'

I sighed and climbed higher, perching right on the top rung of the ladder and bracing my shins against the rust-thin silo. I wobbled but caught my balance and gingerly reached up with the free end of the rope and carefully threaded it over the girder. My heart must have been doing a hundred and sixty by the time I'd lowered myself back down to a less precarious position.

When I got back to the ground we tied the rope under Sean's shoulders and both grabbed the other end and pulled. He was heavier than he looked, and even with the two of us pulling it was tiring work. My arms were burning by the time we got him to the top. Getting him over the edge wasn't too hard, since the rope was pivoted over the silo, but I knew that getting him out again would be a bugger. I'd probably have to climb up there and pull him across. Lowering him down was easier, but Charley let go too early, and left me struggling. I was too tired to hold him for long, and the rope slipped through my fingers painfully. There was a loud echoing clang as Sean fell the last six or seven feet.

'Careful Dick, we don't want to off him if we don't have to.'

'Why did you let go then, you arse? I hope you're going to apologise to him later.'

'I thought you had him. Well no use worrying about that now. He didn't wake up so maybe he'll sleep through until morning. He'll never know. If he's dead, fuck him.'

I blew on my palms to relieve the burning. 'Let's just get over to the bank manager's house shall we?'

Chapter Fourteen

We got there a bit before eleven at night. We'd told the Smallwoods to be there at four in the morning, but I wanted to be inside ready and waiting for when the boys turned up. We knew that the Grossmans went to bed at ten on the dot, and the lights normally went out at a quarter past. We were a bit surprised when the bedroom lights stayed on until almost midnight.

'Ah we forgot that Friday is their special night,' smirked Charley.

'They don't need the lights on for that. I'm sure he knows where it is by now. She must like it with the light on. We'd better give them a bit longer before we go in.'

I pulled at the balaclava I was wearing. 'Where did you get this clava Charley? It must have been made for a giant.'

'It's the normal size. It's just you who has a head a couple of sizes too small, like your dick.'

'Just be ready. Give it a half hour then cut the phone line.'

Charley grunted and crawled off under the hedge to get into position.

When the half hour rolled around I crept to the back door and got out the duplicate key to open it. I stepped inside quietly and the first thing I heard was the old man snoring away. At least I hope it was the man. I did a careful recce and checked the other rooms. They were all empty and confirmed that the Grossmans were in their bedroom, sleeping away. I opened the front door and let Charley in. We settled down in the front room to wait for the Smallwoods to turn up.

At four o'clock Charley nudged me and pointed at the window. It was briefly illuminated by an external light. Then again. And again. Three flashes. That was the signal we'd agreed on.

'I'm surprised they remembered,' grunted Charley and I got up to open the door. In they came, good as gold, and filed quietly into the front room. They were carrying their sawn-off shotguns and wearing masks. Seamus had a couple of sets of handcuffs and some ball gags looped around his belt.

'So where are they?' he whispered loudly.

'Are you eager to crack on?' I asked in a pointedly quieter voice.

'Damn right.' He showed me his yellowed teeth in what I took to be a smile.

'Calm down and take a moment,' I said, 'They are nicely tucked up in bed. You might as well wait an hour or two before going in there. Otherwise you'll be babysitting them all night.'

Seamus thought about that for a bit. He was clearly the brains of the family, but I could still almost see the cogs going round in his head as he realised I was making sense. 'All right,' he agreed. 'Take a seat lads.'

The gang sat themselves down and settled in for a wait. At least it was warmer in here than it was outside.

We managed to hold them off until nearly half past five, and then their patience snapped. Seamus led the way into the bedroom and we heard a sudden explosion of shouts and screams as they went to work on the Grossmans. I started to go and check out what they were doing, but Charley grabbed hold of my arm and stopped me.

'Hang on son. No point in getting involved if you don't need to. They're just putting the shits into the happy couple.'

Sure enough, it wasn't long before the Smallwood gang came out of the bedroom dragging the bank manager and his wife into the front room.

'Lucky for you they're both wearing their pyjamas,' I said to Charley, 'I'm not sure your old ticker could take seeing her in the altogether.'

I moved to the side of the room and positioned myself so I was behind the Grossmans. No point risking being identified.

The bank manager and his wife were reacting just like you'd expect. They were scared shitless. We'd determined that they were both slaves to convention, and that even though they both held jobs where they told other people what to do, they had gained those positions by doing what they were told, so under stress, they would revert to the behaviour that had served them well in the past. In other words, they'd do whatever we told them. We probably didn't need the weapons.

'You'd better listen good,' Seamus was saying to the bank manager. 'You're going to get dressed in your best pinstripe, and accompany me and a couple of my boys to the bank. Your wife will stop here with the rest of the guys until we get back. If you take too long or try anything funny, she's going to find the last few minutes of her life very messy and very painful. Understand?'

Harold Grossman understood. His wife let out a little squeal and fainted. 'Don't hurt her,' he whimpered, 'I'll do what you want.' He started to cry, which was a bit embarrassing really. Even Seamus seemed a little thrown by that.

It took no time at all to get the keys to the Grossman's cars. Mr. Grossman had to help us out with that with that one, since his wife preferred to collapse face-down on the floor. Smiling John took Grossman back to the bedroom to get him dressed. The other boys grinned at each other.

'We fucking did it,' crowed one of the mouthier guys. 'Did you see him go to pieces?'

'This is going to be a piece of piss,' said another. 'What are you gonna spend your share on?'

'Now then lads,' interrupted Seamus, 'Let's play this out first. We can celebrate when we have the cash in a safe place. Not before.'

'Right boss,' came a bunch of replies, but I could see they were all still picturing the flash new cars they could get when it was all over. I was impressed with Seamus for saying that, but he had probably been burned by our little demonstration with his brother and didn't trust us any more. Smart of him, considering the circumstances.

Smiling John came back with Grossman, who looked like he was going to puke. He also needed a shave and a comb. If it was my arse on the line, I'd have made sure he tidied himself up and looked like he was actually going to go into work, but I didn't say anything. The gang was going to get burned anyway. Mrs. Grossman had regained consciousness by then and I saw the mew of disapproval on her face too, but she quickly hid it. Maybe she was smart enough to have the same thought?

Seamus got everyone's attention. 'Myself and you three are going to take Mr. Grossman here on a little drive. The rest of you stop here and look after Mrs. Grossman.'

This is how we'd planned it. Seamus had to be in the bank when the Garda arrived, which was the whole point of this exercise from our point of view. The others were there to drive the car and load it up while Seamus kept an eye on Grossman. I had suggested they leave three guys looking after Mrs. Grossman because she was probably safer that way. One guy on his own couldn't be trusted and two could egg each other on. A third person would screw over all those dynamics and keep them all well behaved. Unless all three were psychopathic rapists, in which case she was in trouble, but there wasn't a lot I could do about that. Casualties of war and all that. Charley and I were on lookout, in another car. We needed to be able to tip off the Garda when the gang entered the bank.

Seamus turned to us and gave Charley an inscrutable look for a few seconds. 'You two had better get into position, and make sure that my brother is ready for when we finish this.'

His words seem to have woken everyone up, because they all did a comedy swinging of heads as if they had only just realised that Sean wasn't there.

'Where is he?' asked Smiling John with a snarl.

Seamus narrowed his eyes and jabbed a finger at us. 'These fuckers decided to hold onto him until the job was done.'

Everyone turned to look at us. They weren't friendly looks. I was itching to reach around to the back of my trousers and grab my gun, but it wouldn't have done me a lot of good. Everyone else had shotguns at the ready. It was going to get very messy if we weren't careful.

'Now then Seamus, we talked about this and agreed it was for the best,' smiled Charley. I wanted to kick him. The man never knew when to keep his mouth shut. He was going to get me killed some day.

'We agreed nothing,' snarled Seamus. 'Except that if he comes back with as much as a bump on his knee, I'll make sure you boys never leave these shores alive.'

Smiling John fingered his sawn-off and swivelled it in my direction. 'We only need one of them to fetch him back.'

'If you do anything to us he'll be delivered back to you in jiffy bags, a bit at a time,' said Charley.

My arse couldn't take any more clenching. 'Let's calm down and do the job,' I said. 'In a couple of hours you'll have your money and your brother, and we'll be on our way. Otherwise this whole thing goes tits up, and no one gets anything.'

There was a long period of silence and glaring. I managed to look cool and relaxed, even though I was about to wet myself. Then Seamus broke into a grin and spread his hands out to welcome us back in. 'Your boy is right. We can have this conversation later, once we have the money.'

The tension eased a little, but from the dark looks flashed our way it was obvious we were never going to be forgiven. Maybe snatching Sean hadn't been such a great idea after all.

'Come on Dick,' said Charley, 'Let's make sure young Sean is comfortable.'

We backed out of the house, keeping our eyes on the gang until we were outside. Then we walked quickly back to the car. It was still dark, which I was grateful for.

'That was a bit close,' I breathed as we got safely away.

'Nah, they were never going to do anything,' said Charley casually. I looked across at him.

'Were you in that room just then? If those boys ever see us again we're dead.'

'Just as well that will never happen then. We'd better go and get Sean. He's more useful to us alive than dead at the moment.'

I swung the car in the direction of the farmhouse. It was a cold, foggy morning and very damp. I wouldn't have fancied a night in the silo. We pulled up and as we stepped out of the car we heard a repetitive dull clanging coming from the barn.

'I think we can assume he's still alive,' said Charley.

As we got closer we could also hear some hoarse cries coming from the silo. He'd probably been yelling for help for hours. Charley went up to the silo and banged on the side of it with his fist. 'Morning Sean. Sleep well?'

'You fucking bastards!' Sean rasped. 'I'm going to fucking rip your balls off.'

'Now now, no need to be crude,' said Charley. 'Have you still got that rope tied to you?'

I looked around for the other end of the rope where we'd left it dangling down from the rafter. It wasn't there.

'You bloody well know I have,' yelled Sean. 'It's all in here with me now.'

Charley let out a short laugh. 'Let me guess, you tried to climb up it and instead you pulled it all inside?'

Sean didn't answer, but it was clear that's what he'd done.

'Well we have a problem now Sean,' said Charley, 'because we don't have any more rope, so unless you can toss the free end up and over again, you're stuck in there.'

Sean came up with some really inventive things that Charley could do with the free end of the rope that I'm sure his dear old mother would have been horrified to hear. We let him rant for a bit but eventually we had to come up with a solution.

'You need something heavy to tie to the end of the rope, then throw it up over the edge,' I suggested. It would be a difficult throw, especially as there wasn't a lot of room in there and the funnel-shaped floor wasn't exactly very flat, but it was the only plan we had.

'Aye, I reckon a shotgun would be heavy enough if you have one,' said Sean.

'Sorry old boy, can't help with that,' said Charley. 'What a fucking fiasco.'

'Is it always like this with you?' I asked.

'It's like this with everyone Dicky. That's why I never bother to plan. No fucking point.'

I rooted around and found an old lifting hook. It would be heavy enough to compensate for the weight of the rope but light enough to throw thirty feet up. I hoped. I climbed up the ladder, which was even harder carrying that bloody thing in one hand.

'All right Sean,' I said as I peered over the top. The stink hit me hard and I struggled not to gag. I could just about make him out in the shadows. Even though it was now daylight outside, not a lot of light was getting in. 'I'm going to drop this down to you. Tie the other end of the rope to it and toss it back. I'll try to grab it.'

Sean grumbled something incomprehensible, but after a while called out 'Ready?'

'Go ahead.'

I heard a grunt as he threw it, but didn't see the rope come anywhere close. Then I heard a cry of pain followed by a clang as the hook fell back on his head and bounced onto the floor of the silo.

'Fuck!' he screamed, and repeated himself about a dozen times.

I waited until he had finished, and said, 'You need to throw it a little harder mate.'

I got a torrent of abuse back, but this time I saw the rope get up to within about five feet of me. It fell back down, but Sean was ready this time and stepped out of the way. It didn't half make the silo ring though. Can't have done Sean's hearing much good. He tried another couple of times, and then managed to get enough height that it cleared the rim of the silo. Trouble was, it landed on the opposite side to me, and I couldn't reach it.

'Okay, Sean, try pulling the rope gently to the side. You need to slide the thing round to me.'

He tugged on the rope, but all that happened was that the rope snagged on the rim and stayed where it was while the hook was pulled up and was in danger of falling back down again.

'Stop! Stop!' I yelled just before it fell. I looked around for something else to use. 'Just hold it there. I'll be right back.'

I climbed down the ladder and scanned the barn. There wasn't a lot in it. All the tools were gone and though there were some scraps of debris and litter lying about, none of it looked particularly useful.

'Here, try this,' said Charley. He had kicked a plank out of one of the doors. It was five foot in length, which was about right, and had a couple of twisted nails jutting out of one end.

I grabbed the board and climbed up again. Half way up, I was so busy concentrating on not dropping it and not falling, that I was careless where I put my foot and one of the rungs gave way. My foot dropped through to the one below and I felt a hot rush of pain in my shin as I left several layers of skin on the broken rung. I barely managed to hang onto the ladder and board and took a few moments until the pain settled down from a fiery burn to a dull throb. I could feel my trousers getting damp with blood.

'Careful Dick. If you fall it'll be a disaster. It'll mean I'd have to go up there instead.'

I ignored Charley and carried on climbing. When I got to the top I used the plank to snare the hook, using the nails as claws. It was a bit of a faff, but slowly I got it close enough to grab. Then I had to do my balancing act again and stand on the top of the ladder to reach the rafter, only this time I had an injured leg which stung every time I tried to put weight on it, and a heavy hook attached to the rope threatening to unbalance me. As I threaded the rope over I toppled sideways. I stopped myself falling by jamming my shins against the top of the rim, which reopened the scabbing wound. I hoped I wouldn't get tetanus from the rusty ladder. As if that were more dangerous than a sudden thirty foot fall onto concrete. I pulled the rope through and the hook assisted its fall down to the ground where Charley was waiting to grab it.

'Got it Dick. Now get back down here and give me a hand. I can't do all this by myself you know?'

A few choice words flickered across my thoughts but I kept them to myself and gingerly let myself down again. Despite what he'd said, Charley had already started to haul Sean up by the time I got down. Sean was groaning in pain as the rope cut into him, but there wasn't a lot we could do about that. I grabbed hold of the rope and helped Charley pull him to the top, which was surprisingly easy with the two of us working together. Unfortunately we overcooked it a bit and Sean banged his head on the rafter as he went shooting up.

'Ow!'

'Careful Sean. You might want to watch out for that.'

There was a bit of scrabbling and swearing, then Sean said, 'I can't reach the edge.'

Charley and I looked at each other, then up at the silo.

'I think you're going to have to go back up there Dick and pull him over.'

'For fucks sake,' I said. 'Can't we just leave him here and just tell the fuckers where they can find him?'

'That's not a bad idea actually,' said Charley.

I really didn't want go back up that ladder. Besides, I wasn't convinced that Sean would be a nice boy and not take a swing at me the second I was in reach. There were better places to have a fight than on the edge of a rickety old silo.

Charley and I grinned at each other, and then started lowering him back down into the silo.

'Hey you fuckers!' Sean yelled.

We got him down to the bottom and then left him there, with the rope still hanging over the rafter.

'You might want to leave that rope there this time,' said Charley. 'It'll make it easier for the next guys to pull you out.'

I was expecting a stream of insults and threats as we walked away, but not the sudden pitying howl of terror, sobbing and pleading that came from Sean. It was still ringing in my ears as we drove off.

Chapter Fifteen

'Do you reckon they've started yet?' I asked. It was nearly seven thirty. We'd wasted almost an hour messing about with Sean.

'They should have, they need to be out of there by eight.'

I looked out of the window at the sky. It was overcast and angry. The fog hadn't cleared and everything was a dark, foreboding grey. 'I can't wait until I get out of this country.'

'Not long now Dicky, then we can be on a plane to Amsterdam and spend a pleasant couple of days being debriefed by some of the finest whores in Europe.'

'Amsterdam?'

'Blondie wants us to decamp there after this is all over instead of going straight back to Blighty.'

'When did she tell you that?' I thought I'd been the only one in contact with her since we'd arrived, and I sure as hell didn't remember her saying anything about it before we left.

'Must have been while you were in the khasi or something,' said Charley a little too casually.

I couldn't give him the stare he deserved, since I was driving as usual, but I flicked him an annoyed glance. He was definitely boning her. She'd probably told him on one of the odd occasions when her mouth wasn't full. 'You got anything else you need to tell me?'

'Don't worry son, I've got your back. Need to know and all that.'

I fumed for a bit, then spotted a phone booth and pulled over. 'Talking of her highness, we'd better call in and tell her the job is on.'

'Good idea.' Charley looked outside. 'Looks like rain out there. You'd better be quick.'

I noticed he didn't volunteer to do it himself. I squeezed past the heavy door and dialled the number using a handful of funny Irish coins.

'I don't mind Whiskey, but I can't stand the Tangy aftertaste.' There's only so many variations of the way 'Whiskey' and 'Tango' can be used in a sentence. It was a stupid code, but rules were rules. I hung up and waited for the ring back. Rain started to fall. Big, fat drops at first, then it became torrential, hammering loudly on the glass panes and cast iron roof. The phone rang sooner than I expected. I snatched it up. I could barely hear the voice at the other end over the rain. It was a man.

'We're on,' I said. 'The brothers Grimm are in the enchanted castle ready for the brave knights to arrive.'

'Where are you now?' asked the man.

I looked on the wall behind the phone and read off the address that was printed there. 'We're about to go off to the airport. Oh, by the way, little brother Grimm is stuck in a silo in the old farm half a mile east.'

There was a pause while the guy at the other end made some notes, then he said, 'Understood,' and hung up. I put the phone back on the cradle and looked out into the rain, trying to work out how wet I was going to get and whether it was worth waiting a few minutes. Charley wouldn't care, but the quicker we were on our way out of the country before the boys started blabbing the better, so I made a run for it.

Back in the car I wiped my face dry and shook out my hair, mainly because it would annoy Charley.

'There's no need for all that,' moaned Charley as he wiped away the water drops.

'It's all good. Let's get to the airport.' I put the car into gear and pulled away. The rain was so heavy I had the wipers on fast and I still couldn't see where the hell I was going. I had to drive at about twenty miles an hour to make sure I didn't put us into a ditch. It didn't help that the car windows got all steamed up inside and the car was such a banger that the heater fan didn't work.

'Open a window, I can't see a fucking thing.'

'Bollocks to that, I'll get soaked. Open your own bloody window.'

I cracked mine open a bit. Rain started pissing through, but I was wet anyway. At least the window started to clear up.

I squinted through a clear patch in the windscreen. 'What's that?'

'Fucking furniture van blocking the road. Must be trying to turn around.'

I looked in the mirror, 'Vehicles moving up behind.'

'Look for a side turning.'

'There aren't any.' I'd been down this stretch many times the past week and knew the road well. 'They're boxing us in!'

There were thick woods on both sides, with a ditch between them and the road. No way could we drive out that way. They'd picked their spot well. 'They must have been waiting for us.' I looked at Charley, 'What do you reckon? Leg it?'

'Leg it or you drive right through the side of that van.'

'Leg it then.'

Behind us the grey fog lit up in a bank of blue flashes. In front I saw uniformed Garda fanning out across the road. 'It's the cops. What did Blondie say about harming any of the local cops?'

'She said not under any circumstances, but fuck her. She used to be a field op. She knows the score. If any of them get in my way I'm not going to hold back.'

I nodded my agreement. 'You got ammo, cash, passports?'

'Yep. Now get out of the car slowly, hands up and move to my side. As soon as you are with me we both run like fuck.'

'Roger that. What's that noise?'

Charley looked up, 'Chopper. That's all we need. There'll be blood-hounds next.'

'Thanks to your bloody silo idea they won't need tracker dogs.'

'Come on, get out. Once we start running they'll start shooting. We're armed terrorists as far as they're concerned. Stay in the woods until that 'copter clears out.'

We slowly climbed out showing our hands were empty. There must have been about thirty cops, all yelling at us to lie on the floor. A lot of unfriendly pistols were pointed in our direction. I sidled over to Charley and wondered if it might be better to give ourselves up. We'd spend a few weeks inside and then Blondie would come through like she did for us in Saudi.

Or maybe not. They might just cut their losses and let us stew in there for the duration. We were both carrying illegal firearms and could probably be tied to the bank job, so we'd be looking at ten to fifteen years. Bollocks to that. We ran.

Shots followed us into the forest. All you can do is run as fast as you can. None of this zigzag nonsense. That just slows you down. It's hard enough for someone to hit a stationary target with a handgun beyond a couple of dozen yards. Harder when you are all wound up and excited because they are real people not paper targets, and harder still when they are moving and you are trying to track them through dense foliage. We'd have to be unlucky to be hit.

I'd forgotten about my injury though. Every other step sent shards of pain up my leg, like someone was running a cheese grater over it. Charley was ahead of me. I chanced a glance behind me to see that some of the younger, more enthusiastic officers had given chase. I put my head down, told myself that the pain wasn't there and ran harder.

We kept inside the tree-line, stretched off parallel to the road for a while, then turned away toward a hill. The rain was still coming down, although the leaves kept most of it away from us. Waterfalls of rainwater poured through the canopy and churned up the ground so it became slippery and muddy. We both had a few dodgy moments sliding into trees, tripping over slimy roots and ending up face down in the mulch. So did the Garda behind us, but they were more precious about their safety and their nice uniforms. We started to leave them behind.

'Up the hill,' panted Charley.

I couldn't hear the helicopter any more. The shouts behind us were distant, but that was no reason to slow up. The ground became rocky which was worse in some ways as it was slick with moss and slime and hurt a lot more when you fell over. My chest was thick with mucous and it hurt to breathe. I'd thought I was fit but made a deal with myself that if I got out of this intact I'd run a lot more, and maybe give up the fags. Yeah right.

'Listen,' gasped Charley.

'Dogs.' I said a few seconds later.

'We need to find a river or something. They'll have been all over that car and got our scent.'

'Have you got that dosh and docs in a waterproof?'

'Yes. And I have bags for the shooters.'

I tried to get my bearings. The rain was still coming down but at least now it was just raining steadily, not crashing down. 'I think there's a big lake over there somewhere. I remember it from when we were preparing our fishermen cover stories.'

'Lead the way Tonto. Those mutts aren't going to hang about.'

I set off down the hill at a run. It was easier than running up it, but more treacherous. You had less time to see where you were putting your feet. After ten minutes I was bleeding from a dozen more places and I'd lost count of how many bruises and scratches I'd picked up. The only thing that cheered me up was that Charley looked worse. He must have run face-first into a gorse bush.

'You're going to struggle getting on a plane with your face looking like that.'

'You don't seem to have any difficulty with yours,' he retorted.

I looked up as we topped a rise and saw a huge lake open up below us. 'There it is! Come on, hustle.'

'I remember why I left the army now. I hate all this tabbing about.'

We sprinted as fast as we dared down the slope to the lakeside. The sound of the dogs behind us seemed louder. They were getting close. At the edge of the lake Charley pulled a couple of plastic bags out of his jacket and passed one to me. I stowed my gun and spare clip into it and sealed it up before stuffing it in the front of my trousers.

'Ready Charley?'

'This is going to be bloody cold isn't it?'

'Yes. And wet.'

'We've got to get out of this poxy outfit Dicky.'

We jumped.

You think you are prepared for how cold lake water will be, but it always takes your breath away. We both surfaced gasping and swearing, but didn't waste any time and started swimming for the far shore. The water was choppy and the rain didn't help but at least they would make it difficult for the Garda to spot us. As long as we got far enough out of course.

The lake must have been a couple of miles wide and after only a third of it I was struggling. I had to ditch my jacket which was dragging me under and I lost all feeling in my hands and feet. I wanted to kick my shoes off too, but the training said that was the last thing you should do. Chances are you'd need to run on the other side.

If I was struggling, Charley was in worse shape. A few times he went under and I thought I'd lost him until he resurfaced sputtering. I grabbed hold of him and tried to keep him up, but he was a dead weight and grabbed out at me in a panic, pulling me under. I dug my fingernails into his wrist until he let go and got behind him, grabbing him under the arms and kicking up with my legs to get to the surface. I was totally confused about which way we were going. We were about half way across and both sides looked the same to me. I pulled Charley onto his back and held his face out of the water.

'Just float and rest,' I panted. He was too weak to reply, but his body went limp as he tried to relax and float. The rain beat down like a fire-hose. I trod water and scanned the shore looking for something I recognised. Nothing on the ground, but as I raised my face to take a breath I saw the distant speck of the helicopter hovering over one of the hills. That was good enough for me. I set off in the other direction, pulling Charley with me. It wouldn't take long before the dog handlers realised we had ditched into the lake and send the helicopter over to look for us.

It took twenty minutes to get to the shore, by which time Charley had recovered enough to make it under his own steam. We flopped onto the side like asthmatic fish, completely exhausted. I knew we needed to get under cover but all that was around was grassy hillside and all I wanted to do was lie there and breathe. It was Charley who moved first.

'Come on shorty,' he said wearily, grabbing my arm and hauling me to my feet. 'I think the airport is off the agenda today. We'd better find a place to hole up for a few days until we can bug out.'

We couldn't run, so we staggered as fast as we could stagger inland. Now we were on land we were wet and cold and I had no jacket. Charley still had his lightweight cagoule with the documents in but it was no protection against the dropping temperature. We looked for a cottage or a barn. Overhead a passenger jet roared by on final approach to Cork Airport, seeming to mock us. All around us was desolate hillside and old sheep-shit, but no sheep today. We kept the airport to our backs and struck out into the countryside. After an hour we hadn't made it too far, but had regained enough energy to start jogging which helped to warm our cores, but didn't do much for the extremities. Then Charley spotted something up ahead.

'Bingo, Dicky. There's a road.'

It was one of the most beautiful things I'd ever seen. Not a big road. There were no lane markings and no kerb, and it was only just wide enough for two cars to pass if they went really slowly and didn't mind clinking wing-mirrors, but it was a road, and that meant the chance for a car to come by. I was shivering violently by this time and recognised the early signs of hypothermia. I needed to get somewhere warm quickly.

'Get down out of sight over here,' said Charley. He was trembling too. We crouched down in the lee of a large boulder which more or less hid us from the road, if not the elements. It was still bloody raining.

The only problem with little rural roads like this one is that no bugger uses them. I kept looking at my nice waterproof watch as the minutes ticked by and absolutely nothing came along.

'N…now Dicky,' chattered Charley 'D..don't get excited, but I think we should get close together. Share our body heat.'

I nodded. Something else I'd learned in training. Really we should have shared a blanket or a sleeping bag and got naked together inside it, but we'd have to make do with cuddling up close. 'Don't tell the missus though, okay?'

Charley was too cold to laugh.

It was almost dark before a car came by, and we nearly missed it. Charley was asleep and I was so disorientated I thought the headlights were a dream I was having. I leapt up at the last minute on legs that were stiff and slow and stumbled into the road in front of the car. I didn't care if it was Special Branch at this point. If we didn't get under shelter soon we would be dead of exposure. The car screeched to a halt and almost took me out. I collapsed to my knees and was dimly aware of the car door opening and someone climbing out.

'Oh my god, are you okay?' It was a woman's voice. I looked up. Young, strawberry-blonde. Short and pixie-like. Very pretty. Our plan had been to hijack the first vehicle that came along and leave the owners standing by the side of the road, but I couldn't do that now. It might be twelve or more hours until the next person came by and she'd be in as bad a state as we were. I spluttered out some story about being fishermen and our boat had sunk and waved towards Charley. She helped me stand up and I led her over to where Charley lay propped up against the rock. He didn't look as if he was breathing and his lips were noticeably blue even in the dusky light. I checked for a pulse but my fingers were so numb I could barely feel his skin, let alone the elusive throb of life in his neck. I slapped him and was rewarded by a low groan from him.

'Let me help you,' said the woman. We each grabbed an arm and half-carried him to the car. I was drawing on reserves I didn't realise I had. I managed to conceal his gun as I laid him into the back seat without her seeing it.

'Will you be wanting to go to the hospital now?' the woman asked in a musical lilt.

I shook my head, 'No, we just need to dry off and warm up. Not too quickly.' That was the rule. If you get cold quickly you need to be warmed quickly. Get cold slow, like we did, and being warmed up too fast would mess you up.

'I'll take you to my place. Get you some soup. I'm Erin.'

'Richard.' I said and the next thing I knew she was rocking me gently and we'd arrived. She helped me get Charley inside and got some rugs for us to wrap up in. The house wasn't very warm, but it felt like a furnace to me. I was coming down with a fever. Never good. We couldn't afford to be comatose for a couple of days. Erin was being a good Samaritan but before long she'd see the news and realise who we were. I probably ought to kill her right now and take her car, but I fell asleep on the floor before I'd finished the thought.

Chapter Sixteen

Erin looked after us for three days. Charley didn't wake up until the third day. I managed to get up the following evening and help look after him. I learned that Erin was a trainee nurse who lived alone. Why she trusted us I have no idea. We'd lucked out.

'Where are you from?' I asked as she gave me some meaty broth and a hunk of bread.

'I'm come across from the West coast,' she said. 'Most of my family has been there forever, but I fancied to see a bit of the world. I thought I'd do my training here then go and volunteer in Africa or some place for a few years.' She looked me over, 'How about you?'

'I'm from England.' It was pointless to pretend otherwise. 'Me and my friend here thought it would be a good idea to spend a couple of weeks fishing on the lakes. We hired a boat but the weather was really rough and the thing capsized.'

She looked at me for a beat too long, then smiled. 'Where are you staying?'

'We rented a cottage on the other side of the lake. If you call a taxi we can get out of your hair and head back over there. I don't want to be an inconvenience and you've done so much for us already.'

'Don't be silly. It's what I enjoy doing. Now eat your broth and I'll get you a nice cup of tea.'

The next day Charley's fever broke and he started sleeping more soundly. It was a Monday but Erin took a day off work to stay with us. At one point she left to get some groceries and I had a crisis of confidence wondering if she was off talking to the police. She didn't have a phone in the house, so I couldn't call Blondie. She did have a television and a radio, and I tried both to get some idea of what was going on in the world.

The radio news came on first. It led with the headline of the arrest of Seamus Smallwood who had been caught red-handed in the bank with a pair of accomplices. So one of the guys had got away then. They had picked up Sean Smallwood as well, after a manhunt for a pair of fugitives who were wanted for questioning in connection. They didn't mention where he had been found, but it was a safe bet that the Garda had carried out a house-to-house and found him banging away and crying for help. Grossman and his wife had been rescued and were both safe, if a little shaken. Made me feel better.

The newsroom had made the connection between the Smallwood brothers and the IRA, possibly helped by an anonymous tip-off, so as far as Blondie would be concerned it was mission accomplished. However, it was clear that we'd been set up and hung out to dry. The Smallwoods could have had us followed I supposed, but it seemed too much of a coincidence that the Garda had pounced on us right after I'd phoned in our position to London. Someone knew we were there and wanted to stop us. Just like in Saudi.

I jumped when I heard a car pull up outside and quickly turned off the radio and television. I looked out of the window, half expecting to see a dozen sets of flashing blue lights, but it was just Erin in her little Toyota Corolla E10, pulling bags of food from the boot. I went out to help her.

'I should give you something for this,' I said.

'Don't worry, you haven't eaten too much.'

She cooked a shepherd's pie for us that night, although she made Charley eat soup. He was groggy and weak, but he still made an arse of himself and tried to flirt with her.

'Knock it off Charley, she doesn't want an old fart like you,' I said. I realised I felt a bit protective towards her. Charley just shrugged and collapsed back into bed and slept.

Late that night Erin and I huddled around a coffee each, perked up with a shot of whiskey, one of her David Cassidy LP's on softly in the background.

'We're going to have to leave tomorrow,' I said.

She nodded without saying anything.

'Thanks for everything. We'd have just been two dumb dead Brits if you hadn't come along.'

She smiled. 'It wasn't all horrible.' She really was beautiful when she smiled, and I got a pang of guilt as Jeannie's face flared up in my memory, spitting and accusing me in that jealous way she has.

'Do you think you'll be able to drop us off at the airport tomorrow?'

She frowned slightly, which didn't make her look any less cute. 'Not really. I can take you to town though. You can get a bus there to the airport.'

'Good enough. Thanks.'

She sipped her coffee quietly for a bit and then stood up and walked over to a side cabinet, opened a drawer and pulled out a couple of waterproof bags. 'You'll be wanting your things back then.'

She put the bags on the table. The bags were transparent and you could clearly see the Republic of Ireland passports and the guns inside them. Sort of threw cold water on my story that we were British. I looked up at her too shocked to think of a decent comeback. She just held her hand up to stop me.

'I don't want to know. Just don't cause me any trouble and I'll help you get away.'

I gave her a small smile, a nod and raised my mug silently in salute. She raised hers to chink against mine and we finished them without saying any more.

The next morning she was as good as her word and bundled us into the car. She had washed and dried our clothes and we felt a whole lot better. I didn't tell Charley about her finding the guns. When we got to the bus station she climbed out to help Charley, who was still a bit weak, although I think he wasn't as weak as he was making out. I checked she wasn't looking, then pulled out a bundle of cash, about a thousand pounds worth, and stuffed it in her glove box with a note that said 'Just my little thank you.'

I even got a hug from her as I got out, which earned me an envious stare from Charley. She smelled really nice. I really had to get laid soon.

'Mind how you go now,' she called as she drove off.

'So did you bang her?' asked Charley without preamble.

'No I didn't.'

'Bloody hell, I would have,' he said. 'I worry about you sometimes Dicky. What with that little incident by the side of the road too. I'm not sure we allow your type in army so it's probably for the best you didn't sign up.'

'Fuck you Charley. She was a nice girl.'

He just laughed. 'Nice girls shag too you know.'

We got ourselves a couple of new jackets from a second-hand shop and headed to the airport.

'Listen Charley, I don't think we should use these passports,' I said.

'Why not? We're respectable businessmen.'

'I just have a bad feeling. Someone screwed us over the other day. It might have been the Smallwoods, as payback for what we did to Sean, but what if it was someone at the Firm? They knew where we were and they know what names are on these passports.'

Charley let that thought percolate around his head for a bit. 'You might have a point, but how do you propose to get off this rock without a passport? I'm not swimming home.'

I looked out of the window at the airfield. It wasn't huge. A lot of the traffic was made up of little puddle-jumpers and private planes.

'I've got an idea. Follow me.'

I wandered around a bit and found the baggage reclaim area. It had one of those rubber conveyors that came out of a hole in the wall shielded by a few thin rubber strips and disappeared into another one a few feet away after making a loop into the room. I waited until the room was clear of people in uniforms.

'Now,' I said, and jumped up on the conveyor near the exit hole and hunched down to let it take me through. There was no one on the other side and we hopped off and found somewhere to hide. We found a room containing a couple of lockers full of maintenance worker overalls. Perfect.

'Here, get into one of these.'

We got dressed but it was a bit comical because Charley's was too small, and mine was too large.

'We look a right pair Dicky. This had better work. We're going to be the laughing stock of the Firm if we get caught.'

'Just shut up and put this on.' I gave him a hard hat and a pair of ear defenders.

'You're not planning on hiding away in a cargo bay are you? You realise they aren't pressurised?'

'We'll be fine if we get on a small plane. They don't go that high.'

'How do you know if it will be going to the right place?'

'As long as it is away from here I don't care.'

'I don't want to end up in bloody Dublin though.'

Charley had a point. We'd have to just mooch about and see what came up. We strolled out onto the tarmac and walked around purposefully as if we had every right to be there. No one gave us a second look. We saw a private plane loading up close by and ambled over to it. There were a couple of guys in the same lurid jumpsuits we'd pinched loading a few cases into the rear.

'Hi,' I said, getting their attention. 'We're new. We were told to come and help.'

The men looked at each other. They were immigrants of some kind. African probably. They just shrugged and gestured to the bags. Charley and I grabbed one each and hefted them up the ramp. I looked at the one in my hand. It had a Harrod's logo on it.

'Where is this plane going?' I asked one of them conversationally.

The guy just shrugged. I guess he didn't have much English.

I caught Charley's eye and he beckoned me over and showed me a luggage label tied to the handle of the suitcase he was holding. It had a Knightsbridge address on it. Bingo. Even better, the two Africans just started walking away once the cases were loaded. I guessed it was someone else's job to close up for flight.

'Are you sure about this Dicky?'

'Not entirely, but we don't have a huge amount of choice do we? We must be due some luck by now though, surely?'

'I only have bad luck Dick. You should know that by now.'

We hid ourselves in the back of the bay behind some crates and sat down to wait. It wasn't long before someone came and closed up the hatch and we heard noises above our heads as the passengers climbed on and found their seats. I was more scared than I admitted and I'm betting Charley wasn't all that comfortable either.

It wasn't as bad as I thought, although considering I thought we'd suffocate and freeze to death that isn't saying too much. It was cold, but it didn't last long. Not as long as the fiasco on the Irish moor anyway. The plane touched down after forty minutes and I stopped praying. The cargo hatch soon opened and we heard sounds of people moving about. I peered outside. There were a couple of ground crew messing about with the offloading ramp, ten feet away. Now or never, while their backs were turned. We dropped to the tarmac and hurried away. The plane had landed at a little airfield outside London and we slipped out without being spotted. It felt good to be home again.

Chapter Seventeen

I wanted to call in straight away and start getting some answers, but Charley wanted a drink and a pie supper first. I didn't take much persuading.

'So how do we play this?' I asked, once I'd downed the first pint and half a plate of food. It was a good old English bitter, none of this dark stuff they call beer over the water. I'd completely gone off the stuff.

'You still think we were set up?' Charley

'It's obvious isn't it?'

Charley shrugged. 'Maybe it is. It's becoming the norm for us. I just don't see how it matters. The whole place is riddled with informers and double agents. If we go in there mouthing off about another one we'll just get told to take a number. I'm more annoyed that the job went off okay. I was hoping we'd screw it up enough to be sacked. Coming to something when we can't even manage to fuck up.'

'Somebody has to put us out of our misery soon. Just a matter of time.'

We finished our meal and I made the call. We were told to come in immediately for debrief, over to the Russian House again. Where I'd first met Charley. I paid up and realised I still had hundreds of pounds of cash left.

'What do we do with all this?' I asked 'Do we give it back?'

'Nah, stash it somewhere. They're not expecting to see it again, and it might come in useful one day if you run out.'

We took a detour to dump our stuff into a public locker in St. Pancreas train station. Nice and anonymous. We left the guns too. You can't go wandering around London with hot guns.

They were expecting us at the front desk by the time we arrived, and wasted no time hustling us upstairs to the meeting room. Blondie was there, and looked us up and down as we walked in. We must have looked like beggars off the street. Charley especially had lost a bit of weight, his Latin complexion was sallow and we were both unshaven. It hadn't seemed right to use Erin's underarm razor on my face.

'Take a seat gentlemen.'

Two men joined us. I didn't know them, but they recognised Charley. Someone had arranged for tea and biscuits, which was nice, since we were going to be in there for the rest of the day. We had to go over every detail of the past couple of weeks. They seemed to know more about what we'd done than I did, but they had their notes from my regular calls and I just had my memory. Charley did a lot of the talking, but they wanted to hear my side too. They were particularly interested in the other characters that Seamus had introduced us to. I managed to hold my tongue until we got to the bit about the Garda turning up to arrest us.

'That was a bloody farce,' I said. 'Someone tipped them off. There was no way they'd have known otherwise.' I let some bitterness into my tone and glared at Blondie.

She looked back at me coolly, 'It could have been the Smallwoods. After what you did to Sean it is highly possible.'

I shook my head, 'Seamus and his brother needed that money. Even if they wanted to get revenge on us, they wouldn't have risked the whole job for it. They'd have waited until it was done, then sent the boys after us.'

'You're accusing someone inside the Firm?'

'You know more than me, but I know there was a connection between the crates in Saudi and the Smallwoods.'

Blondie gave me a hard look, and I could see her weighing up the risks of telling me. 'There is a connection,' she admitted. 'The drugs in the crate were going to the Smallwoods, who would have sold them and used the money to buy weapons for the IRA.'

'That doesn't explain the fuck-ups in Saudi or Ireland.'

'You were unlucky. There could be any number of reasons the Garda discovered you. They could have been watching you for days. I need you to finish your reports before you leave. Then you can take a couple of personal days.'

And that was that. I was deliberately vague about the couple of days we'd spent with Erin. I didn't want to get her into any trouble. Then it was into a taxi and back to Jeannie.

'Richard!' she flung her arms around me and dragged me inside the new home that Lord C had provided for us. It was the first time I'd spent any time in it. After welcoming me home in that special way only a woman can, we lay together and talked.

'How long do I have you?' she asked.

'I've got a few days off at least.'

She snuggled beside me and smiled. 'I love the house Richard. And I just got a big role in a new show at Maida Vale, so now you're back, everything is wonderful.'

'Don't get too comfortable,' I said reluctantly. 'We'll probably have to give it back when I leave the Firm.'

Jeannie pouted, 'Are you still thinking of doing that?'

'I thought we'd decided this already.'

'Well you seem okay this time. Maybe what happened in Saudi was just bad luck?'

I sat up and pulled away from her. 'I'm not that okay,' I snapped, 'I may not have been hurt this time, but you don't realise how much I've been through.'

Jeannie sat up too, and got a face on her. 'No I don't, but you don't think about me either - left behind while you disappear for weeks on end.'

'That won't happen if I'm not doing this job,' I protested.

'What if it does? What if we give all this up, and lose this great place, and I'm left in some hovel and you're still off swanning around with that Charley? Do you even know what you'd do if you left the Firm?'

I didn't really. Just not this. Just then my bleeper went off, so I climbed out of bed to get it.

'You need to come in,' said the man on the other end of the line when I phoned in. He hung up before I could tell him I was on leave. I called Charley, and he'd had the same call.

'What do you think it is about?' I asked.

'We'll only find out when we get there. Don't worry, if they wanted to arrest us, they'd send the police round.'

'That's not as comforting as you might think, Charley.' I said and put the phone back in its cradle.

'What the hell was that about? I thought you said you'd been given some time off?' Jeannie had been listening to my side of the conversation and it didn't take a genius to work out I was going back in.

'They probably just want to check a few more things. I won't be long.' I got the silent treatment for the next few minutes as I threw on some clothes.

I got there just before Charley, but I saw him coming up the street from the other direction and waited for him. He'd shaved and washed and looked immaculate again. I'd got as far as having a quick shower after my reunion with Jeannie, but I'd forgotten about everything else. I looked even more untidy standing next to him.

'Someone looks happy,' said Charley with a smirk.

I grinned but I was still nervous about why we'd been summoned back. 'Shall we go in?'

'Lead the way my friend.'

We got inside and did the usual checking-in routine. This time there wasn't any tea and biscuits and Leighton-Hart had been at the whiskey again.

'Thank you for coming in again,' said Blondie. She was looking a little strained around the eyes.

'What's going on?' Charley asked.

'There's been an incident, and we need everyone to pitch in. Since you two are not currently committed to an operation, you are it until we can recall some more operatives. I'm afraid leave is cancelled.'

Charley let out a deep sigh, and earned himself one of Blondie's glares.

'Leave is overrated anyway,' he said. 'It's not as if I'd be spending it shagging and drinking, unlike Dick here.'

I ignored him, 'What's the incident?'

Blondie picked up a folder and slid it over the table to us.

'Peter Short, MP, Home Secretary.'

I didn't follow politics closely enough to keep up with all the different positions the government ministers had, but I remembered him. He'd been the minister at the briefing that had sent us to Ireland.

'His daughter has gone missing.' The folder contained a photograph of a young woman, aged eighteen. She was brunette, smiling at the camera and had a flower tucked behind her ear. She was wearing one of those long tie-die dresses and sandals.

No offence to his right honourable,' said Charley, 'But so what? She's probably out getting shagged senseless by some pretentious poetry-spouting hippy.'

I might not have said it exactly like Charley, but I agreed.

'We think she has been kidnapped. Mr. Short received a letter this afternoon. It contained a lock of her hair and said he should wait for instructions.'

'Okay, so maybe I buy that she has been kidnapped. Why aren't the police dealing with this instead of us?'

Charley nodded his agreement.

'Well for a start it is sensitive. If this went public then there would be an outcry, calls for an internal investigation and a lot of other things we simply don't want to have to deal with.'

'What else?' I asked. 'You said, 'for a start'.'

'From certain words that were used in the letter, we think there is a connection with the Saudi drug container.'

Charley frowned, 'That doesn't make sense. Why target Peter Short?'

Blondie hesitated a beat before responding. 'He was the minister who authorised the operation which intercepted the container. We think this is a retaliation.'

Charley and I looked at each other. We were both thinking the same thing.

'Who knew he was involved?' I asked.

'I know where you're going with this, and I'm starting to agree,' she admitted. 'We have a mole somewhere. Which is one of the reasons I want you on the job.'

'It's sweet that you trust us,' said Charley.

'More that you are far too careless to be a mole,' she said tartly.

Ouch.

'So what do you want us to do?' I asked.

'Find her and get her back,' she said simply.

'What do we have to go on? Where do we start? She could be anywhere.'

'We think she's still in London. The letter had a Brixton postmark. And they'll want to have her close by for when they are ready to make ransom demands.'

'We can't wander around Brixton asking the locals if they've seen a posh white tart tied up anywhere,' snorted Charley.

'Just get into position and be ready. We'll keep you updated by radio. We don't know how long she's got before they start sending bits of her to us in the post.'

We were given a car and a bag full of pills and expected to sit in the streets of Brixton and await orders. Charley got into the driver's seat, which made me stop and stare.

'Bloody hell, are you feeling all right?'

'Just shut up and get in.'

I'd barely pulled the door closed before Charley was racing away, weaving in and out of traffic wildly. I thought he was keen to get there, but he turned north, which was taking us away from Brixton.

'Where are you going?'

'I need a drink. I know a nice little place where the waitresses bring you your pint while wearing stilettos and a thong, and not much else.'

'Er, I thought we were given pretty clear instructions to go straight to Brixton and wait.'

'Have you ever been to Brixton, runt?'

'Once or twice,' I said, but I couldn't say I'd done much more than drive through it. Quickly.

'How many white people did you see there?'

'What difference does that make?'

'Do you really want to sit in a car on a crappy side street in that neighbourhood and wait until you get lynched? I don't know about you, but I'd rather suck my own balls. Blondie will be hours yet trying to work out where we need to be, so we might as well wait around somewhere pleasant.'

Charley had a way of persuading me.

'One more bloody job,' I said, 'and I'm out. I don't care how much Jeannie likes the house, I'll get another somehow.'

Charley grunted in agreement. 'What do you fancy doing then?'

'I thought a little private security company. Nothing too strenuous.'

'Sounds like heaven. Let's hope you don't have to die to get there.'

The bar Charley knew was a private members club, but I got in as Charley's guest, and then becoming a member only cost a quid, which I thought was well worth it. The beer was a bit steep, but the girls were cute and perky, and didn't expect too much in the way of tips. We spent a pleasant couple of hours there before the portable radio squawked, and gave us a possible address.

We were a bit merry as we left, but I'd tried to pace myself and was in a better state than Charley. He staggered straight to the passenger side and collapsed in the seat.

'I think I'll take a bit of a nap. Wake me up when we get there, but don't drive too fast.'

'You're such an arsehole Charley.'

'I'm training you up. You should be grateful,' he said, and closed his eyes.

I made sure I took every bend as hard as I could, to knock him around a bit, but he kept snoring away like he didn't care. I had to calm it down a bit as we got closer, because the number of police cars seemed to increase. It was dark by now, and the area looked quite unfriendly. Gangs of youths loitered near mini-cab offices and take-away food shops, and gave us menacing looks as I drove by, looking for the right street. It was a residential area, away from the main roads, and the streetlamps were either dim or broken. Knackered old cars lined the streets and it took ages to find a place to park. I found somewhere near some lock-ups a couple of streets from the address, which wasn't great.

'Wake up,' I elbowed Charley.

'Are we there?' Charley opened an eye and looked around.

'Almost. I can't find anywhere to park and still get eyes on the address.'

'Well you'd better get out and walk then.'

I wasn't keen. 'I think I felt safer in Saudi.'

'Just get going. I'll go round from the other side and we'll meet up over there.'

I couldn't argue with that. I wished I'd brought my gun. Still, it was only a gentle stroll around the area to see what was about. The streets were quiet compared to the main roads where the shops were. The address was a mid-terraced property that blended in with other mid-terraced properties in the area and faced an identical terrace of houses with tiny concrete front gardens and pot-plants. It looked like an improbable place for a kidnapping.

I hung across the street a few doors down and watched it for a while. There was a light on upstairs and I checked my watch. Half-past ten. Not too late. I looked at the houses next door and opposite. The ones either side were occupied. They had net curtains in the windows. There was a For Sale sign outside a house opposite a bit further along, which I made a note of.

'What do we have?' Charley strolled up, looking surprisingly sober.

'Not a lot. Looks like a place your grandmother would live in.'

'There's not a lot we can do tonight. Apart from wandering up and down the street, and that'll just attract attention.'

'I've got an idea about that,' I said. We went back to the car and I ferreted about in a bin and grabbed a newspaper. I took it back down the street and made myself out like a tramp near a doorway across the street. With my unshaven face I blended right in. The floor was hard and cold, and I had to stay as still as I could. By the time the grey dawn started to lighten the sky I was stiff and uncomfortable. I hadn't seen anyone enter or leave. The lights had gone out at about eleven. Then at seven in the morning, after the milk-float had hummed down the street, the door opened and someone came out. It was no grandmother.

Chapter Eighteen

The man was your typical Anglo-Saxon Neanderthal. About six-three, broad-shouldered, and walking in that rolling, arm-swinging kind of way that young men do before they realise being tough is a state of mind, not a state of body. I let him get a couple of dozen yards away and then got up and followed. I was grateful for the walk. The guy didn't have a clue. He didn't look behind to see if anyone was following him, so I didn't have to try that hard.

He led the way to a corner store, which was too small to follow him in and remain inconspicuous, so I hung about outside until he came out. He was carrying a couple of bags of groceries. I saw loaves of bread sticking out of the top, along with other staples, like eggs and Coca-Cola. He set off again and I followed him to a Victorian brick-walled warehouse a few streets away. It looked run-down, almost disused, but it had bars on the windows and a new reinforced door, which he banged on with the base of his fist. It was opened by a stoner-type. Hair down past his collar, dazed look on his face, and tatty flared jeans. They both disappeared into the door and it closed behind them. I was just considering sneaking up and trying to look in a window, when it opened again, and Cave-boy walked out, this time with only one bag.

He lurched off towards Clapham Common and stopped at a large house on the edge of the park. Must have cost a bomb. It had three storeys plus some windows in the roof-space, and it clearly went back quite far, but the trees and hedges obscured the rest of it. Again he banged on the door, and it was opened by a woman this time. She was tall, slim, probably in her forties, and dressed as though she was about to go out to a business lunch. The kind of business that required tight skirts, fishnets and stilettos and a ton of caked on make-up. She didn't invite him in, just held out her hand and took the bag.

Cave-boy turned around and ambled back the way he had come. I hung back and let him get on ahead. I had a pretty good idea that he was heading back to the terraced house. I was right. I watched him right up until he went inside, just to be sure, then returned to the lock-ups to meet up with Charley.

'Where the hell have you been?' he asked.

I told him.

'Well while you've been enjoying an early morning stroll, I've been sorting out some extra help.'

'Did that involve getting with Blondie and slipping her one?'

'You've got to do what you can do protect the nation, Dicky. No matter how repulsive it is.'

'Are there enough to cover three locations?'

'Bloody hell, give me a chance. I only knew about one last night. I'm going to have a cock like a side of raw beef after this.'

'I'll take that as a no. We'll have to make do then, until your love wand can work its spell.'

I was starving, so Charley and I drove around the corner and got some breakfast from a greasy spoon café. We should have been watching the house really, but fuck it.

'So what do you reckon?' I asked, mopping up the last of the bacon juice with a slice of cold toast.

'Could be a couple of brothels, by the sound of it.'

'You think Yasmine Short is in there?'

'Maybe. Probably strung out and curled up in a corner somewhere. If she's lucky.'

'How do we find out if she's in there? Break in?'

'Not if you want to keep those precious looks Dicky. We have no idea how many black-hats are in there. You know the routine - we watch, gather intel and make a considered opinion.'

We decided that the first house seemed an unlikely place to keep someone against their will. It was too close to other houses and someone simply banging on one of the walls inside might raise the alarm. It may have been where the kidnap was arranged, however. The other two locations seemed more likely to be where she was.

'So when does the cavalry get here?' I asked.

'Later today,' said Charley. 'There's a team coming down from Manchester. In the meantime, let's split up and watch one of the places each.'

I got the warehouse. Charley wanted the Clapham Common house. Maybe he was hoping to see an eyeful from the girls? The warehouse was a large stand-alone two-storey building with a narrow gate just big enough for a small truck to squeeze through, leading to an enclosed loading area. I could get round two sides of it that faced onto intersecting streets, but the other sides were blocked off by a high wall topped with broken glass to deter thieves. There were windows running along the length at ground level and along the upper storey, all of which were protected by three-quarter inch vertical bars. I could get my fist between them, but not my head.

The surrounding buildings were also industrial, and equally run-down. One of them might be empty, and be a good place to set up a surveillance point, but I'd need a locksmith or a crowbar to get in, which meant waiting for backup.

I found a vantage point and settled down to watch. There was no activity until about midday, when a car pulled up and a couple of skinny men in camel-hair coats climbed out. They looked up and down the street shiftily, completely failing to notice me huddled in a doorway fifty feet away, and banged on the door.

I couldn't see who opened it from where I was. Whoever it was stayed in the shadows while the two wide-boys tucked inside. They left the car on the side of the road and I took a stroll up to check it out. It was empty, a flash Cortina with high-end tyres. Nothing on the back seat, and nice and tidy inside. Even the ashtray was neat. I tried the door and it was unlocked. Too tempting. I leaned in and opened the glovebox. There was a revolver in there. I flipped open the drum and tipped the bullets out into my palm and pocketed them. They probably had more, but it might give me an advantage.

I shoved it back and closed the door. I went over to one of the warehouse windows and tried to look in, but they were so grimy on the inside I couldn't see anything. With nothing else I could do, I backed up to my watching place and waited for them to come out. They were inside for fifteen minutes, and when they came out, one of them was carrying what looked like an old doctor's bag. I was betting it was full of cash. They drove off with a squeal of tyres. I made sure I'd got the number plate. I'd get it checked out later.

It was getting on for seven o'clock in the evening before the first punter turned up. Some bloke in his late fifties, driving a Jaguar which he parked down the street. He was wearing a charcoal suit and carried a sensible brolly and a large briefcase. He checked his watch and waited for a minute before he knocked smartly on the door. It was opened quickly and he stepped inside. He didn't even look over his shoulder, so I guessed he was a regular. He didn't look like a criminal, and at first I thought he was some sort of bigwig, but over the next hour or so a steady stream of men arrived and knocked on the door. They stayed for between thirty minutes and an hour, then emerged and hurried away with a smile still on their faces.

It was nine o'clock before I started wondering where Charley's backup was. I was in a bit of a bad situation. I couldn't leave in case I missed something interesting, but I couldn't get hold of Charley while I was standing here. We'd picked up a radio when we left, but only one. And Charley had it. I made a note to request a second one at the first opportunity.

It started to rain, and that made my mind up for me. I didn't mind being wet and cold, but being wet and cold and wondering where everyone was is not comfortable. I jumped in my car and headed over to the Clapham house. Charley was tucked up nice and cosy in his car in a tree-lined avenue with a good view of the house.

'Mind if I join you?' I asked as I climbed in next to him.

'Evening Dick. How has your day been?'

'Bloody miserable. Where's our bloody backup?'

'Still sitting around with their thumbs up their arses I think. I had a call about an hour ago that said they were delayed.'

'Shit. For how long?'

'A few more hours. Call it tomorrow morning.'

I had to settle for that. 'What do you reckon we should do then?'

Charley scratched his cheek. 'We have to wait,' he said eventually.

'If she's in there then she could be hurt or killed at any time,' I objected.

'I know. What's your bright idea then?'

'Why don't we break in and have a look around?'

'Dangerous.' Charley grunted.

'Let's pick up the shooters from the lockers then.'

'Do you realise the depth of shit we'd be in if we actually killed someone on British soil?'

'They'd only be for a last resort.'

Charley was quiet for a bit and then sighed and I knew I had him. He was as bored as I was. 'Which one first?'

'The warehouse. Looks more secure so that's where I'd stash her.'

Charley started the car and took us back to the warehouse, via the train station lockers. I left my car where it was. I'd come back and get it later.

It was still too early to go in when we got back, being before midnight. Charley found a spot on the street with a view of the warehouse and gave us good eyes on the comers and goers. There was a reasonable amount of traffic to the door and at any one time, there could have been up to twenty guys in there. After about three in the morning the last of the punters seemed to leave and no more arrived. We waited until four before we made our move. That's the best time to carry out an intrusion. We popped a couple of pills each to perk us up and stole over to the warehouse. The side door that was used by the punters didn't have a keyhole or a handle, so there was no way we could get in there unless we used a crow-bar, which would be far too noisy.

'Let's try around the back,' I suggested. Except there was no other door around the back. Only the high wall topped with cut glass. There was the vehicle access gate though, leading to a loading yard, which was secured by a padlock.

'This'll be easy,' said Charley and he set to work while I shielded him with my body and kept watch. Say what you like about Charley - he's an arrogant, lazy son of a bitch most of the time, but he does know what he's doing with a lock-pick. He was done within half a minute and we were inside soon after. We hooked the padlock back in place but didn't lock it, in case we needed to get out quick.

The loading yard wasn't large. A van could get in and just about turn around to get out, but that was it. There was a large roller-shutter door into the warehouse itself, next to a personnel door. This door had a keyhole. There were no windows in the wall, so we crept up to the door and listened. Nothing. It was as quiet as a graveyard and no light shone through the keyhole, so Charley set to work again.

The door opened into a large dark chamber, and I flashed around a shielded torch just long enough to show it was about ten paces a side and was largely empty except for some flattened cardboard boxes leaning against the walls and some bottles of engine oil on metal shelves. The oil stains on the floor just inside the roller-shutters suggested that this was used as a garage. There was a door opposite leading into the rest of the building. I put out the torch and we crossed over to it. We waited a full five minutes to let our eyes get used to the gloom.

It was still as black as a raven's wing in the antechamber where we were, but beyond the door there were windows which would let in a bit of light. Charley gave me a signal and we readied our pistols. I gently turned the handle and pushed the door open. The room beyond was huge, essentially the whole of the rest of the warehouse, and a dim light filtered in from the high windows. Around the walls there were multiple irregular structures and it took me a few moments to realise that they were makeshift tents made out of blankets hanging over ropes. Each partitioned area was about six to eight feet a side and I had a pretty good idea what was inside them.

There was no movement and no lights that I could see. Charley and I inched our way over to the nearest tent, and looked inside. The light didn't penetrate the blankets and it was too dark to see, but we could hear low breathing and the stale smell of cooked heroin and musky sex hung around like a wet fart. I wrapped the torch in my shirt to dim the light and turned it on. Even though it was heavily filtered, it still seemed dazzling to our dark-adapted eyes. It was enough to be able to see the inside of the tent. There was a rough mattress on the floor covered by a grimy blanket, and between the two lay a sleeping woman. She was heavily made-up, although it was smeared across her cheeks and had probably fused her eyelids together. She had that hollow-cheeked look of malnutrition and drug-addiction. It wasn't Yasmine. Around the floor were used condoms, tissues and needles. And rope. One of her wrists was visible above the blanket and it showed signs of rope-burn. I didn't think it was self-inflicted.

'Fucking hell,' whispered Charley.

'Let's check on the others,' I said. I felt bad for the girl, but it wasn't our job to get her out. The police could do that at the end of all this. Our job was to find Yasmine Short. We split up and went from tent to tent, looking at the girls. They were all in a shit state - bruised, dirty, wild hair and most of them stank. I didn't know what lowlife scum would want to get intimate with these women, but they were clearly fucking sick in the head. I guessed that sex with them wasn't really what it was about, given that most of them looked like they'd been gagged or tied up or whipped.

It took half an hour of careful creeping to get round all the tents. I didn't think any of the ones I saw were Yasmine, but to be honest she could be unrecognisable from the pretty young woman in the photograph we'd seen.

At the far end of the room there was a door with 'Offices' written on it. There was a band of light showing under the door, but the only sound was snoring. I guessed they didn't expect any of the girls to run away. Charley and I pulled back to the garage area by the roller-shutter door.

'Anything?' I asked.

'She wasn't in there,' confirmed Charley. 'Let's get out and lock up. There's nothing we can do right now.'

I agreed, though I felt bad about leaving the girls there. I didn't suppose another couple of days would make much difference to them though. Charley locked the door and the padlock behind us and we sloped off down the street to find a place to eat. We'd got as far as half-way down a mug of tea in a little all-night café, when the radio squawked.

Chapter Nineteen

'Charlie Papa Hotel Quebec - RV back home PDQ,' came a distorted voice. Charley had turned the volume low, so only he and I would hear it, although the only other person in the place was the short order cook, who was busy in the back frying up our bacon.

'Hotel Quebec message received,' Charley replied, and stowed the radio away again. There wouldn't be any more messages. Hotel Quebec was HQ.

'Looks like our backup has arrived,' I said. Charley grunted and twisted around to check on the progress of our breakfast. We weren't actually that hungry because the pills killed your appetite, as well as giving you a few other fun side effects like constipation, but it had been drummed into us to get into the habit of treating your body like a machine and refuelling it regularly, even if the warning light wasn't flashing.

We shovelled down the bacon and eggs, washed it down with more tea, then jumped in the car. I was driving this time. HQ was the Russian House, and we were waved through the arched entry into a private car park by the security guard. There were a couple of vans parked there, marked up in the colours and logos of British Gas. Inside the building we were greeted by a large hall decked out with a couple of dozen people in plastic chairs facing an overhead projector screen. Blondie was sitting off to the side, and noticed us as we arrived. She gestured for us to take a seat at the back. The presentation was being given by a man I didn't recognise, and he was going over the roles that the teams would have. I counted twenty-two people in the audience, not including us.

It was to be a standard surveillance. We'd be split into two shifts, made up of an electronics man who would install listening devices, a couple of leg-men to do foot surveillance and one or two security officers trained in unarmed combat and firearms to act as anti-personnel operatives. There were drivers for the vans and motorcycles and the rest were 'watchers'; normally older ex-military men and women, who would gather information without engaging. We were the two intelligence officers assigned to the case and were introduced as Whisky and X-ray. Everyone else had already been assigned a codename starting at Alpha and working up through the alphabet.

I leaned over to whisper to Charley, 'Great planning by someone. There are no black operatives here. We're all going to stick out like a sore thumb.'

'You'd struggle to find any ethnic groups in the Firm other than white Anglo-Saxon protestants Dick. Just be glad there are a few women. Anyway, once you're all dressed up in your fancy boiler suit, no one will look twice.'

The guy at the front continued his briefing by handing round maps of the sewers and aerial photographs of the roads around the warehouse and the two houses. We were a bit thin on the ground to cover all three properties. They were only expecting to deal with the first terraced house when they assembled the team, before Charley had radioed in the other two locations, so a lot of talk was around how to split the teams up to manage it. We stayed at the back, pretty much quiet the whole time except to stand up and make ourselves known when we were asked. I was pleased when they brought out a big crate of radios and handed them all round. I snagged one.

'He hasn't told them what this is all about,' I mentioned to Charley as the briefing was coming to an end.

'They don't need to know,' replied Charley. 'All they have to do is watch the place, take notes of who comes and goes and do what we tell them. Anything more than that and they'll want paying too.'

I snorted out a laugh, but I did wonder what else was going on that I 'didn't need to know'. Finally the orders were completed and the men and women got up and filtered out, heading for their assigned posts. Charley and I went over to talk to Blondie for any additional orders.

'Good morning boys,' she smiled, leaning in for a kiss on her cheek. Charley took the offer, and I'm sure his hand slipped down onto her arse for a quick squeeze. If it did, she didn't say anything. I gave her a cursory kiss because it was expected, but I felt weird doing it since she was my boss. I thought it was inappropriate the way she constantly flirted with us, especially with Charley, but I wasn't about to say anything. She could have me disappear if she took a dislike to me.

'What have you got for us?' asked Charley. She reached down to the side of her chair and lifted up a sports bag. Charley took it and handed it to me. I opened it and saw several bundles of cash inside, a first aid kit plus a few bags of amphetamines and a couple of keys.

'Two thousand pounds for sundry expenses,' she said, 'Plus some supplies. There is a lock-up near Waterloo with a few more things you might need.'

'Much obliged,' said Charley.

I looked at Charley, wondering whether to mention the hall of whores we'd found. He caught my eye and must have guessed my thinking, because he shook his head imperceptibly, a barely visible hardening of his eyes, warning me off. I kept my trap shut. Seems that secrets were kept in both directions.

We went to the lock-up in Waterloo first. It was one of those storage places which contained lots of little secure box-rooms inside a large building. One of the keys we had let us into the building and the labyrinth of narrow corridors between the storage bays. The other key opened a padlock on the lock-up itself. It contained a couple of camp-beds, some tins of food, bottles of water, and another large bag. The large bag contained a couple of Beretta automatic pistols, a sawn-off shotgun with box of twelve-gauge, some stun grenades and a bottle of chloroform with pads to administer it.

'Our Great Aunt has come through for us again it seems,' said Charley. He took possession of the shotgun and gave me the chloroform. I took one of the automatics and a couple of clips of ammo. We divided up the stun grenades, which created a bright flash and loud bang to disorientate anyone within a few yards. In one of our training sessions, we'd had to stand in a small room while someone tossed one in so we knew what it felt like. It was pretty humbling. I remember coming round some time later and seeing that the instructors had marked a big 'x' on my chest, forehead and each leg with a piece of chalk while I was affected. I hadn't even realised anyone was near me. It took a full twenty-four hours before I could see anything except a big black negative image when I closed my eyes and another day before I could hear properly again. It wasn't an experience I was looking forward to having again.

I drove us back to the warehouse we'd broken into the night before. Gamma team were there before us and they had already found a good spot near the place and had parked up one of the British Gas vans. Beside it they had erected a roadwork barrier and signs warning of gas leaks. There was a little red and white striped tent on the pavement with a great view of the warehouse.

We got into the back of the van. Inside were a couple of guys, codenamed Golf and Lima. Golf was the electronics man and Lima was his security.

'What do you know?' Charley asked.

'We've got watchers all round the place,' said Golf, 'And a bike in place down the street in case someone leaves in a car. We've not been able to get inside yet. I'm still waiting for the watchers to report in.

'Okay, don't get impatient,' said Charley. 'If you don't get a chance today we can pull the gas leak scam on them tomorrow. That'll clear them out.'

We left them to it and went to check out the crew watching the terraced house. There were only five of them here, because some of the team had been sent home to sleep, ready for the evening shift. No gas van on the street this time and we couldn't see anyone either, which was a sign we'd been given some professionals. Charley had to get on the radio to learn that they had broken into one of the houses for sale across the street and set up an observation post in one of the upstairs bedrooms.

'I think it's a waste of time watching this place,' I said. 'She won't be in there.'

'Maybe not, but there is still a connection to those other places, so we might be able to learn something. Surveillance is all about patience, Dick. You can't go gallivanting around saving the world like James Bond.'

We couldn't go in through the front door, because that would alert the neighbours that something was going on. There was a back door that could be reached through the gardens, so we used that. We had to be careful not to be seen, but the high fences on either side were a good screen. The house was empty of furniture, but it was carpeted and clean, which was a luxury compared to a lot of observation points. They were normally in dusty old attics or run-down husks. There were two operatives in the house at the time, Romeo and Kilo, and just to be confusing, Romeo was a woman. That's what happens when you assign codenames randomly. Charley was all over her like a swarm of ants.

'Hello sweetheart, are you comfortable up here?' he asked.

She was in her thirties and kept herself trim. She had short dark hair and carried herself like she had been in the military. She took one look at Charley and had him pegged from the off.

'It's perfect,' she said in a hushed voice. She pointed at a camera that had been set up some distance from the window but still gave a good view of the house opposite. 'You just make sure you keep the noise down in here and when you leave. The walls are pretty thin. We've already heard the couple next door arguing.'

The man called Kilo was even shorter than I was, and built like a racing snake. He could only have weighed seven stones dripping wet. 'We've seen a couple of people moving about downstairs. They are watching the telly. Can't tell about upstairs because all the curtains are closed.'

'What about round the back?' I asked.

'We've got a watcher walking her dog and a couple of legmen in position,' said Romeo. 'We should get some reports back soon.'

There wasn't much to do after that. Charley kept smiling at Romeo, and she kept pretending she didn't notice, so eventually he gave up and we left. 'Fucking lesbo,' he muttered as we got back to the car.

'Maybe she just has a conscience and good taste,' I said. 'Didn't you see the wedding ring?'

'Girls like that just wear those as an excuse.'

I gave up. 'Come on, let's check out the last house.'

I took the wheel and made the short drive round to Clapham Common. I was hoping to get my car back, and was relieved to see that it was still happily sitting where I'd left it. Just up from it was another of our gas repair vans and its little red and white tent. We parked Charley's car and invited ourselves inside. There was only one guy in the van, going by the name Bravo.

'Where's the rest of the team?' I asked. Normally you'd have two people in the van at all times in case things got dicey.

'It was getting towards dinner, so he went out for some takeaway.'

'We'll stick around then. I could do with some chips,' said Charley.

'Have you managed to get inside yet?' I asked.

'Not yet. We thought we'd try an entry in the early hours.'

That seemed reasonable, so we sat down in the back of the van, taking it in turns to watch the house through the windscreen. Delta came along half an hour later with a load of fish and chips. He was surprised to see us, but he'd bought enough food to last all night, so there was plenty to go around. We stayed there for a few hours. Bravo and Delta were ex-military, probably SAS. I didn't ask specifics and they wouldn't have told me, but they were good blokes. They viewed the whole thing as a bit of a laugh and a lot less miserable than sitting in a wet field all night.

'You can even boil a cup of tea,' said Delta, showing us a hot plate that had been installed in the back of the van. 'Bloody luxury.'

As the sun went down, a couple of other members of the team joined us and relayed what they had learned.

'The house is full of a bunch of prozzers,' said Foxtrot, an older gentleman not far off retirement. 'Seen a couple of John's lurking about but it'll probably get more interesting for the rest of the night.'

'Have any of the girls left the house?' asked Charley.

'Not that I noticed, but you can see them through the windows. Got a right eyeful I did, thanks to these old things,' he hefted a large set of binoculars.

'It's going to be hard to get inside to bug the place then,' I said. 'Too many people wandering around and staying up late.'

There was general agreement, but no one had any credible suggestions. The best started out as a joke and came from Bravo.

'What if I went up pretending to be a punter? I bet I could hide a bug in there while I'm inside?'

'Inside who?' asked Charley. That got a laugh, and degenerated into gags about strapping cameras to knobs. Boys together.

'Actually you might have something there,' I said, when the laughter had calmed down. 'What do you reckon the chances are that someone could get in posing as a customer?'

'They'd probably have to be expected,' said Charley, 'Which means knowing their phone number, which we don't.'

'Worth a try though? You could say a friend told you about it.'

Charley grinned at me, 'Go and give it a try then.'

'Me?' I hadn't been thinking that I would go.

'No one else looks as desperate as you do shorty. They'd never believe that someone like me would have to pay for it.'

I gave him the vee's, but now he'd said it, everyone was looking to me to step up. 'Fine. It's worth a go,' I gave in.

They set me up with a tool bag in which I put the listening device and the screwdrivers. I'd pretend to be on the way back from work and wanting to get a bit on the side before getting home. I had my boiler suit on, which was clean enough. At least we weren't greasemonkeys. I wasn't looking forward to it even so.

'Come on Dicky. You've got to take one occasionally for your country,' said Charley. 'Just close your eyes and try not to think about all the infections they'll have crawling around down there.' He was enjoying himself far too much.

I grabbed a slack handful of fivers and got out of the van. I walked away from the house first and double-backed round the side-streets to approach it from a different direction. It was fully dark by now and the streetlights were off too. Probably the council trying to save power due to another miner's strike. All the windows in the house were lit up and welcoming. I saw someone up ahead loitering around the gate at the foot of the stairs leading to the front door. I slowed my pace, wondering if he was a customer and wanting to get an understanding of how they dealt with visitors. He walked up and down for a few strides, then turned purposefully toward the house and marched up the steps and knocked on the door. It was opened by a young woman in a thin satiny nightgown, who let him inside without even a word. Either he was expected or recognised or they got clients inside first and then talked business. I was hoping it was the latter.

It was my turn to stiffen up my nerves, which was stupid really. It was only a bunch of women in there, and the chances were none of them was the one we wanted. Hell if Yasmine was in there it would be easy. I'd just walk out with her.

I walked up to the gate and was pushing it open when the door opened and bright light spilled out. I turned my head to avoid being blinded, and that may be what saved me. Down the steps came a short Arabic man with a trimmed black moustache who hardly looked at me, but I took a side glance at him as he passed. Part of the training. You look at everything. It can be a pain sometimes. This time though I was so shocked I missed a step and had to catch myself from falling on the railing. I couldn't breathe for a while. By the time I turned around the man had passed through the gate and was hurrying away down the street. He hadn't recognised me, but I'd never have forgotten him. The long weeks in Saudi with a salt-soaked cane had seen to that. It was Black-Eyed Susan.

Chapter Twenty

I hurried back to the van, keeping an eye over my shoulder at the retreating back of Black-Eyed Susan. He was just turning the corner towards the high street when I slammed open the door and leaned in.

'Charley! I got eyes on an old friend. Jeddah. Old Black-Eyes.'

'What?' He looked at me in confusion, but tinged with anger. Not at me. At him. Charley had had his 'meals' a lot hotter than I had.

'Come on. We've got to stay with him.' I grabbed a radio, dumped the tool bag and sprinted off after him. I felt a fire in my chest I didn't recognise. It was anger, excitement, fear, all wrapped up in uncertainty. I heard the van door slam shut and Charley taking to his heels following me. I reached the end of the road and pulled up before I turned the corner and Charley slammed into the back of me.

'Where is he?' he hissed. 'I'm going to rip his fucking head off.'

'Wait! Not yet,' I held him back, and peered around the corner. I saw him, walking quickly, head down. He was wearing a Saville Row suit instead of the Safari gear but I still knew him.

'That bastard is going to die!' Charley snarled.

'Yeah, I agree, but let's follow him first. Find out what he knows.'

Charley grabbed my arm and squeezed hard. I grabbed his and squeezed back warningly. We hung there against each other until Charley got a hold of himself and calmed down enough to grunt and nod.

'Standard pattern,' he said thickly. We split up and I crossed the street to tail him from there. Charley kept behind Black-Eyes, about thirty yards back. I ducked into a doorway and got on the radio.

'Bravo X-ray. We need assistance. Suspect on foot, heading east on high street.'

'X-ray Bravo, copy. On route.'

'Bravo X-ray, call back-up to assist.'

'X-ray Bravo, confirmed.'

I put the radio away and continued the tail. Hopefully the teams would get in touch with each other and coordinate around us. I wouldn't know because I'd turned the volume off. I couldn't risk it being heard by the target. The radios came with an earpiece, but it was so bulky and obvious it was a liability.

Following a target on foot is different to tailing them in a vehicle. There are more places for them to go, more chances for them to surprise you by stopping, or turning around suddenly. I was expecting him to show some counter-surveillance knowledge and give us a hard time, but he clearly had something on his mind, because he seemed oblivious to the possibility of being followed. I kept an eye on Charley too, in case he looked like he was going to change his mind and take a pop at him. He was behaving himself for now. After a couple of streets, we switched, and I took the side behind Black-Eyed Susan, and Charley took the other side of the street.

I was expecting our Arab friend to jump into a car, which was another reason for calling in the team in the van. I was surprised when he ducked down into the newly opened Brixton Underground station. Charley and I had to close ranks to keep in sight. Following someone on the trains is difficult. There is nothing for people to do on the trains apart from look around at all the other passengers, which meant more chance of being spotted. You really needed a whole team to do this, and all we had was the two of us. I hung back at the entrance just long enough to send a message to the other teams about where we were going and to stand by. The radios wouldn't work underground so they wouldn't know where we were going until we got there. The tube only went one way from Brixton, as it was at the end of the Victoria Line, so we knew at least which direction he'd be going.

The platform was almost empty, so Charley and I kept close to the walls and tried not to move. There was only a half a minute wait until the train arrived and the Arab got on the nearest carriage, towards the middle. I got into the same carriage at the far end and slunk down into a seat with my collar hunched up. I was still wearing the boiler suit. I'd need to ditch that at some point. It was a marker. Charley waited on the platform until the doors started to close, then leapt onto the carriage behind ours. It was risky because the train might leave without you, and your movements might also be seen by the target, but it was necessary in case the target was conducting counter-surveillance and planned to jump off as the doors were closing. This is why you needed a large team.

He only stayed on for one stop, then switched to the Northern line, heading north. On the platform there was a three minute wait, so I took the opportunity to step aside and strip off the boiler suit. Charley kept eyes on him while I was doing it. I stowed the overalls under a bench, then sat on it. Black-Eyed Susan was standing on the platform, near to the edge, waiting patiently.

When the train came we did the same routine, except we switched, and Charley rode his carriage. We stayed on the train for several stops and followed him off at London Bridge. If he'd been going any further, we'd have switched again. Five stops is the typical time people stay on a line before changing, so anything longer than that and your chances of being remembered increases.

He led the way out back up to the street, and Charley dropped back so I was nearest. Once outside he turned along the river and started looking up and down the street as if expecting to see something. He stopped once and looked back. I had to keep walking so I put my head down, and twisted to check the road as if I was about to cross. I saw Charley some way back tucked behind a flower stall making a radio call. Reporting in our position. There was a gap in the traffic, so I had to take it. I looked back up the street towards Black-Eyed Susan, as if I was just checking the traffic, and I saw that he had gone. Shit. I was half-way across the road at that point, so I hurried to the other side, spun round and dropped down as if to tie my shoelace. It gave me the chance to scan the other side of the street for him.

There were a few men in sharp suits, but none of them was our guy. Then I saw his little beady profile in the passenger seat of a dark Mercedes as it pulled away from the kerb. I looked back at Charley. He was scanning the street too, and his eyes met mine. I pointed at the car and got a nod of understanding. He got straight on the radio. I took off after the car, running down the pavement to keep up with it. That wasn't as hard as it sounded. The average speed of the traffic was only about fifteen miles an hour, once you took into account the traffic lights, pedestrians, buses, and those maniac cyclists who weave in and out like they own the place. I still had to sprint though.

The car took a left at the next junction. It was a one-way road, like a lot of streets in London, and I dashed across the path of a black cab to keep up, causing him to brake hard with a squeal of metal. I didn't hang around to apologise. He probably had a few choice words to say to my back.

The Merc came up on a queue of traffic which gave me a chance to slow down and catch my breath. I pulled the radio out and turned the volume up to find out what was going on. I heard Charley's dulcet tones snarling away.

'…do you mean, you've been pulled?'

'Whiskey Bravo, orders just came in to stand down. We're turning back now.'

'Fuck the orders!' Charley's radio etiquette wasn't great at the best of times. It seemed to have gone out the window.

I shoved the radio back in my jacket as the cars started moving again. I didn't have time to chat, or to ask why our back up had been pulled. It was unexpected, given the amount of resource that had been drawn together at short notice, and the apparent priority Blondie had placed in it, but it wasn't unusual for orders to change from hour to hour.

I didn't give a shit about the orders right now though. I wanted that black-hearted bastard. I didn't know what he was doing here, or why he was coming out of a house we were staking out, but it was too improbable to be a coincidence. The Merc turned right and the road took it around a small green park. I changed direction and jumped over the low fence surrounding the park and sprinted through it, meeting the Merc as it rounded the corner and continued north. They were getting closer to the river and the warehouses along the docks area. Traffic became lighter as they got into a more industrial area and they picked up speed. I had to give it a whole lot more to keep pace.

They got about eighty yards ahead of me and then turned to the right into a warehouse complex. I didn't know if there was a longer road down that way. It could have taken him all the way to the coast for all I knew. I had no choice but to dig deep and get to the corner as fast as I could. I nearly fell round it, gasping. My chest burned with acid, and I knew I'd not be able to go on for much longer. I didn't need to. The car was parked next to a warehouse about thirty feet ahead on the opposite side of the wide road. I pulled back and hid round the corner, then peered round a bit more carefully.

The driver was getting out and walking across to the passenger seat. He didn't open it though. He just stood there, facing the warehouse, with his back to me. He was wearing a leather bomber jacket which made him look wider than I was tall. I got on the radio and dialled up Charley.

'Whiskey X-ray. They've stopped. South bank of the river near some warehouses.' I looked around for a street sign. There wasn't one obvious. So I gave him the name of one of the businesses nearby.

'Got it. I'll be there in a minute,' came the reply. Like I said, his radio etiquette needed some work.

I tucked the radio away and settled down to watch. A door in the side of the warehouse opened and a man stepped out, looked around and then nodded at the driver facing him. The driver opened the door and Black-Eyed Susan got out and walked purposefully inside, followed by his new host. A security light over the door illuminated the area by the car, so I had a good view of what was going on. Until they went inside. The driver got back into his seat, but he didn't drive off, which was encouraging. That probably meant the Arab was going to return. I hoped Charley got here by then. I didn't fancy running back across London.

I heard a car behind me and looked to see a taxi pulling up. Charley got out, had a word with the driver and hurried over to me.

'What do you know?'

'Our man waited for a bit then went inside. I didn't see who he was meeting. I'm guessing it wasn't the guy who opened the door. The driver is still in the car waiting.'

We looked across at the warehouse, scoping it out. There weren't any lookouts or guards outside that we could see. There weren't any windows either. But there was a ladder tacked to the side of the building going right up to the roof.

'What do you think about the roof?' I asked. 'Skylights?'

'Could be,' said Charley. 'A bit risky though. They might come out when we are up there.'

'You'd better stay down here then with the taxi,' I said. 'I'll shinny up and see if I can see anything. I'll keep in touch by radio.'

'You do that. Don't get spotted.'

I grinned, 'Care for my well-being? I'm touched.'

Charley scowled and muttered something about paperwork. I got ready to dash across the road, then paused and asked a question.

'What happened with the back-up?'

'Fucking wankers. I opened my mouth too wide is what happened,' Charley said. 'I told the B-team back there that we were following a contact from Saudi. They must have been on the blower while we were underground and reported that back. By the time we got topside again someone had decided that we were off-message and ordered a stand-down.'

I frowned, 'I don't like the sound of that. Don't they normally let us make those kind of calls? We're the ones on the ground.'

'I think the whole thing stinks, Dick. All I know is we're on our own on this one. Talking of which I'm not getting any younger or better-tempered. Get over there and up that pole.'

I kept low and made a wide circle behind the car and crossed to the other side of the street. Once out of sight of the car it was easy. I went round the back of the building next door and got to the ladder from the shadowy darkness in the opposite direction. The driver wouldn't have been able to see me if he'd been staring in my direction. The ladder had a safety loop to give you a fighting chance to grab something if you fell off. I wasn't planning on doing that. I was more concerned in case it was all rusted away and whether the rungs would snap. That silo experience in Ireland had made me cautious. The rungs were strong enough though, and I was soon scampering up them like a monkey.

At the top, it let out onto a series of iron walkways suspended above the corrugated roof. I didn't think the roof would take my weight, but the walkways branched and went close to several skylights that dotted the roof like little pyramids. There was light emanating most strongly from the ones nearest the road, so I went over to them first. The walkway rattled and I had to walk carefully to keep the noise down. I got to the skylight and looked inside. I could make out some figures thirty feet below. About half a dozen sitting around a table. One of them was Black-Eyed Susan.

'I'm in position,' I said into the radio, putting the earpiece in to keep the noise down.

'What do you see?'

'He's in there. Five others. Four in suits, one in a pullover. Can't see the faces too well.'

'What are they doing?'

'Just talking for now.' I shifted position, something making the hair on the back of my neck stick up. I glanced around to make sure no one was creeping up on me, but I was alone on the roof. I needed to shift position to get a better look at the other people in there. I shoved the radio back in my pocket and leaned out over the railing attached to the walkway. It was no good. I'd have to step out onto the roof and look in from the other side of the skylight.

I swung my legs over the railing and hung there, looking for a place that was strong enough to support my weight. The wooden frame supporting the skylight windows was my best option. It was a couple of feet away, so it could be a one way trip. I wouldn't easily be able to pull myself back if it wasn't strong enough. I took a breath and went for it. No guts no glory. I placed my foot where I aimed and balanced there, weight equally spread between the frame and the walkway. It felt sturdy enough, but there wasn't much to hold onto and the window frame was only a couple of inches wide. I pulled the other leg across and got both feet onto the frame. I carefully supported my balance with a light hand on the pitched window. Thank god it was night-time. I'd have been a really noticeable silhouette in the day.

I gingerly shuffled around to the far side of the skylight and made sure I wasn't about to slip off. My legs were strained and warming up nicely. I couldn't hang about here too long. I looked down into the warehouse and had a much better view of the other players at the table, especially the guy in the sweater. I just about caught myself from falling as the second shock of the night hit me. I pulled out the radio and toggled it on to raise Charley.

'You're not going to believe who's in there with him.'

'You'd better fucking tell me then. I'm not psychic.'

I took a steadying breath. 'It's our old mate from Ireland. Smiling John.'

Chapter Twenty-one

Charley didn't say a lot to that, which I took for a bad sign. He just grunted. Maybe he'd half-expected it? Maybe nothing surprised him any more?

'You'd better get your arse back down here, Dicky,' he said finally.

'What's up?'

'We're going to break out the stun grenades and the shotgun and redecorate the inside of that place, and you can't do that from up there.'

'On my way.' I toggled the radio off and carefully put it way, making sure it wouldn't fall out of my pocket and give my position away. I was still on the wrong side of a torturous route back to the walkway, and was beginning to regret being so bold. Slowly, I eased around the skylight, my entire world now focused on a one-inch beam under my feet and a flimsy glass window to the side. The leap back to the walkway was easier. At least I had a railing to grab on to. It made a loud clattering when I lurched onto it, and I froze, waiting to see if there was any reaction from inside. I didn't hear anything, so after several more breaths, I eased my way over the railing onto the walkway. From there it was just a case of walking softly and trying not to run. I retraced my steps back around the building to Charley.

'About bloody time,' he grumbled when I reached him.

I ignored him, 'Are they still in there?'

'Unless they've slipped out the back while you were pansying around.'

'Got the stuff?'

Charley held up the sports bag containing the grenades and sawn-off. 'Right here. Did you see any sign of our girl in there?'

'No. I could only see a small bit of the room. The rest was all dark. What's the plan? Wait for backup?' I asked.

'I don't think backup is coming.'

I had to force myself to close my mouth. 'And you seriously want to march in there and take on six guys - seven including the driver?'

'Piece of piss. Pop a few flashbangs in first, then follow up and take them down. Easier than convincing your old mum to swallow.'

'Sounds easy,' I muttered. It was never easy.

'I'm not letting that bastard get away,' Charley said coldly. I knew him well enough by now to realise there was no changing his mind. If I backed out he'd just go in on his own. I wasn't going to let that happen.

'Fine, I'm in there with you. Remember we're looking for civvies as well though.'

Charley didn't exactly smile, but for a few moments his expression was slightly less bitter.

We checked on the driver. He had given up standing around and had climbed back into the car. We could see his head nodding up and down as if he were listening to music. I checked my pistol and arranged some grenades around my pockets for easy access, then held one in my hand to start the ball rolling. Charley did the same, but favoured the sawn-off. He was going to be point man. I didn't want to be in front of him when that thing started going off.

The driver was our first target. He was distracted so it was easy for us, crouching low, to cross the road behind the car and get close to it. Charley circled around to the passenger's side, staying below the window line, ready to open the door and engage while I went for the direct approach.

I stood up and approached the driver's window. He was completely unaware of me. He was reading a magazine of some kind and listening to some thumpety-thump music I didn't recognise. I knocked on the window, and he nearly hit his head on the roof as he jumped. He quickly recovered and glared at me, and wound down the window with his right hand. He opened his mouth, but I didn't give him a chance to tell me where to go. A swift gun butt to the temple and he was down, slumped across the passenger seat and nicely out of sight.

I gave Charley the all-clear and we took up position by the door to the warehouse. This was going to be the tricky bit. I shoved my pistol into the front of my trousers and got a second grenade out of my pocket. The room where I'd seen the men should be on the other side of this door, and they would be about twenty feet further in and off to one side. Unless they had moved in the last ten minutes since I'd last seen them. Which was possible.

At a nod from me, Charley flicked the handle and pushed the door open. It wasn't locked.

I triggered the grenades, stole a glance round the door frame and saw the table with men around it. I tossed the grenades in together, watching them arc over towards them for long enough that I was sure they would land in the right place, then pulled my head back and looked away. There was a clatter as they hit the concrete floor, cries of surprise and anger, then two sharp cracks and flashes, like a mini-thunderstorm.

Charley was straight inside and unloaded both barrels before I'd snatched up my pistol and followed him. Thick white smoke swirled around us. I could make out some silhouettes staggering about where I thought the table was, and levelled my gun, ready to fire if they looked threatening.

Charley didn't bother reloading the shotgun, but pulled out his pistol and cast around for a target. We pushed deeper into the room and saw several men rolling around on the floor moaning. The table was illuminated by an overhead light, but the rest of the warehouse was dark. Rows and rows of shelving and stillage stretched into the darkness, and stopped us seeing much further.

I covered Charley while he went in and searched the men. He found a couple of pistols and several knives, and flung them in my direction for safekeeping. As he did, one of the men on the ground managed to pull out a revolver and waved it desperately in my direction. He pulled the trigger a couple of times. I flinched, but all that happened was the hammer clicked uselessly on empty chambers. It was one of the camel-hair coat guys I'd seen collecting money. I stepped over and relieved him of it.

While they were still stunned, Charley pulled out some tape from the sports bag to use as a gag and bound their wrists behind them.

'I only see four,' I said.

'I know,' said Charley tightly. Neither Black-Eyed Susan nor Smiling John were among them. One of the four had a large red stain on his chest slowly seeping through his shirt. Charley got to him last, and swore under his breath.

'He's dead.'

'Shit.'

Charley didn't reply, but kicked the body twice in frustration, a little more enthusiastically than necessary. 'Fucking claret everywhere!'

He knew we were both in deep trouble now. We'd get away with a lot under the umbrella of the Firm, but murder of British citizens wasn't one of them. We should have known better than to barge in with weapons drawn, but when the blood was up, reason tended to take a back seat.

'We need to find the others,' I said.

Charley made sure the three others weren't going anywhere, and reloaded his shotgun. It might have been my imagination, but he looked a bit paler than normal. 'Let's go,' he said.

There was an office nearby, which seemed the most likely place they'd have gone to. Charley went first, kicking the door down with his size twelves. No point being subtle now. The room beyond held a couple of large desks and a row of filing cabinets. In the far corner was a fire escape door, but some helpful person had padlocked it shut.

'They didn't get out this way,' I said. Charley was already backing out and peering into the darkness of the extended warehouse.

'Round the sides,' he muttered quietly, and gestured for me to take the left hand side. He waited for my nod, then set off in the other direction. They could be hiding in the middle, but the chances were they'd have bolted for an exit. By splitting up we'd double the chance of catching them.

I jogged quietly alongside the walls, pistol ready to fire. The darkness swallowed me up and I had to reach out with my hand to run it along the wall to work out where I was going. The dim light from the skylights and the table behind me didn't penetrate this far and I couldn't see anything at all. I stopped, hoping my eyes would adjust, and listening hard. Apart from the groans of the goons we'd taken down, I couldn't hear a thing. I started walking again, flinching at any shadow that seemed a bit darker than the rest. This was stupid. Chances were I'd bump into Charley and we'd shoot each other. I stopped again and turned back to the lit-up table. Charley could piss about in the dark if he wanted. I stayed in the shadows beyond the pool of yellow light. No point making myself a target.

I kept straining my senses into the darkness, trying to see or hear anything. Susan, Charley, anything. On a whim I drifted over to the main door we came in by. I looked out just in time to see the door to the car close, hear the engine fire up and the car screech away.

I swore and brought my gun up, unloading half a dozen rounds into the back of the vehicle. The rear window exploded on the third shot and the car swerved, but it just accelerated away. I don't think any of the shots hit anything vital, such as the driver.

Charley was beside me seconds later, and was there to see the car veer around a corner in the distance.

'Was that them?' he gasped.

'I think so. I didn't get a good look though.'

'Shit!'

He repeated that word for about a minute, shouting in denial and kicking at the walls, the ground, the table, anything in his way really. I stayed well back and let him vent. The guys on the ground were staring at him with wide, panicked eyes. Even I didn't know if he would turn on them.

Eventually he seemed to run out of steam and I got back in his face.

'Are you done?' I offered him a cigarette.

Charley muttered something, then nodded and took the fag. It was about as much of an apology as I was going to get. I crossed over to the guys on the ground and squatted next to one, holding my gun carelessly in front of his face.

'Have you got a girl here?' I asked, slowly, letting my anger and frustration bleed into my tone. He was gagged, and couldn't say much, but his head started bobbing up and down enthusiastically. He was eager to please.

'Good boy,' I said, and hauled him to his feet. They were bound together, but he could still hop. 'Lead the way,' I said and poked him with the gun.

He mumbled something, but started to hop comically towards the far side of the warehouse. He did pretty well. He only fell over two or three times, and only once landed on his face. By the time we got to the opposite side, Charley had wound down and sauntered over to join us.

'What are you doing Dicky? Taking him for a walk?'

'He's showing me where the girl is. Aren't you my friend?' More mumbles and reassurances. The goon was getting tired and nearly collapsed against the wall. He gestured wearily with his chin towards an unassuming door nearby, fastened closed with a couple of sliding bolts. Someone had brought a white transit van inside and parked it nearby.

'In there?'

More grunts and nods.

Charley put him to sleep with a quick jab to the back of his head.

I listened at the door. Anyone in there would have heard the gunshots and would probably be trying to be really quiet, so I didn't think I'd hear anything. I certainly wasn't expecting to hear snoring.

I frowned and beckoned Charley over. He listened too and started to chuckle.

'If that's her she must be three sheets to it. Either that or she's having it away with an industrial vibrator.'

You could always rely on Charley to lower the tone.

I slid the bolts back. No way to do it quietly, so I did it quickly instead. Charley kicked the door open as soon as I was done and barged in, gun at the ready. The smell of cooked heroin hit me first. Then the delightful tang of piss and vomit mingled together, dusted with an underlying layer of stale sweat. A makeshift bed made of a rank mattress was shoved into the far corner, and on it lay a pile of elbows and rags that turned out to be the once respectable Yasmine Short.

'Wake her up, runt.'

'Fuck off. You do it,' I replied.

'And ruin my one good suit?'

Charley wasn't going to budge, so I stuffed my gun into my jacket and went to check on the girl. She was totally out of it. God knows what they had done to her, but she was in danger of overdosing on the horse. Her eyes were rolled right back in her head and I could only get a low moan when I slapped her.

'She needs a doctor,' I said.

'I'll get on the blower. We need to secure this place fast.'

'Aren't you forgetting about something?'

Charley cocked his head and looked at me.

'The dead Raz Clarke back there.'

'Shit. We can't leave him there.'

'What do you suggest?'

Charley looked around helplessly, then a slow grin spread across his face and he darted out of the door, leaving me cradling the girl. His head reappeared a few moments later.

'Bingo. We'll shove him in the van. Once he's out of sight, we'll call for backup, off-load the girl, then take off in the van and dump him somewhere.' He was well pleased with himself.

'All right Einstein,' I admitted, since I didn't have a better plan, 'Let's get going.'

Charley hopped in the van and started it up. I carried the girl out, and Charley followed after me in the van. I laid Miss Short on her side on the ground and tried to make her comfortable. I didn't want her suffocating on her own vomit after all the effort of finding her. Charley hopped out and went over to the dead body.

'Give us a hand over here will you?' he said.

Charley had already bagged the legs, which left me with the heavier, soggier end.

'He liked his pies didn't he?' I grunted as we hauled him around to the back of the van. I opened the doors and looked inside. It was stacked with unmarked cardboard boxes of various sizes. There was just enough space to shove the body if we folded the legs up around his ears. We both had to lean on the door to get it to close. It wasn't pretty but it worked.

Charley leaned back against the van, panting. 'Now let's call this in.'

I got on the radio. 'Bravo X-ray. We have the package.' I was half-expecting there to be no answer after being ditched earlier, but I got a reply immediately. I told them where we were and got a curt 'Hold tight,' in response.

'They're on the way,' I told Charley.

'I'll move the van round the corner. Once they've collected the girl and pissed off, we'll take the van somewhere and dump the body.'

Sounded like a good plan. Nothing could go wrong with that.

Chapter Twenty-two

Within twenty minutes the place was a confusion of activity as it seemed all our backup converged on the warehouse at once. The woman operative, Romeo took charge of the Short girl.

'What the hell did they do to her?' she demanded, as if I knew. She didn't really expect an answer. She was just ranting.

'Will she be okay?' I asked.

'I don't know. If she pulls through it will be no thanks to men like you.'

'That's a bit harsh. Men like me rescued her.'

'That's your job though. I don't see you making a habit of it. Girls like this are abused by men every day and no one thinks anything about it. If they stop to think about it at all they just blame the girls for dressing like sluts.'

I glanced at Charley, who rolled his eyes.

'No love, you have us all wrong,' he said, 'We love sluts.' Women's lib was an alien concept for him. I knew I wasn't going to get anywhere with this conversation so I pulled away and joined him near the door. The other thugs were being led away by our boys. They'd get the third degree for a while then get handed over to the police if we thought it was worth brownie points. Otherwise the pigs or incinerator were in for a feed. I favoured the incinerator or we'd have to drive down to the farm in Kent. I was worried about them blabbing about the one we'd shot. We didn't need anyone bringing that up. Chances were they'd keep their mouths shut. They thought we were cops after all.

The bloodstain on the floor was like a beacon to me, but everyone was walking around it obliviously.

'We'd better get out of here soon,' I whispered to Charley. Knowing the body was in the van only a few feet around the corner was like a festering sore in my mind. It made me twitchy every time someone stepped outside.

'Relax,' said Charley. 'I'll sort it.'

He strolled over to a couple of the guys who were sorting out an ambulance and had a quick word with them. They nodded absently and he turned toward me and cocked his thumb over his shoulder, in the universal gesture for us to get going. I followed him to where he had parked the van. If anyone noticed us leaving, they didn't say anything, and even if they had, we were the senior officers at the scene.

I pointedly jumped in the passenger side, forcing Charley into the driving seat. The adrenaline was washing away now, and the magnitude of what we'd done was starting to break through to me.

'What the hell did you do back there?'

'I just told them we had something better to do,' Charley seemed to deliberately misunderstand me.

'I'm talking about our friend back there with a sucking chest wound.' Anger was bleeding out through my words. 'You didn't have to kill him. He was already down.'

'Don't you have a fucking go at me, runt,' he snorted back, 'What did you think was going to happen when we danced in there all tooled up?'

'A neat take-down?' I knew what had happened. Charley was hoping to see Black-Eyed Susan so much, that he'd convinced himself the goon he shot was him. The swirling smoke and shadows hadn't helped. I took a breath and we sat in silence while Charley drove and we both tried to calm down. There was no question that Charley had fucked up, but there was also no question that I was going to help him sort it out.

'What's the plan then?' I asked eventually. 'We can't take it to the usual places without the Firm finding out.'

Charley shrugged. 'I'm still thinking.'

'What about a building site somewhere?' I suggested. 'Bury him under the foundations?'

'Not a bad idea that. I know just the place.' Charley grinned. The cocky bugger was back. He took us south, off towards Blackheath, where they were digging up the road and laying the foundations for a new office block. It was the early hours of the morning when we got there, and the place was dead. Quieter than a mime convention.

There was a low fence surrounding the foundation work, but it wasn't going to be a problem. Charley parked the van as close as he could and we hopped out to get the body. It was heavier than I remembered and the cardboard boxes were crushed. I didn't look too closely at the contents as I struggled with an uncooperative set of arms and legs. Charley was 'supervising' and keeping watch. He did give me a hand hoisting the body over the fence and we waddled our way across the mud to the nearest pit filled with concrete. At the edge we looked down at it. The surface was about four feet below us and glistened in the dim moonlight.

'Do you reckon it's deep enough?' I asked, pausing for a breath.

'Yeah no problem. These foundations go down six feet at least.' Charley sounded very sure of himself. I didn't ask why.

'Ready?'

He nodded and we lifted the body and swung it into the pit.

It hit the concrete with a thud and completely failed to sink. We stared at it for a while, then Charley sniffed and coughed.

'It must have set already.'

'No fucking shit, Sherlock,' I said. 'We can't just leave it there.'

'No, you're right,' agreed Charley. 'You'd better get down there and hoik him out.'

I didn't even bother to argue this time. I slid down the steep bank and gingerly set foot on the concrete. It was still a bit damp and sticky, and I left footprints where I stepped, but it was solid enough. Getting the body up to Charley was a complete arse. I had to get under it and lift it as high as I could for Charley to reach down and grab it. I took some satisfaction in seeing Charley have to get on his hands and knees in the mud, and between the two of us, we got the body back up out of the pit. Charley gave me a hand out, but we were both knackered by then and had to take a break. We stared at the body for a while, before we attempted to put it back in the van. I had blood all over me now, which didn't improve my mood.

'You're a bloody liability Charley. Has anyone ever told you that?'

Charley grunted and nodded, 'Once or twice.'

I had no answer to that, so we just took and arm and a leg each and marched the body back to the van. God knows what we'd have said if someone had walked by at the time.

'Next brilliant plan?' I asked as we climbed inside again.

Charley frowned. 'Could dump him in the sewers. He'd get flushed out to sea. Or a meat grinder. Turn him into a pie.'

'I know a few places that would buy that meat, no questions asked.'

'Is it too late to take it down to the pigs?'

We were tired.

Charley put the van into gear and drove. We didn't know where we were going, but it was best to keep moving.

I looked over my shoulder at the body sprawled unceremoniously over the boxes and for the first time wondered what was in them. I twisted in my seat and reached back to open one. At first there was just a bunch of packing paper, then a flash of familiar brown paper which made my breath catch. I dug deeper and uncovered a stack of bundles half a foot deep.

'Uh, Charley,' I said quietly, reaching for another box.

'What have you found?'

The second box contained a bunch of plastic bags filled with white powder. I grabbed one and a bundle of the paper and turned to show Charley.

'We've got a shit load of tenners and god knows how many kilos of smack in the back.'

Charley's eyes widened and he swerved the van as he turned his head to look.

'Watch where you're going!'

'Christ, let me look at that.' He pulled over to the side of the road and we both jumped out and dashed round to the back to get a better look. Sure enough there were dozens of boxes of cash and dozens of other boxes of nicely packed heroin.

'There must be millions of quids worth here,' Charley breathed.

I picked up a couple of handfuls of the money. 'It's all used notes. Mostly tenners, but there are bundles of twenties and fives too. Untraceable.'

We looked at each other.

Charley started to grin. 'Untraceable eh? Someone could set themselves up nicely with that lot.'

'We can't just pocket it,' I said weakly. It was tempting.

Just then the radio squawked. I went back to the cab to get it. As I was reaching for it, I heard the broadcast message that was going out to all the rest of the team and my hand froze.

'…be advised that X-ray and Whiskey are in possession of a white transit van containing drugs and money. They are believed to have stolen it and should be apprehended immediately. Cooperate with police to coordinate pursuit.'

I frowned, picked up the radio and returned to Charley, who was ferreting through the other boxes.

'We've got a problem. They know about the money.'

Charley shrugged, 'Someone at the warehouse must have told them. They won't know how much there is though. We can still take a bit.'

I waved the radio at him, 'They think we've stolen it deliberately.'

'That's bollocks. Why would they jump to that conclusion?'

'Well it does look a bit suspicious doesn't it? First we went off-piste chasing some unrelated mark who as far as the team knew, had nothing to do with the case. Then we break normal operating procedure and storm the place rather than waiting for backup. Add in the quick getaway with the van and for all we know, they were trying to get hold of us while we were trying to dump the body, but as I left the radio behind we'd not have heard it. It all stacks up wrong.'

'Just get on the horn and tell them we're on the way in.'

'We've still got the body to sort out.'

Charley swore.

I thought hard and toggled the radio. 'Hotel Quebec X-ray, negative on that. We have the van and are bringing it in. We'd just stopped for a piss.'

The response was almost immediate. Almost. 'X-ray Hotel Quebec proceed immediately to RV.'

There was nothing more. I looked at Charley. The look in his eyes was the same as mine. Something felt wrong.

'Hotel Quebec X-ray Confirmed.' I replied and turned the transmit off.

'We haven't got long,' said Charley. 'They still think we're dirty. We've got to dump this stuff somewhere and fast.'

'What about the lock-up?'

'Too risky. Blondie knows about it. We need to find a deserted garage or something. We'll have to dump the body there and deal with it later.'

A police car cruised by, then slowed as it passed behind us and flicked on its blues as it started to turn in the road.

'Shit!' I said, and raced for the cab. We couldn't be caught with a body in the back. I got there first and slid over to the drivers seat to start the engine. Charley piled in behind me and slammed the door shut. 'Drive!'

Chapter Twenty-three

I crashed the gearbox into first and wheel-spun away, checking the flashing blue lights in the wing mirror. We'd got the jump on him, but he was rapidly closing the gap. I swung hard left at the first intersection, sending the boxes and the body sliding around in the back of the van. Charley nearly ended up in my lap but managed to brace himself on the dashboard.

'How the fuck are you planning to lose this guy?' asked Charley.

'No idea,' I gritted my teeth. The agile saloon used by the police was going to run rings around the clunker transit we were in. 'I'm going to have to get inventive.'

This early in the morning there weren't many cars around. I came up behind a night-bus in the next street and swerved to the opposite lane to pass it. The cop had his siren on now and followed. Charley fiddled with the radio and tuned into the police band. We were all over it. I concentrated on not slamming us through any walls while Charley listened to what they were saying.

'They're calling in more cars,' he relayed. 'They haven't mentioned us by name. Sounds like they were only given a description of the van and told to bring it in.'

'Great, except our fingerprints are all over this thing now. We'll have to burn it or sink it if we can get away.'

Charley looked mournfully over his shoulder at the bundles of cash sloshing about in the back. 'We could have had such a good time together,' he said to them.

A fresh set of blues and twos appeared up ahead, turning to block the road. I braked hard and skidded around a corner into a narrow street. There was a rapid series of thuds as I scraped the van along a line of parked cars and took off all of their wing mirrors. A trail of destruction and broken glass decorated road in my wake.

'I think you missed one,' said Charley.

'I'll get it next time,' I spat back.

Charley checked behind us, 'We've picked up four now. You'd better do something or I'm not going to let you play with me any more.'

All I could do was to keep my foot flat on the pedal and pray nothing got in my way. I could hear our location being updated over the radio as the police coordinated themselves around us.

I swung out onto a wide road and took the opportunity to check my mirrors. I saw a line of blue as the police fanned out behind us. I couldn't see how we were going to get out of this.

Suddenly the glass window in the doors behind us exploded with a loud crack.

'What the–'

'Are they shooting at us now?' I yelled, trying to control the swaying van.

Charley swung round in his seat and squinted into the flashing blues and the headlights. 'It isn't the filth. There's another car back there.'

I glanced to the side and saw a black sedan in the wing mirror. It was trying to come up alongside and its passenger window was open. I saw the barrel of a pistol emerge, and pulled on the steering wheel to get in front of them.

The chit-chat on the police frequency went nuts. They reported the newcomer and ordered the cars to back off a bit. They couldn't risk any of their guys becoming targets.

'Who they hell is it?' I asked. 'It's not Blondie is it?'

'Nah, that's not our style. It must be the fucking Arab. They must have been listening to the radio and found out where we were.'

Another gunshot thudded into the side of the van. I felt a cold draft and looked down to see a ragged hole in my door. Another couple of inches higher and Jeannie and I would have had to adopt.

'Fuck this,' I swerved to the side and slammed on the brakes. The sedan overshot and his brake-lights came on as the driver tried to stay with us. I dropped gears and accelerated into the back of him. He tried to swerve out of the way, but it just gave me an easier target. I caught the back end of the sedan and pushed my way through, spinning it one-eighty degrees. For a brief moment the driver of the sedan and I were side by side, facing opposite directions, and we locked eyes. It wasn't Black-Eyed Susan or Smiling John, and neither was the passenger. Must be just hired help.

I hit the pedal and aimed for another intersection. A no-entry sign informed me that it was a one-way street but I didn't give a shit. A little Mini was pootling towards us, so I hit the horn and got over to one side of the road. The stupid driver, some beatnik-type with a polo-neck and poncey hairstyle panicked and slammed on his brakes instead of getting over. I caught the corner of his car and burst past it with a tremendous rending of metal and glass. The Mini was forced back into the parked cars and spun around, but the transit was a beast and apart from some panel-work, didn't even notice.

'Oops,' I said, 'I feel bad about that.'

'Don't,' said Charley, 'Serves him right for driving a girl's car.'

'How are we doing back there?'

Charley was checking our tail. 'Sedan is still there but the Mini is in the way, giving him a hard time. Cops have dropped well back though.'

'Things are looking up then.'

A milk float turned into the road up ahead.

'I need to learn to keep my mouth shut.'

The milkman was a bit more switched on than the beatnik, and tried to squeeze into a gap leading to a driveway. There was a bit of space between his rear end and the parked cars so I aimed for it and tried to hold the van steady. With all the stuff in the back sliding around it was like juggling water balloons. The milkman saw what was going to happen before I did and leaped from his cab to the safety of the pavement just before I hit the back of the float. More thuds as more wing mirrors were ripped off the parked cars on one side and the smashing of glass on the other side. Milk showered the side of the van and all over the road behind us.

The one-way street came to a t-junction and I had to brake nearly to a stop to take the turn. The sedan took the opportunity to get really close. There was another gunshot, but I think he missed the van. I turned left onto a two-lane divided highway and glanced at a road sign. I had an idea. I kept the van in the left hand lane and eased slightly off the accelerator. The sedan followed and started pulling up alongside on my right. I kept the speed steady and kept an eye on the sedan. The passenger had his gun out and was trying to get a good bead on me. I glanced ahead. Just a few more seconds. It took all my self-control not to swerve away from the sedan. Any moment he might decide to take the shot, but I was gambling on him being frustrated at his past misses and wanting to be sure this time. The sedan got nose to nose with us and I looked down to find myself staring right down the barrel of an ugly automatic held by an obscenely grinning raghead.

I slammed on the brakes and swerved around the roundabout, taking the racing line to cut them off and force them into the raised concrete embankment. The driver was distracted trying to keep his line so his partner could get a bead on me and realised his mistake too late. He had no time to react and slammed into the concrete at sixty miles an hour. The sedan flipped end over end and cleared the top of the roundabout. It was surreal to look out of the window and see it keeping pace with us upside down and flying through the air. Then gravity did its thing and it smashed into the ground, crushing the slimy bastards. I hauled on the wheel and took the opposite exit. Behind us the sedan skidded across the road on its roof. Blue lights were closing fast but they'd be distracted by the carnage behind us. I took a couple of rapid turns, tucked the van under a railway arch and killed the lights.

Charley and I ducked down. The flashing blues headed down a different street. We lay panting for several minutes, listening to the police report the RTA at the roundabout and reporting that they had lost the van.

'That wasn't bad,' Charley admitted.

'You're welcome.'

'We've still got a body to get rid of.'

I looked behind at the mess of boxes. White powder was everywhere where some of the bags had burst. It was mixed with blood and a confetti of used bank notes.

'We'll have to launder it,' said Charley.

'Very fucking funny.'

I sat up and looked out of the windscreen. We were parked across the street from a breakers yard. I had an idea.

It was nearly five in the morning by the time we were done. Charley and I had carried the body across the road and dumped it in the boot of a car in line to be fed into the crusher. Hopefully within a few hours the dead goon would be a lot smaller and encased in a three by three by three metal cube on the way to China to be melted down.

We got back into the van and broke out the fags. I was hungry and tired. My mind was turning things over and not getting anywhere.

'You've got that 'I'm in pain' look on your face,' said Charley, 'You're not trying to think again are you?'

'I am actually. I can't work out why the Firm would jump to the conclusion that we'd stolen the van so soon after we'd taken it. Or why they got the police involved.'

'Yeah I was wondering that too. And it was a bit convenient that the rag heads were listening in and made the connection to us.'

'The whole thing stinks. Someone in the Firm is batting for the other team.'

Charley grunted his agreement.

We sat in silence for ten minutes or so, each lost in our thoughts. Eventually, Charley stirred and turned to look in the back. 'I'm going to sort through that crap and see if I can find any notes not covered in blood and shit.'

'Just leave it,' I said. 'It's more trouble than it's worth.'

'You realise this is your pension runt? The Firm isn't going to look after you once you start dribbling in your soup.'

It still felt wrong. The money was dirty in more ways than one. I let Charley crawl back there and started planning how to get the van back to the Firm. The last contact we'd had I'd promised we were coming in. That was an hour ago. God knows what they were thinking now. Whatever we did we'd better do it quickly. The darkness of the night was fading into the grubby grey of dawn. It wouldn't be long before the streets were busy and make it harder to move around. The van was bashed up, dented, with broken windows. It would attract a lot of attention.

The radio crackled again. We'd left it on the police channel, just in case, but most of the chatter was mundane stuff. Then a chance couple of words caught my attention, and I reached over to turn the volume up.

'...Jeanette Frame reported missing by a colleague in the middle of a performance at the theatre earlier this evening...'

'Jeannie!' I listened to the rest of the report but it was almost over and pitifully short of details. Just her description and that she'd last been seen at the end of act one. Someone had taken her.

Chapter Twenty-four

'I need to get to a phone. See if she's home.'

Charley shook his head. 'No point trying to call her. Her mates and the police would have done that already.'

'I've got to get over there then.'

'Not in this van. It's too hot.'

I slammed my fist into the dash. It hurt but I turned my yelp of pain into a growl of anger.

'Calm down and let's think this through,' said Charley. 'We've got to make peace with the Firm first. We're not going to get anywhere stuck on the outside like this.'

I took a deep breath. He had a point. 'Fair enough. I'm not using that though,' I gestured to the radio. 'Let's get to a payphone and call into Blondie direct.'

'I've got a better idea,' smirked Charley.

It turned out he had her home phone number.

'So you have been drilling that hole after all?'

'Maybe I just overheard her telling someone once? Or happened to find her personnel file?'

I didn't dignify that with an answer.

'The point is she'll just be getting up soon and won't have left home yet. We can get hold of her directly and not have to worry about some agency mole intercepting our call.'

'Charley, how can you spend most of your time being a knob, and then come up with something this brilliant?'

'If I did it all the time someone might start expecting things of me.'

He gave me the number. It was scribbled on the back of a receipt in his wallet.

'You go and wake her up. I'll stuff as many Florence Nightingales as I can into a bag, then we'll torch the van.'

I was trembling as I jumped out. Fear? Rage? Excitement? I didn't know. All three probably. I wanted to sprint down the road, smashing in every door I passed until I found Jeannie.

I raced back to the main street and found a payphone. I considered reversing the charges, but I was already going to be in the deep stuff for calling her at home. We always carried a handful of coins for the phone, so I laid them out on the tray in front of me and made the call.

'Hello?' she answered after two rings. She sounded as if she had been awake for a while and her voice had a wary tone to it.

'It's Delta Foxtrot and Charlie Papa.'

There was a tiny pause while she registered that. I pressed on. 'Sorry for calling you on this number, but we don't think the normal lines are safe.'

'Where are you?'

'Not far. We've got some heat on us though and we need to come in. They've got my girl.'

Another pause. At least she wasn't balling me out. 'I'm not going to talk on an open line. Get yourself to the Russian House.'

'No, I don't trust anyone in there. I want to meet somewhere else.'

'Where did you have in mind?'

I thought for a moment. 'There's a café called Mike's Bites that serves breakfast south of the river near Tower Bridge, on Tanner Street. We'll meet you there.'

'I'll find it. When?'

I checked my watch. 'An hour from now. That should give us time to get there.'

'Okay. I'll see you there. Don't worry, I'll be alone.'

I hung up and looked across the road at Mike's Bites. It was empty, apart from a tired waitress putting out the sauce bottles on the tables.

I hurried back to Charley. He had dug out the sports bag that Blondie had given us and had filled it with as much cash as he could. All mixed up now, but we could go through it later. I told him about my conversation with her.

'Good work. I'll just set this thing burning then we'll go to the café.'

Charley used some fivers to start the fire.

'Oh that's just wrong,' I moaned. It didn't take long to get going, especially as Charley had siphoned off some petrol to help.

'Come on then, let's get some breakfast,' he said.

We headed towards Mike's Bites, but we didn't go inside. Instead we went to a newsagents across the street and bought some crisps and chocolate and a fizzy drink. Not the most nutritious of meals, but it would keep us going for another couple of hours.

We took up positions on the opposite side of the street to the café and waited. We stayed away from each other, and pretended to read newspapers. It wasn't that I distrusted the lying cheating bastards in the Firm, but as the Russians like to say, 'doveryai, no proveryai'. Trust but verify. I monitored the radio, flicking regularly between the usual frequencies the Firm used. There wasn't a lot of chatter, but it was only early morning. The sun was up now, but it was still grey and threatening drizzle.

Blondie arrived ten minutes earlier than scheduled. She walked in from the north, wrapped up in a long wool coat and a fur hat. She walked slowly, checking her surroundings and doing her counter-surveillance. Her eyes flicked over me then moved on and while she might not have recognised me, I knew she'd marked me out. She was good. She walked past the café first and went right to the end of the street. Then she crossed over to my side and started walking back. I tucked into the newsagents and positioned myself at the back where I'd be difficult to see from outside, but where I could see out onto the street though the door and window. It was a narrow view. I'd only see someone who walked directly past the shop.

I started counting. She had taken seventy-three steps past my point before turning back. If she kept the same speed, she'd reach the shop in forty seconds. I reached sixty before concluding that she had changed her pattern. She was very good. It was almost time. I moved to the doorway to get eyes on her again. I'd been stupid and forgotten the first rule of watching someone. Don't take your eyes off them.

I saw her within seconds. She was talking to Charley next to a bakery a few doors down. They both noticed me and I crossed the road to the café without acknowledging them. I didn't see anyone else in the area. She must have come alone after all.

I went inside and made sure it was a good place to talk. There were no customers yet and the pretty brunette waitress almost fell over herself to help when she hopped off her seat as I entered.

'Hello love, cup of tea?'

'If you keep talking like that I'm going to have to marry you,' I said, taking a seat at a table at the back. She smiled and pulled out a mug.

'Menu's on the board,' she said, tilting her head toward it.

'I'll have the full English thanks. Better make that three, I'm meeting some friends.'

'Coming right up,' she said, and placed a mug of tea in front of me.

I stirred in six sugars and by the time I'd taken a well-earned mouthful, Charley and Blondie arrived. They took the seats opposite me after confirming my order with the waitress. We waited until she went into the kitchen before we started talking.

'So Charley gave me the basics,' Blondie said quietly. 'But I still don't know why we're meeting here and not at the office.'

Charley stayed quiet, so I had to explain. 'There have been a few times when things haven't gone right. I know that you can get a run of bad luck occasionally, but this feels different.'

'Everyone gets that…'

'It doesn't add up,' I interrupted. 'It started with the Saudi job. There was no way they could have found us so easily, unless they knew we were there and where to look. Then Ireland. Those brothers couldn't have organised the Garda like that, just from an anonymous tip-off. The Garda turned up instead right after we'd called in with our location and sit-rep. We get here and find a connection between Saudi and Ireland, and now someone has pinched my Jeannie. There's no way any of those guys could have known about her unless someone on the inside told them.'

Blondie stirred her tea, one sugar, before answering, 'You don't know her disappearance is related.'

I stared at her, 'You don't really believe that do you? After the night we've had?'

She shrugged, 'Maybe not. Okay, I'll grant you they might be related, but it might not have been a leak from the Firm. These people have ways of getting their own information.'

'Either way, give me the benefit of doubt, and keep the Firm out of this for the moment. Until I get her back. Right now the only one I know I can trust is Charley. No offence.' Our waitress breezed in with three plates of food and conversation stopped. It gave Blondie a chance to consider her options, and I let her. I'd rather she came to whatever decision she was going to make on her own terms, rather than rushing it.

'All right,' she said finally, after we were alone again, and she had taken a mouthful of toast. 'I'll give you twenty-four hours. I'll call the hounds off and let you do your thing. After that you tell what you know to the police and let them do their job.'

'That's not a lot of time-' I began, but she cut me off with a shake of her head.

'I've already got a lot of covering to do for you over the business of that drugs van, which I notice you still haven't brought in.' I think I did pretty well keeping my face straight and not glancing guiltily at Charley, but she'd guessed what we'd done and to her credit, I don't think she really cared.

'I'm in the good books at the moment because you somehow found the Short girl, and because amazingly she's still alive, but there is a lot of heat to bring you in, if only to give you a pat on the head.'

'Don't worry,' smoothed Charley, 'We'll have Jeannie back in Dicky's bed in no time and check back in to pick up our medals.'

She nodded, her point made and pushed a bit of greasy bacon around her plate. I didn't have anything else to say, but I was itching to get up and start tearing up the town looking for Jeannie.

'I can't give you much in the way of support,' she said, 'But if you do find her and need a hand, I'll see what I can do.'

'Thanks,' I said.

She stopped moving food around and stood up to go. Charley eyed the plate possessively.

'Tomorrow morning. My office. Nine.'

'Understood.'

She left. She didn't even leave a tip.

'Eat up shorty, we're going to need it today.'

I ate. Charley finished his own plate, then started on Blondie's. I managed to swipe one of her sausages, but I was too wound up to feel much hunger.

'What now?' asked Charley, pushing the plates away from him.

'It has to be the Arab and the Mick,' I said. 'Nothing else makes sense.'

'Why do it?'

'What?'

'Say you are right for a change and it is them, why bother snatching her and taking her somewhere? If they knew there was a connection to you and wanted to hurt you, they could have just shot her right where they found her.'

I hadn't thought of that. To be fair, I hadn't thought a lot of anything since I found out. My brain was all fuzzy and numb. I was making stupid mistakes and dumb decisions. Like thinking I could do a better job of finding her than the police. I knew why I wanted them out of the picture though. I wanted to find those bastards with her and rip their throats out with my bare hands.

'I don't know,' I said finally.

'Well if you're lucky you can expect a ransom call sometime today. If you're unlucky, you'll be seeing her again a bit at a time every time you open your mail.'

I almost took a swing at him at that. But he was just being Charley. When things got tough his attitude just got bleaker.

I forced a smile. 'I've always been lucky. When it mattered.'

'Good for you,' Charley nodded. 'However, both of our cars are still bloody miles away,'

'I think we should check out the houses we were staking out earlier anyway. We know there is a connection to Black-Eyed Susan there. They may have taken Jeannie there.'

'Not a bad idea.' He turned and waved at the waitress, 'Hey love, can you phone for a taxi?'

'Of course,' she smiled. Charley could get women to do anything. She came back a few moments later with another couple of mugs of tea.

'Taxi will be ten minutes. Time enough for another cuppa. Can I get you anything else?'

'No love, you've been the best,' Charley smiled.

We drank our tea and paid for the breakfast, leaving almost as much again for a tip, and waited for the taxi.

Chapter Twenty-five

We'd left our cars at the Clapham Common brothel, so we went there first. It was after seven in the morning by the time we got there, and traffic was starting to build up. The fake British Gas van had gone. Now that the Short girl had been found the team had been stood down. Our cars were still where we left them. Charley left me to pay the taxi driver and hefted the bag of cash, which also contained the shotgun, into the boot of his car. We sat in his car facing the house, which now seemed lifeless and quiet.

'Looks like everyone has gone,' I said.

'Nah, there'll be someone inside,' said Charley. 'They'll be rinsing out their tender insides and cleaning up all the jism.'

'You've got such an elegant way with words.'

Charley shrugged. 'So what do you want to do? It's your party.'

I'd been thinking about that. I'd been trained for exactly this, and the proper thing to do was to stake the place out, maybe get a listening device in there and gather intel so that the backup we ought to call knew what they were walking into. That was the proper procedure.

'Fuck procedure,' I said. 'Let's bust in there, tear the place apart and make the whores tell us what they know.'

'First sensible thing I've heard you say since I met you,' agreed Charley.

We moved the cars a few streets away. They'd been there all night already. Mine for longer. Someone might remember them, or realise they were not local and call in a complaint. Also if things went Tango Uniform in the brothel and we had to bug out fast, we didn't want to have to return to the same street to collect them.

The house had a long, obscured garden that backed onto Clapham Common, and because it was daylight we decided to make the entry from there. We didn't have time to wait until dark. Blondie had made that clear. The back garden was shielded from view by trees and ringed by a six foot wooden privacy fence, topped with carpet grippers - nasty metal strips with sharp spikes jutting upwards. It was a simple and effective deterrent to casual intruders, capable of ripping someone's hands to shreds, even through leather gloves. We were far from casual intruders, however.

'Have you got a knife?' Charley asked, after a careful inspection of the top of the fence.

I pulled out a short bladed sheath knife and handed it up to him. He carefully worked it under the gripper, easing the nails out while I kept a watch on the park behind us. There were a few people in the distance walking their dogs and one of those mad fitness freaks in a track suit jogging along the path, but they were too far away to see us through the trees.

'Done,' announced Charley after about ten minutes of patient effort, interspersed with the occasional muttered expletive-laden rant. He had removed three of the strips, giving us plenty of room to climb over.

The house looked quiet and all the curtains were drawn upstairs. I suppose if your job kept you up until three in the morning you deserved a lie-in, even if you had spent most of the night on your back. Talking of which I was struggling to keep my eyes open. Waiting around for Charley had dampened the adrenaline a bit.

'Have you got any gear on you?' I asked.

Charley fished in his pockets and pulled out a small tub of the blue pills. 'I was just thinking the same.'

We grabbed a small handful each and swallowed them down without water. They tasted like someone had pissed on some chalk and left it to dry in cat litter but I forced them down anyway. I hated taking the pills on a dry throat.

One last check over the shoulder, then we went up and over. The garden was mostly lawn and flowerbeds. Not much cover. So we hugged the surrounding hedge and jogged quickly to the rear of the house, staying away from the French doors and windows. There was a door leading into a kitchen, a simple white-painted wooden affair with a glass upper half. It had a traditional tumbler lock instead of a Yale lock, which was a lot easier to pick. We squatted either side of the door, listening for any sounds inside. There was nothing for five minutes, and then we heard footsteps. Leather soles on tiles. Flat soles, not high heels. Probably a man, judging by the heavier, longer stride. Women don't normally swing their legs so long.

We heard him potter about for a bit, put the kettle on and then wander off.

'You'd better get cracking on that lock,' I said, 'They'll all be getting up soon.'

Charley got his picks out and set to work. It didn't take very long. The door swung open quietly.

'I like a well-oiled door,' I said.

'I like all sorts of things well-oiled.'

We crept in. We'd be making enough noise soon enough, but without knowing how many we were going to be up against it was worth being cautious. The kitchen was wide and modern and clean. All stainless steel and wood-effect veneer. Everything you'd want from a kitchen. I couldn't help thinking Jeannie would like it, which just made me more angry. A doorway at the far end opened onto a lavishly carpeted hallway with dark wood panelling and high ceilings, leading to the front door. A set of stairs was off to the side. Another door just beyond the kitchen led into a dining room. The sound of someone slurping a drink.

I nodded to Charley. I couldn't hear anyone else. There was a risk he wasn't alone, but we didn't have time to piss about. I slid round the corner, hands spread. A man was sitting at a table big enough to seat twelve. He was side on to me, facing the back of the house and he jerked his head toward me as I entered, but I reached him within one step and put an elbow into the side of his head. The skull is hard, but the elbow is harder. He went down immediately, head on the table and knocked his tea all over the expensive walnut table.

I pivoted around and checked the room as Charley came in behind me. It was empty. Heavy sideboards held silver bowls and candlesticks and no doubt fine china plates hidden away in cupboards. This wasn't a regular knocking shop. This was a high-class joint frequented by politicians, toffs and civil servants. What the hell was it doing getting involved with kidnapping?

'You hit him too hard,' said Charley. 'He'll be out for ages.'

'There must be someone else around who knows what's going on.'

We quickly scouted the rest of the rooms downstairs. They were all empty, but there were clear sounds of movement upstairs. Light tread. Probably a woman.

'You stay down here and keep an eye out,' I said.

'I'll cut the phone lines while I'm at it.'

'Good idea.'

The deep carpet made it easy to move around quietly and I got up the narrow stairs without a squeak. There were lots of bedrooms of course and the smell of oils and perfume was heavy. A door opened and I found myself face to face with a startled woman, maybe ten years older than me. I stepped forward, put my hand over her mouth and pushed her back into the room. We ended up on the bed with her beneath me. She was only wearing a flimsy satin nightgown, but I wasn't interested in that.

'Stay quiet and you won't get hurt,' I hissed. I didn't feel too good about threatening a woman, but she'd probably suffered worse. 'I'm looking for someone. A woman. Someone brought here against their will. Or failing that,' I added seeing confusion in her eyes, 'An Arab or an Irishman.' Recognition. She tried to say something so I moved my hand.

'Not here,' she gasped. 'I don't know anything. The girls here all want to be here.'

'What do you know about the Arab?'

She shook her head, 'Nothing. There was one here last night. He spoke to Sharon, the boss. Then he left.'

'Is Sharon here now?'

She shook her head. She didn't know anything. I let her go and stood up. 'Stay in here.' She nodded.

I checked the rest of the rooms. She was telling the truth. There was no one else in the house. I went back downstairs.

'Anything?' Charley asked.

'Dead end. Let's try the warehouse.'

We left the way we'd entered, over the back fence.

We took my car to the warehouse. Charley did his thing with the padlock on the gates and I stood behind him and casually shielded him from view, although all anyone would have seen from the street would be someone struggling with a padlock, and who hasn't done that before?

It was mid-morning and more people were up and about. The roller-shutter door was down and the back door locked. I didn't wait for Charley to pick this one. I just raised my boot and kicked it in. Charley rushed in ahead of me and crashed through the inner door. I followed him into the dark room and was temporarily blinded by the contrast to the bright light outside. I heard screams up ahead as Charley burst into the main area and a couple of male voices shouting. I ran after him. It was dim inside, but enough daylight to see three guys closing in on Charley. The blanket tents were still up around the room and girls in various states of undress were cowering behind them.

Charley took the first two out before I got there, and my quick kick to the outside of a knee dropped the third. He was writhing around screaming like a pig, clutching his shattered kneecap, so I tapped him out with my heel. Some of the girls started wailing. Most were just watching listlessly.

'Same routine,' said Charley, 'Let's check them all out.'

We split up and went round to take a look at everyone.

'Jeannie!' I shouted a few times, but I already knew that she wasn't there.

The women started clustering around us all talking at once. One or two started edging towards the door. I waved them towards it.

'You can all go now. Run. Get away from here.'

A few of them took off straight away. Some hung about, unsure if it was a trick and then carefully left. Some were still passed out in their beds and couldn't be roused.

'Nothing you can do for them right now Dick. They'll have to be carried out by social services.'

'She's not here,' I said tightly. I clenched my hands, digging my fingernails into my palms painfully. I was struggling for options.

'We could try the terrace house,' said Charley. I shook my head.

'I don't think so. They'd have taken her somewhere different. Somewhere they'd think we wouldn't know about.'

Charley didn't say anything, but I saw him glance at me in a way that said, 'She's probably dead, mate'. I pretended I hadn't seen it. Think!

I stalked away and rechecked the beds, just to stem the frustration. Then I knew what to do.

Chapter Twenty-six

'Get the girls over the far wall,' I said. 'Keep them away from the doors.'

'Why?'

I told him.

We herded the stoned ones and carried the unconscious ones and set them up in a new set of blankets at the far end of the room. There were six of them in total. The rest had fled.

When it was done, I left Charley to make a few preparations, while I slipped out into the street and went to the phone box on the corner. I dialled into the usual number. The one that always came up on my bleeper. The one that was burned into my memory after god knows how many interrupted nights.

'It's never a good idea to drink a bottle of whiskey then try to tango,' I said, and hung up. Usual protocol. The phone rang less than ten seconds later.

'Situation?' said the man at the other end of the line.

'Message for Big Bird. We've located Snuffleupagus and request backup. Could be multiple black hats there with heat.' I gave him the address of the warehouse across the street. 'It'll take us about forty minutes to get there. Hold off until I call again.'

There was a pause while notes were taken, then a short, 'Understood, anything else?'

'Not yet. I'll be in touch.' I put the phone down.

The message would be hand carried to the duty officer who would decode my opening nonsense about whiskey and tango, and call it through to the senior case officer at the Russian House who dealt with me. He would then assess the criticality of the message, maybe discuss it with his colleagues and ultimately, if considered important enough, push it up in front of Blondie who would make the call. Sounds complicated but it all happened pretty quickly. By the time I'd left the phone booth and squeezed back through the gates to join Charley, it would already be with the case officer. Less than ten minutes after that it should be in front of Blondie, who wouldn't appreciate me calling her 'Big Bird', but I could apologise later.

'Charley, get out there and lock up that padlock again would you?'

'Do it yourself,' he said, and tossed me a set of keys he'd taken from one of the unconscious men. He'd been hard at work tying them up to make sure they wouldn't be any trouble.

I went out and locked the padlock. Locked us in. I regretted kicking in the outer door now. The frame around the lock was all splintered and useless. I didn't have much time. I pushed the wood back into place as best as I could, wiped away the tell-tale boot-print in the middle of the door and used one of the keys to unlock it and relock it gently into place. It should hopefully pass muster if you were trying to be quick and were distracted.

'How long do you reckon we have?' asked Charley.

'Maybe twenty minutes?' I replied. 'Any longer than that and we'll know I'm wrong.'

'I hope to god you are,' Charley circled his head on his neck, causing it to make an unnerving popping sound.

I didn't think I was wrong. My blood was boiling and I needed an outlet. I was hoping this was it.

I pulled out and checked my Beretta. It was the latest model, a 92, which fired a nine millimetre Parabellum round at twelve hundred feet per second, the same as the World War Two German Luger. The name came from some Latin phrase meaning 'If you seek peace, prepare for war'. I had seventeen little parcels of peace, double-stacked in the high capacity magazine.

Charley had his pistol stuffed in the front of his trousers, ready for quick access, but he cradled the shotgun. Said it gave a good first impression.

Sixteen minutes after I'd hung up on control, we heard the rattle of a padlock and the clang of gates opening outside.

Chapter Twenty-seven

They didn't batter their way in, so they weren't our backup. In any case they wouldn't make the entry until they were told. The only people who would carefully unlock the padlock and bother to use a key to open the side door would be the kind you wouldn't want to introduce to your prospective mother-in-law.

They hustled in, seven of them, all tooled up and prickling with suppressed excitement, talking tough. Charley and I were hidden behind the blankets, one on either side, but staggered so we wouldn't be in each others' line of fire.

One of them called out, 'Oi, Ray! Where are you?'

It was the last thing to leave his mouth before his face was rearranged and pushed out the back of his head by Charley's shotgun. Difficult to be gentle with a sawn-off at close range. I popped up and took out a couple more. Two taps each. Head shots. Four rounds.

The shotgun roared again and Charley emptied the second barrel and smeared some poor bastard across the far wall. I thought of Jeannie and let another four rounds go.

It had taken less than six seconds. Mr Number Seven had spent the first four of those staring dumbly at us, probably wondering if someone was pranking him. In the last two, he'd realised his mates were going down like skittles next to him, managed to soil his unmentionables, and turned to run for the exit. Some of the more awake girls behind us started screaming. Charley tossed away the shotgun and leapt after him. I put my gun up and released the trigger. We didn't want him dead. Not yet, anyway.

Charley reached him before he made it to the outer door and tackled him to the ground. By the time I got there, he'd rolled his not inconsiderable weight onto the guy's back and had him flat out like a bit of roadkill. I quickly frisked him and relieved him of a flick-knife.

'Hello sunshine,' beamed Charley, grabbing the guy's arms and forcing his wrists together back between his shoulder blades.

'Don't kill me, please!' he wailed.

'We've just got a couple of questions-' Charley broke off as we heard the gate outside opening again. Someone else coming in. Charley clapped a hand over the guys mouth and hissed in his ear to be quiet. I jumped up and slid over to the side of the door to wait for the latecomer. When he stepped inside I thought all my Christmases had come at once.

It was our old friend, Black-Eyed Susan.

I put him down with an elbow to the side of his head and hauled him fully inside the dim garage.

Charley put Mr Number Seven to sleep with a knock to the back of his head and came over to join me.

'About bloody time. How do you think he likes his meals Dicky?'

I smiled grimly. 'Hot, I should say. Very very hot.'

Saudi had been hell on earth and I still wake up a trembling mess, sheets wet, throat dry and shaking from the memory. I don't know if Charley was the same. We don't talk about it. Stiff upper lip and all that. But I bet he does. He had it much worse than I did for some reason. And the cause of all that anguish was now curled up at our feet in an effectively deserted warehouse surrounded by soggy bits of his hired goons. Black-Eyed Susan had known an awful lot about inflicting pain, and like it or not, you couldn't help being on the receiving end of that without learning a thing or two.

'Now then, my lovely,' started Charley, and smiled down at him, with more than a touch of insanity dancing in his rich brown eyes.

'Don't touch me Dog!' Black-Eyed Susan barked, showing a lot more bravado than I'd have expected. He glared from Charley to me and sneered, 'I knew you were Dog-Spy. Both of you.'

I glanced at Charley, then fixed a glare on the Arab, 'That's the part I find most interesting actually. I'm thinking that we were caught pretty quickly over in Saudi. Almost as if someone knew we'd be there.'

'Who told you?' asked Charley.

The Egyptian turned his dark eyes up in a parody of a wronged man and shook his head, 'There must be some mistake. I am merely a humble soldier-'

Charley interrupted him with a savage kick to his ribs. Then another. And another. I let him vent for half a minute or so, then put up my hand. Charley was panting a bit by then and took the opportunity to stalk a few paces away to cool down. Black-Eyed Susan was curled up like a newborn and whimpering like a dog stuck out in the rain.

I squatted down near his head and talked softly, but there was iron in my tone. 'We know you are lying. Someone tipped you off that we were here. Someone in the Firm. Who was it?'

He just clutched himself and sobbed.

'What are you doing with the Irishman? Was he buying your drugs?' I knew he was. I just wanted him to know that I knew. The route was obvious. Heroin from Afghanistan, routed through Saudi, bought by the IRA using money from protection rackets and bank robberies, then sold or traded for American guns. And somewhere in the middle was someone in Whitehall taking a cut.

I gave him a couple of gentle slaps.

'Charley, our friend doesn't want to talk to me.' I looked Black-Eyed Susan in the eyes and watched the pupils shrink to the size of my remorse. 'Would you be so good as to give him a little encouragement?'

I went outside and got through half a packet of fags. It wasn't that I was squeamish. I enjoyed hearing the screams and the begging. It was part of the technique. The sadist and the saviour. Good cop, bad cop. By staying out of sight I separated myself in Black-Eyed Susan's mind, so that when I came back and intervened, I could act as the protector. I can take away the pain, I'd say. I don't want to see you suffer any more, but I'm not sure how long I can restrain my colleague.

I went back inside something like an hour later. Charley had stripped down to his bare chest, partly because he was sweating, but mostly to keep his shirt clean. Blood was splattered all over his chest and face, and his hair was lank and in disarray. He'd been working hard.

I hardly recognised our guest. One of his eyes was completely swollen shut and the other he could barely open. He had been stripped naked and was partly suspended upside down by a rope strung over an overhead beam and tied off around his ankles, pulling him up so his shoulders were still on the ground. There were discarded bits of metal packing banding nearby which explained the weals on the soles of his feet. Charley hadn't even asked him any questions.

I took him to one side, out of earshot. 'How was that for you?'

'He's all yours,' Charley smiled grimly, but at least some of the insanity was gone. Therapeutic, perhaps, but I can't see it being rolled out on the NHS.

I went over to Black-Eyed Susan and pulled out a knife. He saw it and began to squirm and sob, yammering away in Arabic. I picked out a couple of words, but I wasn't minded to be as merciful as his god. I had a role to play, and used the knife to cut the rope and let his legs drop to the floor. They'd start burning soon enough as the blood rushed back into them. It would be agony. I knew all about that, thanks to him.

'Marhaba sidiki,' I said. 'Hello friend'. 'I just want to find my wife. Where is she? Where is Jeannie?'

'I tell you, I tell you,' he wailed. 'Please no hurt.'

It was easy after that. He sang any old tune I wanted, and he'd have danced too if I'd asked. People say that information gained through torture is unreliable and inadmissible. It all depends how you do it. It's true that people will do and say anything to make the pain stop, and they might make up any old thing they thought you wanted to hear, but the skill was in the questions. You ask a leading question like 'You are a spy aren't you?' they'd tell you yes, as long as they thought it wouldn't make things worse for them. They'd happily admit to things being someone else's fault, that they were weak and manipulated or misguided or tricked. Anything to deflect the anger of the questioner away from them.

The way to do it was to ask open questions, that don't have a simple yes or no answer, and not to react to the answer. Don't show pleasure or anger. Just keep your Grey Face on so the victim doesn't know which answers are the ones you want to hear. So yes, it could be plenty effective. As to the inadmissible part, well that was an ethical and moral issue, about which I didn't give a shit. I just wanted to find Jeannie.

'So what did you get?' asked Charley when I had finished. He had taken himself outside for much the same reasons I had and so he could smoke in peace.

'I got that he likes to spend his weekends with underage boys, and he likes his liquor and bacon, and doesn't seem to realise that would displease his god. I got that he's been running the Irish racket for a couple of years and the shipment we intercepted was the biggest yet, and we've pissed off a lot of people.'

'Anything about the mole?'

I shook my head, 'Not really. He kept mentioning the name 'Grandfather', but he didn't know if he was in Five or Six. He just said 'British Intelligence'.'

'What about your missus?' Charley asked quietly.

'The theatre. Where she was working. They've got her there. He said they wanted to use her to get to me. To draw us out. Like I said, we've upset a lot of people.'

Charley cast a glance back towards the mess we'd made inside, 'What do you want to do about him?'

I sucked on a fag and let the smoke do its mischief on my lungs. I took my time answering and by the time I'd flicked the butt away I knew I'd reached my limit. 'Leave him for the cops. By the time they've gone through all the information we can dig up about him and extradited him back home, he'll be all used up and no good to his masters. He'll have a bullet in the back of his head the day after he lands. And he'll know it's coming.'

Charley grunted his agreement. He'd have been happier leaving a bullet in the back of his head right now, but he accepted my suggestion anyway. Hell it was probably a worse fate than a simple quick death.

'Make the call,' he said. 'I'll tidy up a bit. Make it look like a retribution thing. Then we can ride across town and pick up your old lady.'

I'd never heard him say anything sweeter.

Chapter Twenty-eight

'Where is this theatre?'

I was driving, and I wasn't being too careful about the niceties of the highway code, or speed limits. The sun had dipped below the tops of the trees and was painting long shadows across the road.

'Not far. Maida Vale.'

It used to be a small-time, flea-pit cinema that had been converted into a small-time, flea-pit theatre. It had been built out of sturdy, unlovely red brick in the forties, and still had most of its original features. I'd been there a few times, dropping off or picking up. Once, Jeannie had persuaded me to stay and watch a performance. It was some experimental piece I didn't understand. One of the more obscure of Shakespeare's plays acted out by a small cast wearing bin-bags in bare feet. Jeannie had only had a small part, but she'd been proud of it.

I was going over the place in my head, trying to remember the layout. Jeannie was rehearsing for some show they were about to put on. I was away so much all her shows blurred together in my memory into the kind of mess you find at the bottom of an old jerry can, but I knew it hadn't started, because I recalled she'd told me that opening night was going to be on her birthday. That was in two days. Which meant they'd probably have the place all kitted out ready. Complete with props and lighting.

It was dark by the time we got there. The kind of dark where the sky is deep ink-blue and the stars weren't quite visible. I pulled up across the street, a couple of doors away. I didn't know if anyone would be watching the road, but caution had been literally beaten into me. It was a hard habit to break.

'Plan?' Charley asked.

'Find her. Talk to the Irish about his attitude.'

Charley nodded. 'Know where she'll be?'

'Not a clue. Backstage maybe? There's a few rooms back there that might have locks.'

'Any civvies likely to be in there?'

I looked across at the ugly square, two-storey building. There were no lights on, and the foyer was dark. 'Doesn't look like it at the moment, but there's no guarantee someone won't wander in any minute.'

'How many black hats?'

'Susan didn't know exactly. But 'some', he said.'

'So the only way we'll know if anyone we meet in there has murderous intentions, is when they pull out a shooter?'

I nodded grimly, 'Well that or they pull out a frilly scarf and call you darling. That'll be a good sign they're a luvvie.'

Charley muttered something about ponces I didn't bother to listen to.

'Let's go.'

There were two entrances. The main oak-panelled, glass-paned double doors facing any curious onlookers on the street, or the nondescript, plain plywood-covered stage door in a narrow, deserted, rubbish-strewn alley at the back. Guess where we went?

There was a simple tumbler-type lock on the stage door and Charley had that open before I'd finished adjusting my pants.

The door opened into the back of the auditorium, under the gallery seats. It was only a small place. Seating for about two hundred down in the stalls and maybe another hundred in the gallery overhead. The lights were out and once Charley pulled the door closed behind us, it was totally dark.

'Shit, it's blacker than the inside of a badger's arse in here,' muttered Charley.

I put my hand on his shoulder to shut him up and listened. There was nothing at first then the faint strains of pop music coming from behind the stage. I started creeping toward the stage, or at least to where I thought it ought to be, down the slight slope from the auditorium. Charley circled in the opposite direction and I immediately heard a dull thud and a muffled curse as he nearly went arse over tit on something. I gritted my teeth and resisted the urge to hiss at him to be quiet. It wouldn't help any.

I carried on down toward the stage, letting the lumbering oaf sort himself out. It was slow going, but there was a certain inexorability in my movements which kept me steady. I crouched down, and as I got nearer, the ramp started to flatten out, so I hid behind the seating. I listened again. Charley was doing a better job now. Either that or he was drowned out by the tinny beats coming from a small transistor radio in one of the rooms backstage. No way of knowing if it was owned by Smiling John or a keen dramatist. If it was Smiling John and his merry men, they'd be all squirrelled away in a small room together, probably with Jeannie tied up between them. Too closely packed to risk firearms. We needed to draw them out somehow.

I heard Charley fumbling around at the foot of the stage and sent a distracting hiss his way. He joined me between the first and second rows.

'Anything?' he whispered.

'Not this side. They'll be backstage somewhere.'

'Can we get any lights on?'

I shook my head, then realised Charley couldn't see me, 'Not really,' I said, 'The stage lights are all locked up, and you'd need a degree in lighting to get them turned on without blowing anything. There are some working lights, but god knows where the switch is. Anyway, the dark might help us out. We need to liven things up a little.'

I left the row of seats and crawled blindly toward the stage. My head found it first, despite all the flailing my arms were doing.

It wasn't very high. Maybe four feet. I could have crawled up on top of it, but I knew there were steps to either side, which would leave me less vulnerable if anyone suddenly decided to come out. I told Charley to head off to the left, and I tracked around towards the right. The steps led up to a set of narrow fixed curtains which stopped the audience seeing into the wings. Jeannie had called them tormentors, something to do with the frustration you'd feel if you were in the side seats and they were blocking your view. I slipped in behind them and wondered if I could risk a light. It was narrow and treacherous. There was a narrow path all around, behind the scenery boards, and I stubbed my foot on a hard, immovable object that I realised must be one of the weights that stopped the scenery from moving. I bent down and touched it. It was steel with a helpful grab handle and must have weighed about thirty pounds. I could lift it, but not for long, and if I could throw it a couple of feet I'd be happy. I threw it a couple of feet.

It made a satisfactorily loud bang as it landed on the thick wooden boards of the stage, and the acoustics took the sound and amplified it wonderfully. The radio shut off abruptly and I slid behind the tormentors to wait. I heard several sets of footsteps, then a click and a buzz and a series of dull strip-lights started to flicker on overhead. I squinted against the brightness, which wasn't that bright at all, but after all that time in the dark it was bright enough.

For whoever switched them on the effect was reversed. After sitting in a well-lit room for god knows how long, and walking into a dimly-lit, open-spaced auditorium, it would be like peering into a fish tank that hadn't been cleaned for a month. A door six feet from me opened and a couple of men came out. They didn't see me, and looked around, pulling pistols from their waistbands. They weren't luvvies then.

One of them headed toward the rear of the stage, away from me, but the other walked in my direction. He was making for the steps at the side of the stage, and I let him pass me before I jumped him.

The whole thing took less than two seconds, and I ended up with a shiny new gun and a comatose, but still breathing body at my feet.

I left him hidden in the tormentors and peered out to check on number two. He had reached the far side of the stage, and was looking out into the shadows of the auditorium when Charley rose up behind him and delivered a strike to the back of his head and still had time to catch him and his gun before he hit the boards. Say what you like about Charley, but he knew his stuff.

Charley stowed the body in the wings and disappeared round the back of the scenery. I edged over to the door and listened. I couldn't hear any more movement, or talking. I crouched down and flashed a look round the corner at knee height. There was a narrow, white-walled corridor down a few steps with a couple of doors on the left and two more on the right. The second on the right was open and light was streaming out and papering the opposite door. I didn't see anyone.

I still had thug number one's automatic in my hand, so I slid out the magazine, checked that there were a dozen or so round-nosed friends nestled inside it, eased it back home quietly, muffling the sound with my body and checked the safety was off. I reeled off a little mantra in my head - don't put off until later what you can fuck up now - and spun round the doorway and down the steps into the corridor. The wooden floor had a narrow threadbare carpet tacked down the middle, which was enough to deaden my footsteps. Not enough though. I stepped across the open doorway, gun up and ready, but before it came to bear, a foot like a sledgehammer drove into my chest and thrust me backwards. I had a glimpse of the room beyond and a figure sitting on the floor by a cast iron radiator, before I smashed through the flimsy door behind me and landed on a porcelain throne.

I couldn't breathe. At least, I couldn't breathe out. Breathing in was easy, but unless you can get rid of that nasty CO_2, you might as well not bother. I looked up to see Smiling John standing across from me, staring down hard. Then, slowly, his rock-hard features twisted like the ground had heaved and he drew his lips up into a sort of grimace. I won't go so far as to say it was a smile, but he was clearly pleased with himself. He took a step forward, ready to finish me off, then I saw a blur as Charley piled into him and they both vanished from my sight.

I rolled off the toilet and the fittings rolled away with me, sliding to the floor by my side. It took me ten or fifteen seconds to persuade my lungs to work again, and when the exhale came, it was like someone was dancing a jig on my chest all over again. I could hear sounds of close-in fighting round the corner, but my eyes rested on the room opposite. Jeannie was the figure on the floor, her arms tied to her sides with rope, a gag made of her fake silk scarf across her mouth and a couple of pounds of plastic explosive, complete with wires and a tilt-switch, strapped between her legs.

I stumbled across the hall and dropped to my knees in front of her. She looked at me with eyes wide and wet and panicked.

'It's okay,' I wheezed, kidding neither of us. 'Let me take a look.'

I'd been taught about bombs, of course. Mostly how to make them, but also how to defuse them, because our friends across the Irish Sea enjoyed using them so much. You were supposed to approach them calmly, with no distractions around you, and take your time. So much for rules one, two and three.

I leaned over the device and took a careful look. It had been packed into an old metal treacle tin, with a hole pierced through the top so a couple of wires could be threaded through to a detonator inside. Taped to the outside was a large battery which provided the energy to set off the detonator, and a couple of wires ran from this to a pager, and then to a glass tube about an inch long mounted to the lid. Inside the glass tube was a shiny bead of mercury, pooled at the end furthest from the wires. It was a primitive tilt-switch, a nasty little anti-handling device which meant that if Jeannie moved or even fidgeted too much, the mercury would roll the short distance up towards the exposed wires, complete the circuit and, well, two pounds of C4 would mean we'd both be a lot less bothered about the fact she'd be another year older next week.

I got the circuit pretty quickly. None of this nonsense about blue wires and red wires. Improvised bomb makers used whatever they had to hand and since they knew what they were doing, didn't need to remind themselves which wires were going where. All of Smiling John's wires were black. The thing could be triggered either by jostling the tilt switch, or calling the pager. Cutting any of the wires between the battery, pager, tilt-switch or tin would be enough to make it safe. Trouble is, I didn't have any wire clippers.

Charley was getting the crap beaten out of him in the hallway outside, and someone might decide to call the pager. I didn't have much time. I looked around the room for something to use to cut the wires, but it was a simple dressing room. There were lights and mirrors and clothes hanging on rails, but no wire cutters. Not even any scissors. I'd have to go in the hard way.

I pulled out my knife and looked up at Jeannie reassuringly. 'Don't move.'

She started to nod, then just blinked her eyes. Good girl.

The lid was one of those press-fit affairs that you have to lever off with the edge of a knife. If I could get it off without triggering the tilt-switch, I could pull out the detonator and make the thing safe. I lay down on my belly and started on the side furthest from the mercury. I gently levered up one side, keeping a close eye on the switch. Any jerking movement and it might roll back to the electrodes and ruin our day. The sound of the pounding started slowing down. I willed Charley to hang on, and got half of the tin lid clear. Working my blade carefully around the sides I got the whole lid loose and held it in sweaty fingers while I carefully put my knife down.

I couldn't get the lid much higher than about an inch because the wires from the battery were so short. I looked in between the gap and saw a pair of wires dangling down through the hole in the lid into the back of a metal tube, about the size of a nail. That was the detonator. I reached my fingers into the gap and gently eased it out of the oily explosive. One last thing. Detonators were still pretty nasty on their own and I'd heard of people losing fingers through mishandling them. It was still connected to the battery and the tilt-switch. I eased it over the side of the tin, picked up my knife, and used it to direct the detonator toward the ground, away from me, Jeannie and the explosive. Then I uttered a little prayer, looked away to shield my face, gave the lid a little shake and there was a sharp crack as the detonator did its thing.

It took a second or two to realise I was still alive and the device was safe. I let out a big sigh, then wished I hadn't as a band of pain tightened across my chest. I knelt up, kissed Jeannie on the forehead and left her, still tied up and gagged, to go and help Charley. I'd get an earful for that later, but your partner is your partner.

The fight had made its way back up to the stage and as I turned to follow, I stepped on thug number one's gun and slipped, falling to the floor and winding myself again. I recovered quicker this time, grabbed the gun and limped up the stairs. I got to the stage just in time to see Charley take a boot to the thigh he couldn't block which dropped him to the floor. Smiling John levelled a kick at Charley's head, but my shout stopped him.

He turned around. He didn't have to worry about Charley any more. Charley was alive, but was probably wishing he wasn't.

'There you are lover boy,' said the Irishman. His face was definitely contorted into an expression of pleasure. He glanced at the pistol in my hand. 'Are you going to need that?' he sneered. 'I thought you boys had balls of steel. Don't you fancy your chances with me, man to man? Or are you chicken-shit and weak, like I always thought?'

He was goading me. I narrowed my eyes, staring into his ugly, smug face. Charley had given it a good going over. There was blood running from one ear and down his chin from a couple of broken teeth. As he shifted his weight I saw he was favouring his right foot. Apart from a couple of bruised ribs, I was in pretty good shape. I could probably take him. I'd get into less trouble if I captured him alive too. Might even get a commendation.

Then I thought about the easy mess he had made of Charley, and then about what he had put Jeannie and Yasmine Short through, and I put a bullet between his eyes. He fell to the ground, still wearing that attempt at a smile.

Chapter Twenty-nine

Charley was still conscious. Battered, bruised, a few broken bones and he wouldn't be taking up trampolining any time soon, but he'd live.

'Did you get him?' he said, around a swollen tongue.

'I got him.'

'About time. I was getting bored softening him up for you.'

I helped him to sit up and left him poking at various bits of himself while I went to find Jeannie. She held herself together pretty well until I'd pulled off the gag, untied her and set the remains of the bomb off to one side. Then she burst into tears and held me tight. It hurt my ribs, but I didn't complain. I held her tightly in return and let myself come back from the dark place I'd been for the last few days. Make that the last few months. That was it for me. No more, no matter what. I was getting out and so was Charley.

We had a few things to tidy up, and after Jeannie had stopped sobbing I eased away from her.

'We need to get you home. You'll be safe now.'

She sniffed and nodded. Her eyes took on that look that meant she'd made up her mind about something. 'They said they were going to kill you,' she said.

'They missed.'

She raised a hand to brush my cheek, 'Is this how it is for you?'

'Not any more,' I said. 'I'm going to put an end to it. We'll find some other way.'

She nodded.

'Do you want me to take you home?'

'No, I can do it myself.'

'Take a taxi,' I pulled out a few notes and passed them to her. She hesitated for a second, then took them and nodded.

'I'm going to give Charley a hand. I'll see you later.'

I kissed her and she kissed me back, with that fiery urgency she threw into every aspect of her life. She was tougher than me in many ways.

Charley had made it to his feet by the time I got back, and had dragged the two thugs we'd taken out into the middle of the stage so he could watch them more closely. They were still out, but they'd recover soon enough. The body of Smiling John still lay where he fell, in a slowly spreading pool of blood.

'You realise he was our last lead on the mole, don't you?' said Charley slowly. He was doing everything slowly at the moment.

I nodded. I didn't say anything.

'I checked his pockets,' he continued. 'Nothing in there to help us.'

'We'll find him,' I said.

'I don't care one way or the other.'

I looked at him, 'Time to go?' We weren't talking about leaving the theatre. He nodded.

'Then let's call this in and finish it.'

I used the phone in the office to call Blondie. She sent a clean-up crew round that included a car to bring us back in. I don't know what happened to the two thugs, and I never bothered to ask.

Ten minutes after we limped into the building we were sat in a pokey old conference room nursing a mug of hot sweet tea and getting debriefed by Blondie and a couple of men in fine wool suits.

'We got your call about the Arab in the warehouse,' she said, and then waited a beat to look us both in the eyes. I was expecting her to give us a lecture on the responsible treatment of prisoners. I didn't expect her to say that Black-Eyed Susan had gone.

'What do you mean, gone?' I growled. 'He was trussed up nicely, and in no state to walk anyway.'

'All we found were a few strung out hookers and a handful of dead goons.' She gave us a cold look, 'You wouldn't know anything about that, would you?'

'They were like that when we got there,' muttered Charley. His face was swelling up alarmingly. His charm and good looks weren't going to help much now.

'Someone must have waited outside until we left, then went in and snatched him,' I said.

'We will find him,' she promised.

'You'll find him all right,' My tone sounded bitter, even to me. 'You'll find him in a ditch with a bullet in the back of his head. He may not have known much about the mole, but he knew plenty about the operation. Enough to make him dangerous to someone.'

She didn't have much to say to that.

'We want out,' I said abruptly.

Blondie narrowed her eyes but it was one of the men who replied.

'We say when you can get out. You're ours until we're done with you.'

I nearly took a swing at him, 'You know you've got a mole in here somewhere? Maybe dozens. Do you think I'm going to trust anything you tell me ever again?'

'I'm not convinced about the so-called 'mole',' piped up the other suit, looking up from a copy of my statement. I flicked him a glance, but I was too tired to argue. I let him spout on for a bit about incompetence and bad luck, and shrugged it all off. My lack of reaction annoyed him, which made me feel a lot better.

We spent the next couple of hours going over what we'd done, starting from the initial deployment to watch the terraced house and ending at the theatre. Charley and I hadn't had much of a chance to check our stories with each other, and we weren't about to hold our hands up to everything we'd got up to, so there were a lot of holes in our account which we didn't bother to fill, and which the suits kept fussing over.

Blondie didn't stay for the whole thing, and once she left we became a whole lot less cooperative. Charley gave up the pretence entirely, and sat there with his eyes closed, wincing at the pain that was no doubt throbbing through his body.

It was after midnight when things drew to a halt. The suits were all settling in to stay until dawn, but Charley and I were exhausted. Charley even snored a few times.

'Let's go back to the van,' said the first suit.

I rolled my eyes, but before I could let him know what I thought of him or the van, the door opened and Blondie strode in, looking fresh and efficient as always.

'Thank you gentlemen, you can be done now,' she said.

'Ma'am there are still a few things that don't add up,' protested a suit, but she cut him off.

'We have everything we need.' She turned to us, 'You'll be pleased to know that Miss Short will be okay. She has been taken to a very exclusive and very private hospital where she will receive the best care we have to offer. She is expected to make a full recovery.'

I felt good about that. The poor kid had made a mistake, but you're supposed to make mistakes when you're young. Accepting a joint from a stranger isn't supposed to be something you end up dying over.

'And you two,' Blondie continued, addressing us, 'Get yourselves down to the hospital, and get checked over. You get the second best care we have to offer. Take some time off. You can finish the debrief next week.'

We got up to leave, stiff from the sitting and the bruises and hobbled to the door.

'I don't think we're coming back,' I said softly as I passed her.

The expression on her face didn't waver. 'We'll be in touch.'

Chapter Thirty

It only took a couple of days in Jeannie's bed for me to recover. I only had a few bruised ribs to deal with. Charley would take a month or more to get back on his feet. He'd taken quite a pounding all right, and he never let me forget he was taking it on my behalf.

'I really don't know what you were thinking Dicky,' he said when I visited him at his home. 'You could have come and given me a hand, instead of fussing over that girl of yours.'

'I knew you could handle it, a big boy like you. Then again,' I added, 'you are getting on a bit.'

'I'm not that old, runt,' he snapped. 'I can still run rings around you.' Then he collapsed into a wheezing fit, and had to take a moment to recover. I nipped out to get him a drink of water and when I came back I caught him staring into space, a lost and haunted look in his eyes. He'd had a bellyful of this. Much more than me.

I went to see Lord Calveley the following day. Denman set it up, but I had to beg for it.

'I've got important business to discuss with him,' I'd said, 'Firm business.' But Denman didn't budge. He knew more about the inner workings of Five than I did. He'd have taken tea at Claridge's or Grosvenor House with one of his old Oxford chums and received full chapter and verse about what we'd been up to over the past few weeks. For an organisation built around secrecy and 'need to know', it was a leaky bucket of a place. No wonder the mole found it so easy to operate. If ever they found him there would be a collective intake of breath and cries of 'but he's one of us!'. The old boys' network was still going strong, despite the battering it took in the sixties with the 'Ring of Five'. The usual response within the Firm about the discovery of the Soviet spies was a turned up nose and a snooty 'Well what would you expect from *Cambridge* men?'

That's another reason I'd never fit in. To be a poor orphaned yid was just about excusable when papered over with the decent grammar school my grandmother had sent me to. But to duck out of education at the first opportunity marked me out as a no-hoper. I'd forever be a foot-soldier, never an officer.

'I need this meeting, Denman,' I pleaded. 'I'll camp out on the doorstep if I have to.'

There was silence, followed by a rustling of papers. 'He has a slot in two weeks,' he started.

'Not good enough. Tomorrow.'

There was the ghost of a sigh, just enough to let me know I was tiresome, but not enough to hang an accusation on. 'Come by just after breakfast. Eight forty-five. You'll have fifteen minutes. No longer.'

I hung up. I made sure I was there at eight. I'd wait as long as it took. I wasn't going to risk being late and getting bumped. Denman would love that.

He showed me into Lord C's study like I was a workman dressed in oily rags. He didn't offer me a drink. That was fine. At ten to nine, Lord C strolled in with a newspaper in his hand and tossed it carelessly on his desk.

'Richard my boy,' he greeted me warmly, with his kindly uncle face on.

'My Lord, thank you for making time for me.'

'Anything at all for you,' he said and indicated a leather and mahogany visitor's chair by his desk for me to sit in. He sat in his normal position and spread his hands towards me. 'Now what's on your mind?'

'I think you know sir.' I'd gone to jelly again. Funny how I could face down a small army of gangsters, all armed to the teeth and hungry for payback, but I was still scared of the man who had plucked me off the streets and given me a home.

He looked at me keenly, assessing me. He knew perfectly well why I was here. The only question left was whether he was ready to let me go.

'Still yearning after a bit of outside security work eh?' It was said with a lightness of tone, but there was steel behind the words.

'I don't think the service is quite me, sir,' I said.

'Nonsense, you've acquitted yourself admirably,' he said.

I blinked in surprise. 'Ireland didn't go so well.'

'You underestimate yourself my dear boy. You gave us exactly the outcome we wanted. And that business with the Short girl. Brilliant. Her father is overjoyed. Sends his regards. Doesn't know who you are of course, but that's irrelevant.'

'It was a fiasco, sir. Nothing went to plan. We were betrayed, abandoned-'

He waved me to silence. 'These things happen, but the important thing is that you delivered, and you are sitting right there telling me about it. Chaps like you are hard to find. Harder to keep.'

I wasn't expecting any of this. I shifted in my seat and took a moment to reflect. Maybe I'd not done so badly after all. Then a cold suspicion grabbed at my heart. Was this another carrot dangling in front of me, like the Mini and the house? Was I getting a pat on the head and a treat for bringing back the stick? I sat up straighter, ready to argue my case, when he opened a drawer and pulled out some papers.

'However,' he said, placing them in front of him, 'I am a man of my word. I promised you I would set you up with your own company, and I have.'

My mouth hung open and when I realised, I closed it. 'Really?' I croaked.

'Absolutely. I think you've learned a lot and are ready for the next step.' He slid the papers over to me. They were letters of incorporation for a company called 'Associated Security', with a Mayfair address and my name on the Managing Director's line.

I found my voice again, 'I want Charley Parnarti too.'

He looked up and I saw a flicker of disapproval dance across his brows, but it was quickly replaced. 'I'm sure that can be arranged.' He passed me a gold fountain pen and watched me as I pretended to flick through the papers, but I was too dazed to think straight. He looked at his watch discreetly, but not so discreetly that I didn't get the hint. I signed the papers and slid them back.

'I've managed to get a few investors to set up some capital to get you started. Not a huge amount, but sufficient to be going along with. As shareholders they'll have an interest in the direction the company takes of course, so I'll set something up next week for them to meet you.'

I looked up suspiciously. 'I get to call the shots though?'

'Of course. It's your company now.' He reassured me. Then Denman came in and that was my signal to leave.

'I'll have the papers sent over, along with the keys to your offices,' Lord C called as I was leaving.

I invited Charley and his latest squeeze over for dinner the next night with Jeannie and I, and announced the good news. Charley stared at me like I'd grown another head while Jeannie squealed with delight.

'Are you sure this is kosher?' asked Charley. His busty blonde girlfriend looked between us, bemused. Poor thing probably wouldn't be able to tell the difference between a director of a company and a director of a movie, but Charley didn't pick them for their brains.

'Seems to be. We'll both be on the board and we can pick and choose our clients. And we can tell the Firm to take a hike.'

He shook his head. 'You don't *leave* the Firm, Dick. Unless it is feet first in six feet of pine. There's got to be something squirrelly about this.'

I pulled out the papers which had been amended to include Charley's name, and pointed out the solicitor's signature making it all legal and binding. 'We're out Charley. We're really out!'

It got through to him finally. We toasted our cleverness and started talking about all the things we wanted to do. Jeannie and the bimbo listened for a while, then went off to talk about plays and drama, or as the bimbo called it 'actressing'. Charley and I got ourselves very drunk and Jeannie set up the spare room for them. By the time I stumbled to bed I was too far gone to show my appreciation for the way Jeannie had stuck by me all this time and I passed out, half-undressed beside her. I remember waking briefly beside her and hearing Charley and the bimbo pounding away at the bedsprings in the next room. Maybe he was ready for trampolining after all?

A week later Charley and I strolled up to our new offices, all suits and ties, feeling like businessmen. I'd even brought a briefcase, but all it contained was my lunch.

'Look at the state of you,' joked Charley, 'Did you dress yourself this morning?'

'I might have had a little help,' I grinned. 'You don't scrub up too badly yourself. Are you ready for your new life?'

'Lead on runt, let's see the place.'

It was a first floor office in an exclusive, marble-fronted building in the posh part of town. The rent would be enormous. I hadn't asked Lord C how long he would cover it, but probably not long. He was a big believer in letting people do things on their own.

The main door opened into a small waiting room, large enough for a three seater leather couch, an armchair and a desk for a secretary to file her nails at. The walls were panelled in walnut and the carpeting was deep and patterned. Three other doors led to a small toilet and sink, a meeting room containing a six-seater oval table and an office with two desks set across from each other. Charley claimed the desk nearest and put his feet up, looking out of the window at the busy street below. I set my briefcase on the other desk and sat down. We grinned at each other across the small space. Each desk had a telephone, a blotter and a brass table-lamp with a green hood.

'I'm going to buy myself a fedora,' announced Charley, and I laughed.

Then a buzzer went off, and I scrambled up to work out where it was coming from. It went off again before I found an intercom set into the wall near the secretary's desk and I thumbed it.

'Yes?'

'Richard my boy,' came the warm tones of Lord C, 'We're here for the board meeting. We're coming up.'

My heart sank. I didn't expect to get away with owing him nothing, but I thought I might get a bit of freedom. I poked my head into the office and said to Charley, 'Look lively, the shareholders are here.'

Charley went into the board room and I stayed back to be secretary and meet our benefactors.

'There's even a bloody coffee machine in here,' called Charley, and I heard him setting it up. Nice.

The door opened and Lord C walked in, all smiles and handshakes. He was followed by Denman, who just nodded at me and didn't offer a hand. Behind him came a man in a suit and waistcoat I didn't recognise. He was in his fifties, silvered hair, trim moustache and had the air of a colonel about him. Take away the cabbage gear and the rank markings and what you are left with is still an officer in a suit. Spot them a mile off.

'Good Morning Mr. Frame,' he said, holding out his hand. Good guess? I doubted it. 'I'm Reginald McCoy. Call me Reg.'

'Dick,' I shook his hand.

Then the door swung again and in walked our last shareholder. That's when I got the joke. We'd been let out of our cage, but still had a lead attached. It was Blondie.

'Hello Dick. Good to see you again.' She pressed her cheek to mine in a parody of a kiss and breezed across the room to offer the same to Charley. He stood, rooted to the spot as she left him to take a seat in the boardroom, and our eyes met in mutual realisation.

They had us locked up tight. They knew about Smiling John and the mess I'd made of his brain-pan in the theatre. Operatives aren't above the law, and if they kill, there has to be an investigation. The Irishman had been injured and unarmed. It wouldn't look good. Then there were the bodies in the warehouse full of slugs that could be traced to handguns in our possession. If we didn't do whatever they wanted or we stepped just a little out of line, everything I had would come tumbling down around me. It was an ideal situation for them. They had all the capability and talent they had before, but this time with all the deniability they could ever want. We were going to be looking forward to some interesting times.

I allowed myself a bitter smile, straightened my tie and joined the others in the board room, closing the door softly behind me.

CPSIA information can be obtained at www.ICGtesting.com
Printed in the USA
BVOW08s1004180515

400802BV00001B/14/P